SUDDEN
SEX

SUDDEN SEX

69 SULTRY SHORT STORIES

EDITED BY
ALISON TYLER

CLEiS
PRESS

Published in the United States by Cleis Press, Inc., 2246 Sixth Street, Berkeley, California 94710.

Printed in the United States.
Cover design: Scott Idleman/Blink
Cover photograph: Timothy Shonnard/Getty Images
Text design: Frank Wiedemann

First Edition.
10 9 8 7 6 5 4 3 2 1

Trade paper ISBN: 978-1-57344-900-7
E-book ISBN: 978-1-57344-961-8

Love is a sudden revelation:
a kiss is always a discovery.

—Anonymous

Contents

INTRODUCTION

My favorite shorts are frayed. You can see the tips of the pockets poking through, pale white against the sublimely faded denim. Strands dangle from the thigh holes, leaving just the right amount to the imagination. What would happen if you pulled a thread? Would the entire pair of shorts unravel, leaving me naked?

My favorite short stories are totally different—brand new, rather than well-worn. Crisp and focused, taut and tight. The pieces in this collection are waiting for you to slide them on, button the fly then turn and admire how well they fit your kink.

Because—as everyone who knows me understands by now—I'm all about the kink. This collection features BDSM, spanking, toys, tools, girls gone bad and men who need it just as bad. I've assembled stories from writers I've worked with for nearly two decades as well as wordsmiths who are new to me. What do the pieces have in common? Each one maxes out at fifteen hundred words. That's not a lot of small talk. We've cut the awkward getting-to-know-you phase and instead parked you right up at the point. We're past first base, past second, on our way to third. His hand is under your skirt; her palm is on your cock. We're all adults here—no need to fight the fact that sometimes what we crave is simple: *Sudden Sex*.

Take a breath. Bite your lip. Get ready to get off.

Nothing can get more sudden than the stories in this book.

XXX,
Alison Tyler

BOOKED

Alison Tyler

There. Finally. Thank fucking god."

Gina's parking skills were tested to the maximum in order to force her Karmann Ghia into the tight space between two SUVs across from the restaurant. She was visibly trembling when she exited the little citron-hued car and started to walk to the café. This was a big deal—a meeting she'd been prepping for all month. Unfortunately for her, lunch was scheduled for one of those high-end, chichi restaurants that made her tense simply looking at the menu. She'd hoped to arrive early enough to stake her place at a table and get comfortable, but the restaurant wasn't opened yet.

She dug into her purse for her datebook to make sure she had the time right. Most of her friends used iPhones or BlackBerries to track their daily lives, but

Gina preferred paper. Nothing beeped in her purse to let her know she'd missed an appointment. She had to grab the leather-bound calendar and flip the pages to find out where she was supposed to be. Her calendar was filled with words in red. Jesus, she was booked. She couldn't see an inch of free time for the next month.

But at this moment, for once, she was early.

Next to the restaurant stood a used bookstore, a throwback to a simpler era. On a whim, Gina pushed open the glass door, thinking she'd be able to peruse the shelves for half an hour and calm her nerves. Maybe she'd grab a novel to keep her company, something she'd read before that would feel familiar and safe. The man behind the counter hardly looked up at her as she walked in. She caught the fact that he was youngish and cute with a pair of '50s-style black glasses and curly dark hair. He put his finger on his page to mark his spot when she paused to breathe in the smell. Used books. She sighed, feeling more relaxed from the moment the scent surrounded her.

"Vanillin," he said.

"Excuse me?"

"The aroma of old books. It's actually lignin—related to vanillin. It's why used bookstores have that fragrance they do. I read about it"—he motioned to a book on a shelf to his left—"in a book." He grinned.

She looked him over—maybe a little older than she'd original thought, slightly scruffy, T-shirt with something about obscenities on the chest.

"What sort of books do you like?" he asked.

She thought for a second. "Ones that have happy endings."

"A romantic?" he asked.

She never considered herself one. "I like noir—but the stories where the boy gets the girl in the end. Or vice versa."

"Top shelf," he told her, indicating the back room. She went there and waited. What if he followed? What would that mean? She'd been out of the dating loop since she'd landed her current job, the one that had sucked up all her time, her mind, her soul, her life. Her fingers trailed over the broken spines of misused paperbacks, and she hoped he would follow her. But what would she say? What would she do?

She went to a corner of the room and sat on the edge of a short wooden ladder that must have been there for stocking purposes. For just a moment, Gina closed her eyes and breathed in that used-book scent once more. Then she heard the man say, "I locked the front door."

"Why?"

He lifted her to her feet and kissed her rather than responding verbally, and she felt a flood of emotions all at once. She had to go to lunch. She had an important meeting. She had to remain professional, un-mussed; oh, fucking god, his hand was in her hair, his lips tasted so good, sweet, dreamy. Her back was up against the wall of books. She stepped out of her spectator heels and he picked her up in his arms and held her to the stacks. He was hard. She could feel his erection against her. It had been so long, *too* long. When had she last let her fingers wander over a favorite book? When had she last let her fingers slip under her waistband and into her panties?

He roughly pushed her neat gray skirt to her hips, groaned when he felt she was wearing stockings and suspenders. "Noir," he smiled at her. "Femme fatale." No, she wasn't. She was the good girl. The secretary in the pale pink sweater. The gal Friday the detective always treated like one of the guys, never seeing the sex appeal beneath the prim, petal twin set. Why did the good girls always have to finish last?

She wasn't going to finish last this time. Gina groaned when the man probed beneath her bikinis to find how wet she was. Suddenly, undeniably wet. His fingers circled her clit, the rough pads of his fingertips brushing against her most sensitive spot, creating a delicious type of friction. He undid his jeans and let the head of his cock find her slit, and entered her with one forceful thrust. Gina felt her body tighten around his. She hadn't been fucked in so long. She couldn't even remember how sweet the pleasure felt. When he tripped his fingers over her clit as he worked her, she moaned out loud.

The sound surprised her and Gina opened her eyes. She was by herself in the back room, pressed up against the bookshelf, hand in her knickers, lost in an unexpected fantasy. Oh, god. What if someone had seen her? She took a few steps so that she could peek through the doorway and down the aisle. The clerk was still reading his book at the front as if he hadn't heard a whisper. What had caused her to daydream like that? Too much stress. Clearly. She was losing her cool.

She grabbed *High Window* in her slightly sticky fingers and carried the novel to the front desk. Her cheeks felt hot.

When the clerk rang her up, Gina was still slightly breathless. She couldn't find her wallet in her satchel. The clerk patiently watched her take out her datebook as she rummaged for her billfold. He peeked into the gaping mouth of her purse with obvious interest. "No cell phone?"

"Can't stand them."

"Then how will I call you?"

"Call me?" She was too shaken to follow his conversation.

"Slow down." He put his hand on top of hers. Warmth flooded through her whole body. "I saw what you were doing back there." He indicated the round silver mirror at the top of the doorway, one angled to see everything going on in the back room. "It's supposed to catch a thief," he explained matter-of-factly, "but it caught you."

Her heart raced. She flipped her datebook open, already knowing. "I'm booked," she said helplessly. "This month is insane." Besides, how could she go out with someone who'd caught her touching herself? She felt more embarrassed than if he'd caught her shoplifting.

He reached for a bookmark from a small stack at the counter.

She started to wave him away. "I always bend the corners," she said.

Undaunted, he wrote his name and number on the back of a bookmark and slipped it between her pages. The action made her think of the way he'd fucked her in her fantasy, his cock sliding easily inside of her. What he said next changed everything in Gina's world.

"Girls who bend corners should be punished," he said, and she sucked in her breath before she could stop herself. Her visible discomfort seemed to please him. He didn't rush to put her at ease. "You'd like that, wouldn't you?"

Nothing like this had ever happened to Gina before. She didn't know what to say, how to respond. "Yes," she managed to whisper. "God, yes."

"I'd like that, too. I'd like to put you over my lap and give you a good, hard spanking for what you did back there. Touching yourself in my store…" He let the sentence linger between them, so that they could both imagine what she'd looked like back there—untamed, out of control. "What were you thinking about?"

"You," she said, the truth tumbling forward unbidden. "You fucking me."

"You can find the time," he said, "if you want to."

She slid the book into her purse and hurried to her meeting.

FRANK

Donna George Storey

I made Sean take care of registration at the inn, even though I'd booked the room. While he exchanged pleasantries with the pretty receptionist, I stood back and pretended to study the rack of brochures advertising limousine tours of the wine country, rinky-dink local museums and a geyser that was no longer so faithful after the last big earthquake. As we stepped out of the foyer, I caught the young woman studying me curiously. Obviously she hadn't yet realized that some guests prefer not to be seen.

Sean and I carried our own overnight bags back to our cottage suite, hurrying along the path through the perennial garden as if to avoid prying eyes. We closed the door behind us and exchanged a smile. The sitting room was just like the photograph online—marble fireplace, luxury sofa, furnishing that suggested both elegance and self-indulgence.

My husband headed to the bedroom.

"This has potential," he said, nodding toward the four-poster bed.

"Don't get ahead of yourself," I teased. "Why don't you go get a glass of wine or something? I need to freshen up."

He smiled. "I noticed a place that has tastings on the town square. I'll take my time."

As soon as he was gone, I promptly ran myself a bath in the champagne slipper tub. My lover, who would only come to visit me here at this inn, insisted that I be "clean" for him, which meant my armpits, legs and vulva had to be freshly shaved. If I was sloppy, he'd drag me back into the bathroom and do the job right himself.

Carefully bathed and perfumed with moisturizer, I wrapped myself in the inn's terry robe and curled up on the sofa to wait for him. Already my lower parts were feeling tingly, and my breasts ached for his touch. I ran a finger idly over my satin-smooth labia, checking for any strays. Without thinking, one finger dipped into the cleft and brushed my distended clit. I flicked it tentatively, then with more purpose.

The knock on the cottage door made me jump.

I rushed to the door.

"Eva, my dear, how good to see you after all this time," he said in his usual proper tone. It was Frank.

"Yes, it's been too long," I said, instinctively bowing my head.

He took my chin in his hand and gazed sternly into my eyes. "Is that why you're so impatient? Look at what you're wearing. Does a lady greet her guest this way?"

"I missed you so much, I thought we…" I faltered.

"Hasn't your husband been keeping the home furrow plowed?"

I swallowed. "It's never like it is with you, Frank."

His dark eyes softened. "Since you're in such a hurry, go get the bed ready. I'll join you in a few moments."

My pulse racing, I pulled back the quilt and sheets and spread out the large towel I'd brought from the bathroom. I perched myself at the edge of the bed feeling very much on edge myself. Who knew what Frank would do tonight? I was suddenly aware of the warm slickness between my legs.

Frank could make me wet before he even touched me.

Just then he sauntered into the bedroom, an impressive erection already tenting his robe. I blushed and looked away.

He sat on the bed beside me. "You have something naughty to tell me, don't you, Eva? I know that expression on your face."

My cheeks flamed brighter.

"Are you going to confess or will I need to resort to firmer means?"

I felt another gush of arousal ooze down my thighs.

"While I waited for you, I…"

"Out with it."

"I touch…touched myself."

"Indeed? Do you think of me and masturbate when you're at home, too?"

I nodded reluctantly.

Frank clicked his tongue. "Your poor bastard of a husband has no idea how depraved you are. You know you need to be disciplined for this?"

I nodded again, my heart now thumping against my ribs.

Calmly, deliberately, Frank arranged my body across the bed and tied my wrists to the bedposts with the belts of our robes.

"Now that your greedy fingers are safe from wandering into a dirty place, I'll teach you what it means to be patient."

Straddling me, Frank yanked my loose robe apart and began to kiss my breasts ever so softly for what seemed like an hour until I was squirming and moaning and juicing all over. Gradually he increased the stimulation, twisting my stiff pink nipples between his fingers, nipping them gently.

"Please, touch me. Down there," I begged.

"Patience, my dear. You're going to learn patience tonight."

He suckled my breasts some more, laughing softly at my growing distress.

Finally, I realized what I had to do. "Frank?"

"Yes, my dear."

"I'm sorry for being rude. I promise I'll wear a respectable dress next time. Pearls. I'll greet you like a proper lady."

"Yes, I want to see you in your Sunday best, Eva," he agreed, appeased at last. "Now that you've learned your lesson, we can proceed. Spread your legs." He trailed his fingers over my shaved slit, and I shuddered. "Very nice and clean today, Eva. Not like the last time when you were lazy. Do you still want me to touch you there?"

I groaned assent.

It was then he planted a slap on my tender flesh. I stiffened from the shock, but the sting was immediately followed by a wave of hot pleasure. He spanked my vulva again. This time I sighed and opened my legs wider.

"You are a wicked girl," he announced coolly. "You've deprived your lover of the pleasure of arousing you. There's only one way to control your lust. I want you to get a composition book and record all the times you masturbate while thinking of me. Describe every thought and deed in filthy, explicit detail. When we meet again, you'll stand before me naked and read the entries aloud while I decide how to punish you."

My pussy clenched so hard I whimpered and arched up against my bonds. "I prom...promise," I stuttered.

"Do you want me to fuck you now? Be honest. Isn't that why you came to the door with your tits practically falling out of that slutty bathrobe?"

"Yes, oh, yes."

Suddenly impatient himself, Frank threw off his robe, knelt between my legs and pushed himself into me in a single stroke. Tweaking my nipple just so, he began thrusting into me, with exquisite care, so I could rub my bald lips against his wiry bush.

"Tell me what a dirty girl you are," he hissed.

Panting and sweating, I babbled out the truth of my darkest desires. "I love sex. I love cocks ramming up inside me. I love getting tied up and spanked on my pussy. I love shaving myself so I can be perfectly bare all over just for you."

Frank answered each confession with a deep grunt of pleasure. He was losing it now and so was I. The prim Victorian bed squeaked beneath us. I jerked my hips up and up, desperate in my need, the knot of pleasure in my belly growing hotter and bigger until it exploded, bursting from my throat in a wail of release. Abandoning all propriety now, Frank bellowed rudely as he came into me: *fuck oh fuck Eva fuck*.

Afterward we lay in each other's arms, marveling again that each time brought something wonderful and new.

"That masturbation log is a pretty perverted idea," I said, snuggling close. "We'd better come back soon, or I'll be reading my twisted fantasies to you all night."

"Did I go too far? Be frank now." Sean grinned.

I felt another sweet twinge between my legs. "No, honey, that's your job."

RIDING
THE 5:15

Sophia Valenti

I'd noticed him before, the young man with the dark, searching eyes. Our paths had crossed occasionally in the evenings—that is, whenever I was able to get out of the office quick enough to make the 5:15 train. He'd glance my way the second I'd board the car, and then he'd keep his eyes trained on me for a long while, conveying his interest with his unyielding gaze. I'd catch him out of the corner of my eye and could never hold back my smile. I liked the attention—and our little routine. He'd stare at me patiently, appreciatively, waiting for some sort of hint, a sign that would encourage him to sidle up and talk to me during our thirty-minute ride to the suburbs. But no matter how many times our paths crossed, I never acknowledged him—until last week.

It was the evening before a long holiday weekend,

and it seemed as if everyone in the city had hightailed it out of town by midday. I rushed from my office and through the steamy streets, eager to head home. The air was thick and damp, feeling as if the city were on the verge of one of those violent summer downpours—the ones with heavy raindrops and striking claps of thunder. Electricity seemed to be already coursing through the air. Or maybe it was the sensation of my own frazzled nerves resonating within me. Either way, I soon realized I had three blissful days to unwind and indulge myself however I wanted. And that lit a spark in me, one that set me in a mood for some adventure.

By the time I descended into the station, my thin sundress was clinging to my curves, my skin hot and damp. I hurried across the empty platform, hearing an announcement that told me my train's departure was imminent. Clutching my purse, I hustled down the last few steps and into the train, the doors closing behind me a second later.

I glanced around the car, seeing that it was empty—except for one familiar passenger.

There was my handsome stranger, reclining in his seat, with his tie loosened slightly and the first few buttons of his shirt open. He appeared relaxed and as ready for the weekend as I was.

Boy, did he look good. Rather than ignoring him, I stared directly at him this time. After all of those weeks of one-sided admiration, I felt I'd earned the right. Brazenly, I let my gaze trail from his intense eyes to

his full lips and manly jaw, before taking in his broad
shoulders and legs crossed casually at his ankles. My
eyes then reversed their path, heading upward before
locking with his. His lips quirked up in a smile, and my
cheeks flushed with heat. I felt like all of my senses were
on high alert.

Feeling bold, I sat directly opposite him, and his smile
grew wider.

"Just in time. Lucky you," he said, extending his
hand. "My name's Paul."

I put my hand in his, enjoying the feeling of his strong
fingers wrapping around my palm. "Hi, I'm Maya," I
answered, my voice nearly a purr. "But it remains to be
seen how lucky I'll get."

Paul sat up a little straighter, but his easy laugh let me
know that my words didn't shock him. But what they
did do was add an extra dash of sexual tension to the
attraction that was already sparking between us.

He and I made small talk about our jobs and the
weather, politely filling the time, until the conductor
came by to check our tickets.

"This train's nearly empty," he said to us. "Enjoy the
peace and quiet. I know I will," he added before disappearing.

"Mind if I join you?" I asked, nodding toward the
seat next to him.

"Not at all," he answered, smiling wickedly as I took
my place at his side.

Reaching up to his face, I caressed his stubbled cheek

with my hand. He growled low in his throat, nuzzling my palm. I leaned in close, kissing him and inhaling his scent, enjoying the sensation of his soft lips pressing against mine. Paul threaded his fingers in my hair, tightening his grip and making me gasp into his open mouth as his tongue began to tease mine.

When our car cleared the tunnel, sunlight streamed in through the windows, and as the train picked up speed, so did we. Before long we were kissing wildly, lost in our embrace, as the train rhythmically rocked along the tracks. Paul's hands slid down my body, caressing me through my flimsy dress as he lavished my neck with kisses. Despite the train's air-conditioning, I felt red-hot inside.

When Paul's hand slid up my thigh, I moaned with longing. Not able to wait, I wriggled out of my panties, and then straddled his lap.

"This is a much better seat," I whispered.

"I'd have to agree," he said, his intense stare thrilling me to my core. I felt as if he could see into my very soul, instantly reading the depth of my desire for him.

We resumed our lip-lock as Paul brought his hand up under my dress again, finding the split of my body and using his thumb to circle my clit before flicking it gently. I was on the edge, but I needed more.

"I want you inside me—now. I can't wait," I told him in a heated whisper.

Deep down, I knew there was a chance we'd be discovered, and while that excited me, I knew it might also call an end to our game. And that was something I couldn't tolerate. I was hot and wet and desperate; there was no time to lose.

I reached into my purse to fish out a condom. Paul's face lit up with a half-cocked smile, and he hurriedly opened his pants. His erection sprang upward, and I stroked it affectionately before rolling the latex along his length. Then, with my dress billowing around us, I lowered myself onto his cock, sighing as I took him inside my body.

Paul brought a hand to my hair once more, tangling his fingers in my tresses as I began to ride him. I started off slow but increased my speed, feeling the rhythm of the train pulsing within me as we sped to our destination. Outside, the sky grew dark and fat raindrops slammed against the windows, turning the world into swirls of gray. Paul reached underneath me, his thumb once again finding my clit, and I ground against him lewdly. Working my hips, I quickly sparked my climax, biting my lip to keep quiet, while he grabbed my hips and powered his cock in and out of me. Our mouths met once more, and a few seconds later, a loud crack of thunder came, masking the sound of Paul's orgasmic groans, but I felt their vibrations in our kiss as we rode out the last spasms of our climaxes together.

They say that life's about the journey, and I'd have to agree. But the journey's even better when you have company that's as sexy as Paul.

PEACH-COLORED PANTIES

Thomas S. Roche

About four o'clock, I called Tess into my office and told her to close the door.

"Is that a new skirt?" I asked her.

She brightened. "Yes, Sir. Brand new. Do you like it?"

"Yes," I said. "Lift it. I want to see what you're wearing underneath."

She looked at me shyly, her hands dropping to the hem of her skirt—but she did not obey. Her pale face went pink, working toward crimson.

"Is this really necessary, Sir?"

"Of course," I told her. "Dress code. Remember?"

"Yes, Sir, of course," she said, toying with the hem of her slate-gray, pleated skirt. "But you've never checked before, Sir."

"Oh," I smiled. "I've checked. You just didn't know I was checking. Those little skirts you wear. You tend to forget how short they are. You bend over quite a lot for a secretary, don't you?"

She stammered, "I don't know, Sir."

"One might think you were going out of your way to flash me."

She shook her head nervously, her face reddening more deeply as her ample breasts heaved.

"No, Sir. I didn't realize I was flashing you."

"Uh-huh," I said with obvious suspicion. "You just want me to know what color panties you're wearing every single day, then?" Before she could stammer an answer, I chuckled. "Then again, it's not like I haven't encouraged you, Tess. Why do you think I keep all the client files on the bottom shelf? God forbid you should kneel to do the filing."

"Kneeling bags my stockings," said the blushing secretary. She glanced down shyly at her thighs; for the first time in weeks, the lacy tops of her nude-color stockings weren't visible. I didn't even know for sure if she had a garter belt or stay-ups!

"You were kneeling yesterday afternoon," I said with a sneer.

"That's different," she blushed. "My job duties required it. Besides, the pad under your desk is smooth. It doesn't ruin my stockings the way the carpet does."

"Well," I said. "That's reasonable. But you know the rules around here, Tess. Panties and bra must match."

"Yes, Sir," she said, still toying with the hem of her skirt. Her breath was coming quickly; her lips were parted, glistening with lip gloss and spittle.

"Since I can already see your bra," I said, "I won't ask you to open your blouse—you're half-hanging out of it, you know?"

She glanced down at her tits and bit her lip flirtatiously. Those once-milky, now-crimson mounds could be blamed almost as much as her very short skirt for my calling her in to my office. I probably wouldn't have been so obsessed with what sort of panties Tess was wearing if I hadn't spent half the morning transfixed by her upthrust mounds. The improbable sky-blue satin top into which she had crammed herself was at least a size too small. But it was her lacy bra that made me really curious. Somewhere between a millimeter and an inch of her lacy bra was visible at the edge of her plunging neckline. It was a peach-colored bra; it was not at all far from the hue of her skin.

It made her look naked.

If she was wearing peach-colored panties under her skirt, I wanted to see them.

On any other day, I'd just wait till she did her filing.

But her new skirt was far too long. She could file all she wanted; I wouldn't see a thing.

And speaking of Tess's breasts, they provided me with tangible evidence of her mounting arousal. Her nipples had gotten so hard that they showed right through her red satin top, tenting its fabric. She had been flashing those tits at me all afternoon. She had bent over to deliver me an unasked-for cup of coffee ("Just the way you like it, Sir. Hot and creamy...") or the Jackson report ("So you can see *every* detail of the case, Sir,") or the take-out menu from the Dim Sum Café downstairs ("I know you skipped lunch, Sir, and they've got *delicious buns*.") Every time she did, she made sure that she bent over, tucking her ass up high in the air and placing the document or coffee cup or whatever on my desk with a decided firmness, remembering to wiggle as she did it.

As if that wasn't enough, those nipples—which now peaked the sky-blue satin of her top so suggestively—had been in evidence at various times through her workday so far. Each time, I could see her nipples, dark beneath the rippling, suggestive texture of the nearly see-through blue blouse and the lace, tenting both.

I spent much of each workday getting acquainted with my secretary's under things—often without her "noticing" or letting on that she noticed. But today I was thoroughly transfixed by the way the peach-colored bra offset her lovely, creamy skin.

I wanted to know if she had peach-colored panties.

"Up," I told her, nodding at her skirt.

Tess said, "Yes, Sir," and raised the thing up to her waist.

My eyes went wide. My jaw dropped. I gulped.

My secretary wasn't wearing peach-colored panties.

In fact, she wasn't wearing a damn thing under that skirt. Not even pubic hair—not a whisper of it.

Her red lips twisted in a smile.

She panted slightly, obviously pleased. "I shaved this morning after you left for work," she said. "Do you like it?"

"Y-y—" was all I managed to choke out as I rose from my big leather chair. I came around the desk quickly, as Tess pirouetted and planted her perfect, bare ass on the edge of my desk.

I was on her in an instant.

I had this whole big thing planned out; I was going to chastise her for flirting with me, threaten her with some sort of civil charge of sexual harassment, blah blah blah; I had a whole huge monologue in my head, to be delivered while I bent her over my desk and gave her the spanking she so richly deserved.

But when I saw her complete absence of peach-colored panties, a spanking seemed pointless.

Instead, I kissed her hard and felt her up. Tess held her skirt up to her waist and wriggled against me. Feeling the smooth, easy access to her slicked-up sex, I dropped to my knees.

I buried my face between her smooth thighs. I licked her smooth sex and slipped my fingers up in her, working her clit and her swelling G-spot until she was ready to come.

Then I was up and ready to fuck. She got my pants open, shoving them over my hips. They dropped to my ankles. I entered my secretary easily, in one even thrust. Tess's ardor ruined yet another J. Crew dress shirt—I'm still finding buttons weeks later.

When I was in her deep, buried to the hilt, I kissed her hard, our tongues entangling as I gave her blouse the same treatment she'd given my shirt. Private practice can be murder on a married couple's bank account—because of all the ripped-off clothes.

I lowered and raised my hips till I found just the right angle—then grabbed her hair and held it tight. I looked in her eyes while I worked my cock precisely up and down, reaching between us to thumb her clit as I thrust shallowly at just the right angle—I knew it so well. Her mouth dropped open. She moaned. I gave my secretary slow, jagged thrusts—just the way she liked it, ma'am, hot and creamy. She came in a minute and a half, maybe longer. She shuddered and howled and melted into my arms while her pussy clenched me rhythmically.

I let Tess catch her breath, purring into my ear as she settled into soft, even afterglow.

Then I took my pleasure with my secretary.

It had certainly turned out to be a fruitful professional relationship. Months ago, it had become painfully necessary that my small private practice needed a part-time secretary.

Tess was, at that time, working at home as a contractor; a morning person, she was up at six and done with work before noon. When I left for work at eight or nine, she'd be locked in her office in sweats and a tank top. Afternoon, she relaxed or ran errands.

But even so, I wouldn't have suggested her for the

job if her filthy little mind hadn't gone there right off the bat—suggesting that whatever lucky young slut I hired would end up bent over my desk with great frequency.

And she certainly had—with *great* frequency.

I came with a shudder, Tess's body clutched tight to me, her legs spread wide across my desk. It was the best time we've had since my wife started working for me.

Which is why I'll never forget the day my secretary didn't wear peach-colored panties.

RESERVED

Jax Baynard

The house was one of those old summer homes on the bay: one big room with a porch and two smaller rooms off the back. It was no treat in the winter when the wind blew off the water with a damp chill and the lack of insulation made the house hard to heat, but in the warm weather the rickety house was full of charm. The view was all grandeur: an expanse of water held in the wide curve of the bay, the mountain rising from the foot of the far shore, cloaked now in the brown grasses of summer, with the darker green of oak and bay in the gullies and the lighter green of willows growing in the streambeds.

Jackson didn't own the house. He was renting. Abigail parked on the road and walked up the narrow drive. Common wrens twittered in the bushes and out in the marsh she could see an egret standing on one leg, stately, looking for lunch in the tall reeds. They were friends. They'd met, had a few beers, gone hiking. She liked him, but she wasn't sure how much. He hadn't put on the hard press. He was even-tempered, reserved. Maybe he was waiting for something. Abby didn't know; he hadn't told her. The door stood ajar. The house was quiet and cool. She didn't call out, thinking he was working outside. The house was somebody's second home. When he had time, Jackson paid the rent in labor. He cleared brush, fixed fences, replaced broken windowpanes. He liked to sit in a wooden chair in the evenings with a beer in his hand, watching the marsh and cataloguing his next round of chores.

Abby left her shoes by the door and prowled to the back rooms, curious. In summer, everyone lived mostly out-of-doors. She'd never seen the rest of the house. She was brought up short, silently, in the doorway to the bedroom. She'd found Jackson. Not the man she thought she knew—the modest East Coast geologist with the lopsided smile. This Jackson was naked and held his penis in one hand, working the shaft slowly in his tight fist. He had no hair at all on his body. Except for the hair on his head, a sandy brown, he was shaven smooth all over. And he was wearing stockings, flesh colored thigh-highs that clasped the top of his legs in lacy elastic bands. His eyes were closed. Abby stood, barely breathing. Her belly flip-flopped, the desire surprising her. Looking at the familiar face, reddish color staining his cheekbones, it was as if a finch had metamorphosed into an eagle. Not so modest, nor so reserved. He had a kink or two and that made him interesting. Her eyes went back to his cock. He moved slowly, teasing himself. Near the beginning, then, she thought. She watched the way his hand curled tight around the flesh, viscerally felt the pleasure he was giving himself and wanted it to be her hand. The thought made her go wet in a liquid rush.

He stopped moving and Abby glanced at his face. He was looking at her. Still waiting? Sweat gleamed on the delicate skin below his eyes and on his eyelashes. The grip on his cock did not slacken. "I'm not going to apologize for this," he said evenly, eyes moving to indicate the stockings. She thought it was the stockings.

"Did I say you should?" Abby asked, coming into the room. "I'm wet. I like it." She knelt down between his legs, pushing them farther apart to make room for herself. He said nothing, neither inviting nor rejecting. She ran her palms from his ankles to the tops of his thighs, burrowing her fingers under the elastic. He had them on for a reason. His fingers flexed and his cock jerked in his hand. "Do you mind?" she asked. He still did not speak. He was guarded, Abby realized, waiting to see what she would do. But his fingers opened and Abby's fingers replaced his on his cock. She squeezed firmly. He was hot and silky and slick from a little precome that emerged from the slit on the head of his penis.

All that she knew of him, Abby thought, was drift, flotsam pushed up by the tide and left on the beach. It was politeness and manners and social mores. It didn't do much for her. It made him like everyone else, nodding and smiling at the appropriate moments. But this was a man with wary blue eyes and shaved skin and stockings and a hot erection growing and throbbing in her hands. This, she wanted. She moved closer, shifting her grip to the base of his cock and taking him into her mouth. He made a soft sound, the switch from the pressure of her hand to the warmth of her mouth making him flinch. She sucked him gently, giving him time to adjust, letting him go long enough to lick and kiss her way up the thick shaft and run her tongue around the rim of the circumcised tip. She lifted her head to look at him. "Do you want this?"

"Yes," he finally spoke. "I do." He made a sound that might have been a laugh. "A lot."

Abby nodded, sucking the length of him back into her mouth, as much of him as she could take. She moved her head, pushing him to the back of her throat and breathing through her nose to keep from gagging. His breathing changed, becoming fast and uneven. His hands fisted in the sheet and she wondered if he was reluctant to touch her. Sort that out later, she thought. Or now? "Hold my head," she told him. "Move your hips." He did it with an alacrity that was gratifying. She gripped his legs with her freed hands and let him use her. She held herself immobile and he thrust his cock, hot and purplish, in and out of her mouth, hands tightening in her hair.

Her own fingers curled, pressed, making runs in the stockings, then rents, then great tears. She tangled her fingers in the material and laid scratches into the smooth skin of his thighs. Men were always hairy and this one wasn't. It excited her and she flattened her tongue on the underside of his shaft, soft, soft and wet for him to slide against. He came, stiffening in every muscle, arching beneath her. Slowly he relaxed, breathing like a bellows. Abby rested her face in the crease of thigh and groin, breathing as hard as he was, breathing in the scent of him, licking the salty taste of come from her lips. His hands, open now, rested on her head. "Jesus, Abigail," he said, something like wonder in his voice. "That was no bird-watching hike in the park."

"No," she agreed, smiling and turning her face to kiss his cooling skin. "I think that was much better."

NIGHT VISITOR

Cheyenne Blue

She comes to him in the deepest hour of the night. His bedroom door opens and there's a crack of light from the living area, swiftly extinguished as she closes the door.

He's instantly awake, eyes following her shadowy shape as she moves into the room. In the light of a thousand stars through the window, he can see she's wearing a towel wrapped around her body, tucked tightly between her breasts to hold it in place.

"Are you okay?" The words lodge in his throat, for she drops the towel.

It pools at her feet and she's naked, gloriously naked. She walks toward him, the dark patch between her thighs mysterious and beckoning. She stands by the bed and her smile is a secret, inward one. Then she's pulling back the quilt and sliding inside.

He can hardly breathe. "Thea," he says, and then more urgently, "Thea."

The words are stopped in his throat for she's kissing him as if she's falling into him, her tongue sliding into his mouth, and her hands, oh, my god, her hands, are on his body, running down his chest to his groin. She palms his cock, running her fingers along his length.

He bucks up into her hand willing her to continue, even as some befuddled part of his brain is wondering, why here, why now? They're housemates and their friendship has never included benefits—until now. But he doesn't think too hard, as her hands caress him closer to the edge. He stares up at her as she rears over him, her body gilded with starlight, dusky with shadows. She's beautiful even when she's slouching around the house in manky sweats, but naked, her short spiky hair tipped with silver, she's ethereal and otherworldly.

He has to be sure even though he fears he'll shatter the mood, so he says her name once more, and then when she remains silent, her gaze on his cock, he repeats it again.

She lifts her eyes to his face, tips her head to one side as if she's heard a whisper in the shadows and kisses him. She's not gentle; her lips mash into his and he tastes the copper tang of blood where she's caught his teeth. Without breaking the kiss, she straddles his prone body and her moist pussy is hot on his belly.

He touches her then, his hands stroking up her thigh,

dancing over her waist, fingertips grazing her nipples, and when she pushes her breast into his hand he circles, pinches lightly.

His cock prods her backside, but she seems in no hurry to impale him. So he concentrates on her pleasure—nipples, skin, and when he can no longer stand it, her pussy, slick with arousal. He wishes he could taste her, push his face between her thighs until he's as wet as she, but her legs are tight around his waist and he can't move. So he uses his fingers in light, flickering movements on her clit.

Her face is curiously distracted, as if she's only half in the moment. He feels a twinge of unease—she can't be asleep, can she? But as if she senses his concern she smiles and lays a hand softly against his cheek. He wishes she would say his name, but he's reassured by the touch.

And doubt is blown out the window as her vise grip eases and she rises, positions herself and sinks down, taking him inside her, a smooth movement, no fumbling, no hesitation.

He's wide-eyed with the ecstasy and the completion of a long-held dream. His fingers find her core once more. He knows he won't last, and he wants this to be good for her too.

He grasps her hip, urges her on, and then he's feeling her internal muscles flutter around his cock in rhythmic pleasure pulses. "Oh, god," he starts to say, but he can't continue as the pleasure is so intense. Physical feelings, yes, but they're overlaid with a veneer of caring that he's never let himself show before, not to Thea, never to her with her wisecracks and cocky, independent attitude.

As he pours himself into her, he thinks he might love her. He closes his eyes, winds the words into a tight knot so that they can't escape.

She swings off him, and the cool air caresses his cock to softness.

He opens his eyes and she's once again standing by the bed. She bends and retrieves the discarded towel.

"Stay," he entreats, holding out a hand for her to take and be drawn back to his embrace.

She turns without a word and the sound of the door closing feels like the end.

He lies and watches the numbers on the clock turn over until morning. In the hours before dawn, he's besieged by doubts: maybe he just ruined a wonderful friendship. What will she say in the morning? And he wonders, horrifyingly, what if she *was* asleep all along?

He's sitting at the counter nursing his third mug of coffee when she appears.

"Morning," she trills, and as she always does, asks, "Any more coffee in that pot?"

Not trusting his voice, he waves at the pot and she pours a mug and sits down next to him.

"You're quiet," she says, and her eyes are inscrutable over the rim of her mug. "Did you have a bad night?"

There's a sick, dark feeling in his stomach and he has to swallow hard before he can trust himself to speak. "I had a great night actually."

"Good." Her palm rests against his cheek for a fleeting moment, just as it did in the frantic dark hours past. Her voice hums with satisfaction. "So did I."

TRIPARTITE

Georgia E. Jones

I was new in town, which made me the fresh meat. It was intimidating. As soon as everyone sniffed around and took a turn they'd get bored and go back to whatever they were doing before I moved in, but I'd been through a divorce and wanted no part of it. I needed wingmen, and in Will and Adam I had them.

There was sexual attraction, to be sure. Adam glowed with it. It was the first thing anyone noticed about him because, like a boxer with a solid left hook, he led with it. He propositioned me first thing; I declined, and after that we were friends. Will was harder to read. It took him four months to ask for a hug, but when he made his interest known, there was no mistaking it. I was tempted. Extremely tempted. But I didn't want anyone to get hurt, least of all myself. Instead of friends with benefits, we became friends with attraction.

We met for drinks. We went hiking. They showed me the best places to swim and where to pick berries in the summer when the heat lay low in the thickets and there was no breeze anywhere.

In August they took me swimming at Daylight Beach. It was small and hidden and only the locals knew about it. The tourists congregated on the bigger beach to the east, noisy with kids and dogs and radios. We stayed near the water all day long and past it. It was dark when we started to hike back to the truck.

The path was thin and twisted, lined with the roots of bay and oak trees and the cinnamon-barked madrones. I stumbled twice on things they seemed to see in the dark. "Stop here," Will said, when we reached a small clearing about halfway to the truck. "The moon is coming up."

I stood, catching my breath. Days were hot on the coast, and the nights cool. I shivered, wearing nothing but a thin T-shirt over a damp bikini top. Adam saw it or felt it.

"Come here," he said, and put his arms around me. I leaned against him, grateful for the warmth, ignoring the frisson of desire that sifted through my skin and down into my belly.

"Hey," Will said softly, a protest. He came up behind me, moving closer until I was caught between the two of them. Adam was built solid and low to the ground. Will was taller, his chin resting on the top of my head. I stood still, absorbing the heat and scent of them. Adam's cock rose up, pushing against my belly. He wasn't the type to apologize and I liked it, unequivocally. I canted my hips backward, pressing my ass against Will, an invitation, and got an answer in the sweet rise of his flesh against mine. I was wearing an old cotton skirt and I lifted it in handfuls. If they thought that was a bad idea, they could tell me.

Adam sank to the ground, pulling me with him. I ran my hands across his belly before pulling down his trunks and putting my mouth on his cock. He made a strangled sound, and I sucked on him, hard, crouched between his thighs, not giving him a chance to adjust. Will lifted me to my knees, stripping off my bikini and touching me, spreading me open, nudging me with the head of his cock. He knew exactly how much sex I hadn't been having since the divorce. Then I was filled up; the hot, thick length of Will inside me and hard thrust of Adam's cock in my mouth. It was what I wanted, bone deep and mindless. I couldn't establish any sort of rhythm, clenching around Will and grinding back against him. He said something—the dark voice of a cautionary tale—and held my hips in broad-palmed hands and did it for me.

I sucked on Adam, licking him up and down, cupping his balls in one hand then taking him as deep as I could until he touched the back of my throat. Adam came first, crying out, his hands fisted in my hair. I swallowed and rested my face against his belly, feeling Will thrust harder and harder, my own pleasure rising toward orgasm, but it was going to take longer than he had, so I just tightened around him as hard as I could and held on until he came.

We lay in a warm heap of tangled limbs. I measured my breathing against theirs, first Will's, then Adam's. After a time, Will said, "She didn't come."

Adam sat up. "We'll have to do something about that."

"Let's," said Will.

Adam didn't say anything else, just picked me up and put me where he wanted me, which was straddled across his lap with my back against his chest. "I want you inside me," I said, tilting my head back on his shoulder, and he did me the favor of taking me seriously.

"Give me a minute," he said. He pressed his cock into the small of my back. He reached around and dragged his hand between my legs, smearing the wetness on his cock, then more on my nipples, then on his lips, acting generally like a man with all his favorite foods in front of him who decides not to choose one but to have them all. He lifted me and pushed inside me and I shivered all over, not from cold. It was strange, having two different cocks in quick succession. I arched, squirming on him.

"No," he said, brusque. "Hold still." And he held me down, thighs spread wide.

Will knelt between my legs and touched his tongue to my clit. He licked me all over, like he liked the taste of me, all around my clit, trying different angles until he found one that made the strong tendons in my inner thighs go weak.

Adam was whispering in my ear. "Come, come, come," and I was dying to. I was desperate to move, trying to close my thighs around Will's head, trying to move on Adam's cock, throbbing inside me, and he held me down and made me take it until I broke, spasming around him, against Will's mouth, in waves and waves for what felt like a long time.

I drifted, warm and sated. I slowly became aware that Adam had tipped my head to one side and was gnawing on the spot where my neck ran into my shoulder. "Yes," I said. "I want you to. Do it." He gasped—relief, I felt it—and began to thrust, strong and unrestrained. I gripped his thighs, the muscles flexing under my hands. Will stood up. His cock was hard from making me come and he stroked it. The moon was up, round and full. In the dim, white glow I could see his blue gaze resting where Adam moved in and out of me. I lifted a hand and Will came closer on delicate feet. I pried his fingers apart and wrapped my hand around his cock. "Now do it," I said, and he covered my hand with his and began to pump until he came.

I kept laughing on the way up the trail, drunk with love. I fell once and didn't care and after that one of them kept a hand on me. I sat between them in the truck, the heater blowing warm air on my feet. Will drove. Just before the turnoff to my place he said, "Unless you say different, you're coming to the cabin." They shared an old cabin in the pines above the bay.

I didn't say anything.

Inside, they took my clothes off together, one piece at a time, and rolled me under the covers. The bed was big and soft and I sighed, closing my eyes. "We've worn her out," Will said.

"She'll be fine," Adam said, and he had the right of it. I reached for Will, curling my fingers around the muscle of his forearm at the widest part, where it tapers down to the wrist. "Will this be awkward in the morning?"

He dropped a kiss at the corner of my mouth. "Only if coffee makes you feel awkward, sweetheart," he said.

Adam pressed a kiss to my temple. "We'll be in the other room if you need anything."

I could hear them in the next room, maybe talking about what had happened, maybe just talking like people who can spend all day together and still have something to say to each other at the end of it.

I was naked. I wanted to stand up and go to them and spread myself across their laps and ask for more. But my eyes wouldn't open. My body wouldn't move. I lay quietly in the bed and listened to the sound of their voices, the low murmur of water falling over stones.

LIFT A FINGER

Jeremy Edwards

It's Friday night. Exhausted from her workweek, Glenda intends to enjoy a completely lazy evening alone.

She's a little horny, frankly. But she doesn't even want to lift a finger to gratify herself. It's too much effort. All she wants is a peaceful night.

No, she tells herself once again, as she studiously ignores the clinging caress of her underwear, she isn't going to lift a finger to spread her lower lips—to stimulate those patient nerves or exercise those dormant muscles. She's simply not going to bother. Not tonight.

She's restless down there in her knickers, though, she can't deny it. She's watching TV, but her pussy's itch for attention keeps *getting* her attention, through a game show and another...until, almost involuntarily, her hand drifts lazily between her legs, while she watches a sitcom and tries to focus on her glass of wine.

And now that her hand has somehow made it to her pussy, her precious inertia favors keeping it there. So she lets her fingers lie comfortably upon her panties, but she vows to disregard the tiny throb of her clit against the inert heel of her hand.

The subtle grinding motion of her hips, under the cozy flannel throw, is relaxing at first. It isn't anything she's planned on: it has simply begun to happen while she's been zoning out on the couch, her hand in her crotch.

Soon, though, the pivoting of her hips has taken on an urgency that starts to distract her from her program— and from her resolve to be passive. She answers the petitioning of her hips with soft, yet indisputably deliberate, strokes to her pussy. Then, before she knows it, a lone finger is exploring the edge of her gusset and the tender, moistening flesh beyond.

As the next sitcom rolls, Glenda is thoroughly luxuriating under her sofa throw, unabashedly savoring the horniness she'd earlier shrugged aside. She spreads her legs wide to let her heated pussy radiate, displaying herself to the tight, complicit audience of cotton blanket. Then she slams her thighs closed again, to let her diamond-hard clit tingle where she squeezes herself together. She repeats these maneuvers, over and over, until she's ready to burn straight down through the sofa.

Long before her last television program concludes,

Glenda finds herself parading around her living room, her fingers frantically busy inside her underwear. She diddles herself over to the table, then back toward an armchair. She returns to the sofa and pauses there, putting one leg up on the cushions to finger herself deeper.

She ruts herself against the cheeky corner of another couch—then briskly moves away in a lewd waddle, her palm cupped over her clit, rubbing hard. The TV audio babbles irrelevantly under her moans.

She can't make up her mind where to have her climax, and so she simply wanders, an itinerant living-room masturbator, until the inevitable overtakes her in the middle of the floor.

There she sinks into a knee bend and howls to the ceiling, as a hot wave of undiluted release boils through her frame. Her lifted fingers stretch her pussy open like raw daybreak and twist her clit into fire.

STOPOVER

A. D. R. Forte

He listens while I explain. I'm a road warrior. One of that special breed. Two, three hundred days a year living on restaurant fare; flying double, triple platinum. An existence so bizarre that even in so-called downtime, I have to feel the asphalt under my tires, miles flying by as I go.

Go, and go, and go. Different places, different faces, another night somewhere else I don't belong. Some hotel room echoing with the ghosts of ten thousand strangers, picking up my echoes for a night or three or five until I'm gone again.

Always on the road for money and for love. It's why I'm here now: crappy diner with fluorescent lighting and blue plastic booths, the best this town has to offer.

Any port in a storm though, and boy is it a storm

out there. Enough to run even me off the road, mangle my tire against broken debris sloshing along the asphalt. Fate telling me to stop so that he could find me. With his pretty brown eyes and his blue-checkered shirt, coming out of the dark like a knight in a shining tow truck.

Not that I'm looking for a knight to rescue me. Not at all. I'm out there looking for adventure, for freedom, for the next big thing. Or maybe I'm looking for danger.

Danger. The kind you can't find tied down safely where people know your face. The kind that happens in hotel rooms behind paper-thin walls, sound bleeding through all through the wee hours of the night when decent people are asleep.

Not that I'd ever dare ask anyway, even in those places where the girls *and* boys come cheap and nobody checks ID. Where if you've got American green, anything's for sale. How does that song go? It makes a hard man humble? But not for me.

I never rock the boat, never tempt fate. I just keep hoping somehow...somewhere...

Why am I thinking it would be him anyway? Just because his eyes are the softest shade of brown and he towed my car for free. Called up his mechanic buddy and made him promise to fix the piece of crap by noon, offered to drop me off at a motel. Expecting nothing in return: money or otherwise. Even though by now I've seen his gaze stray more than once. Not obviously, not so I'd be offended. Still a Southern gentleman, even in jeans and flannel.

A gentleman isn't what I need.

But a stranger is.

And he nods like he understands, like he gets it, a knowing something in that gaze. But he can't possibly. Can he?

Because I barely understand it myself.

I slide the scratched plastic key through the lock, surprised this so-called motel even has something so modern.

"Best you're gonna get 'round here," he said when he dropped me off at the lobby, apology in his voice. As if he wanted it to be something better. But I smiled and told him it was just fine.

Now I open the door, go inside, wedge a shoe between door and frame. And my heart beats much too fast.

I turn on the bedside lamp, take in patches of worn carpet, scuffs and scratches all over the corner desk, the coarse blanket on the bed, its off-olive shade hiding age and use. I drop my bag in a corner and my other shoe, and the crumpled bill from the diner falls out of my purse while I listen to the air conditioner hum like a factory and I think...I think this place is perfect.

I hear him come in. I don't turn around.

He pulls my arms behind me and pushes me to the bed. Ties them with something rough, could be rope, but I'm too busy breathing. Too busy panicking. Am I sure? Really sure?

I don't know, but I don't give myself a choice. And

I've asked him not to give me one either.

So afraid he'll do what I've asked.

More afraid that he won't.

I lie on my stomach, hands bound, nose full of the stale smell of the blanket, and feel him lift my skirt. His hands grip my thighs, push them apart, and through my panties his finger strokes my crotch. I hear him breathing hard.

Slowly, he pulls the panties down, stuffs them in my mouth. I gag at the cloth in the back of my throat, something instinctive telling me it shouldn't be there, and I feel him hesitate. But I shake my head.

No. Go on. Let's do this now, before I start thinking. Before I lose my nerve.

He makes a little noise as if he doesn't quite believe this, before he flips me over. If only he knew, I don't believe it either. Why am I here? Why am I doing this?

But I don't have answers. All I know is that it has to be here, with him, in this small-town, godforsaken motel room or else it won't ever be. And I want, I want it so badly.

Brown eyes alight with pleasure as he unbuttons my shirt and unhooks my bra. Squeezing creamy flesh between thick, strong fingers, nails still stained with car grease. Bared teeth on my nipple, pulling at the flesh until I moan. Flicking the dusky red flesh with his tongue, his finger. While I pant and stare at what he does. Feel my muscles clench, thighs wet with sweat and need.

Yes, I do want this. In the very worst way.

He takes my skirt off and spreads my legs wide.

"Oh, babe." As he touches me. One leg between mine, leaning over me, his denim rough against my naked skin. Fingers rubbing my clit and the folds of my slit. Now gently, now rough. Never letting me get a grip on the sensation to where I can handle it and master it. Keeping me helpless.

Faster and faster. He won't let me close my legs; won't let me twist away. I'm flung open and at the mercy of lust. At the mercy of *him* as he watches my crotch.

As he jiggles his fingers on my touch-hungry clit.

As my breath comes shorter and my heartbeat races madly out of time.

As I feel the heat across my chest.

I know what comes next and I can't stop it to save my modesty. To save my pride...

Oh, but he smiles when he sees me come.

Panting and writhing and wordlessly begging for more. Burning up with shame and pleasure and trembling all over. Every helpless twitch of my muscles that I can't hide.

No one's ever watched me like that before.

I see him unbutton his jeans. God, I'm not ready— but *he* is, and I want him.

He lies over me, smelling of cars and rain and coffee and sweat. Grips my hips hard and drives into me, grunting when I arch and grind against his cock. Yanks the panties from my mouth to kiss me.

Tongues twisting wet all over each other. Lips bruising against teeth.

He lifts my legs up in the air and flesh slaps against flesh. Dirty rhythm. I scream as loud as I can, hoping there's somebody to hear. To know I'm being fucked like this, to know I'm loving it.

And to envy *me*.

"I'll pick you up when the car's ready," he says behind me, loosening my bonds.

"Don't," I whisper through dry lips.

He hesitates.

"Please."

He drops my hands, still trapped by rough strands of rope, leaving me to free myself finally once he's gone. He kisses my shoulder, puts his face into my hair for a moment, breathing me in before he leaves and walks out of my life for good. Because once I check out, this whole night is history.

At least, I think so.

I lie still, and the door clicks closed. He's gone and here I am alone. Used and so tired, cum still sticky on my ass and crotch. I crawl under the rumpled blanket to sheets smelling of cheap detergent, ignore the voice that tells me to shower.

In the morning I'll wash it off.

Scrubbed clean and decent again, I'll pack up and be on my way. Clumsily, I turn off the lamp and remember I forgot to tell him "Thank you."

Blind, in the dark, I wriggle and twist my hands until the rope slips off my wrists, leaving behind the memory of knots and fear and sex. I never leave loose ends hanging, never move on without closing the deal. Or minding my manners.

I toss and turn and feel his cock again. His tongue in my mouth. His hands on my flesh.

This place is cheap, free coffee and bagels, good place to stop for a night.

So I suppose I might be back.

Just passing through.

THE POINT OF LEAST RESISTANCE

Saskia Walker

Joe paces the floor, and every step illustrates one thing—he's in control. I, on the other hand, am not. But I can't let him know that. Not yet.

Instead I look at my lover's broad back as he walks away from me, hating the distance it puts between us. What I want is his body against mine, hard, possessive and unrelenting.

The way he looks, so easy in himself, so strong, leaves me awestruck. It always does. His ripped T-shirt is stretched taut over his shoulder blades. The belt on his jeans emphasizes how low they are hanging on his narrow hips—low enough that one finger latched over the belt could ease those jeans down if I wanted to, and I was able. My body thrums with expectation at the very thought of it, but my hands are tied and strung up above my head, leaving me unable to pursue the suggestion that is getting me so hot.

Joe glances back then looks me up and down. I feel more than naked, I feel raw under his scrutiny. My nipples sting as much from his stare as from the pegs that nip them. Eventually, he comments. "You wanted this."

The accusation burns.

I squirm, shifting my weight from foot to foot, my fingers meshing to stop me from working against the rope wrapped around my wrists. The movement makes my clit pound, a maddening sensation, especially because my clit is currently contained by a peg that holds my pussy lips closed at their apex. Sweat breaks out on my skin. I'm close to coming as it is and Joe has barely touched me.

"Yes, I did...want this." Even though it's hard for me to endure it when he owns me this way—when I resent the need to surrender—we are at our most intense this way, closer than ever.

He lifts his brows. "So, why the hesitation...the uncertainty?"

He was pressing me to say more than I could right then. Besides, he knew why.

I glare at him, furious, challenging him back in turn. I want him to break my resistance but I can't say it aloud, and Joe knows that.

His nonchalance is unbearably arousing. To the casual onlooker it might suggest callous disregard. It was anything but that. Joe knows me inside out, better than

I do, and he knows this easy-handed domination of his pushes me along until I'm right at the edge—desperate and ready to beg for him to use me.

"You're a strong woman—"

"I am."

He smiles when I interrupt him. It's a dark smile, echoing his power.

"But you're..." He steps closer and glances up, looking pointedly at my tied wrists. "You're a bit tied up and helpless right now, aren't you?"

I hang my head, acknowledging defeat. My heart is pounding, expectation and longing making me crazy.

That's when he moves in.

One finger under my chin makes me his.

"What do you need?"

Arousal dampens my inner thighs, the pulse at my center pounding demandingly. Humiliation swamps me but there's no going back, not now. "I need you to... handle me. To take control of me."

"And then?"

My head drops again. "To fill me."

My voice is scarcely above a murmur, but he hears me.

"You look particularly beautiful," he comments, one hand moving to the peg on my pussy, "when you beg." He releases the peg.

The pain only increases in the moment of sudden release, leaving me gasping for air. It's dizzying, bound up with pleasure as that pain is.

I hear the sound of his zipper. It makes me wilder still, desperate for his hardness inside me. "Please, Joe."

He unpegs one nipple then the other, casting the pegs aside.

"Oh, fuck." Sensation burns in the peaked flesh as I try to adjust. I'm shaking from arousal and have to grip the rope overhead tighter still to stop myself from buckling.

Lifting me around the hips, he wraps my legs around his waist, encouraging me to lock myself there. I swing into position and my pussy splays against the bough of his erection. He rubs it there, bringing me to my first climax with his cock hard against my clit.

Then, he's inside.

"Crazy girl," he comments, thrusting deeply in and out, fucking me with determination. "Was it so hard to beg?"

I toss my hair back, high on the rush. "Yes, and you damn well know that!"

He grins then shifts and starts moving me back and forth on his cock, holding me easily with his hands under my buttocks, forcing me to give over all control to him. "There's nothing quite like seeing my proud woman brought to her knees and begging for what only I can give her."

How can I not love that? My legs lock tighter around his hips and I squeeze him hard with my inner muscles, elated when he groans in response.

"Careful now," he warns, "or I'll have to find another way to restrain you."

I lean closer and kiss his mouth, hungrily, showing him I want that, I want it all. I moan when his cock swells inside me, inhaling sharply as I feel his orgasm build. His cock arches against the sensitive front wall of my sex. I clamp on him, milking him off, as I come.

He staggers slightly in the aftermath, but still holds me safe.

"One day we'll reach the point of least resistance," he comments, later, as he unties my wrists and carries me to the bed, "but I hope it's not too soon, I do love it when you put up a struggle."

As soon as he lowers me to the bed I swipe at him, slapping him on the arse, hard. "Cheeky bastard."

Joe pounces, of course, but he doesn't chastise me for my reaction. Instead he stares down at me with affection in his eyes then kisses me. Because he knows me so well, and I know he's everything I want.

MISDIRECTION

Victoria Janssen

D amn it, we've got to get out of this somehow," Mil said, pacing the sealed white chamber. "And no, I do *not* have any handy explosives tucked in my pocket." To his right, a port twice the size of his head displayed the alien planet below. The *wrong* alien planet. His hyperspace navigation had turned out to be completely inadequate to their needs.

Lenora lounged against the opposite bulkhead, staring up at what was, despite its bizarre design, clearly a monitor: bulbous orange pods followed their every move and vibrated with each word they spoke. She said, "You might as well sit down. There's no hurry *now*."

He snarled. "If you recall, they've got our ship. The only thing we possess. The only way we have to stay ahead of our former employers."

"These aliens haven't hurt us."

Yet, Mil thought.

As if she'd heard his thought, Lenora made a face at him and said, "There *is* a way out. Demonstrate the human mating ritual, and they let us go."

Mil threw himself into the only available chair, which was pulpy and green, and fumed.

Lenora sauntered over to him.

Mil eyed her, suspicious. "They aren't controlling your mind, are they?"

"No," Lenora snapped. He didn't care if he had annoyed her; it was a perfectly reasonable question, under the circumstances. She sat on the lumpy arm of the chair and traced the rim of his ear with her fingertip. He batted her hand away. She tangled her fingers in the hair at the back of his neck, tugging gently. She had nice hands. Skilled. Also soft. She—

"Stop it," he said. "I can't believe you're even considering giving in to them."

"Can you think of a better way to make them let us go?"

"Several ways. But I *still* don't have any handy explosives in my pockets, so…"

She grinned, trailing her finger down his throat. He felt his pulse thump against her warm fingertip.

He vaulted out of the not-chair. "They're *watching* us."

"You do want to get out of here?" She rocked forward on her toes and kissed him.

It wasn't at all the carnal assault he'd expected. When she pulled back, he sighed. "But—" His words were cut off when she kissed him again, warm and sweet.

She leaned forward until the tip of her nose bumped his. "Yes?"

He couldn't see anything but her brown eyes. "There must be another option."

"Must there?" She lunged.

"Lenora! Stop it!"

He had no idea what he was doing on the deck. No, he did know, but he wasn't sure how she had put him there, flat on his back.

Lenora's warm weight pressed into his cock as she straddled him. "You're not being helpful. I want out of here," she said. "And you know this won't hurt."

He scowled. "Well, the hell with it."

"With what?"

"I don't know. Dignity."

She grinned at him, the mischievous grin that was his secret favorite. She leaned forward and kissed him in earnest. His reluctance steamed away within seconds. Moments later, his hands were firmly gripping her arse, and she was muttering into his ear. "You *sure* you don't have any handy explosives tucked in your—"

"*You* did this to me," he said, in mock annoyance. "You broke it, I think."

Lenora dissolved into shaking peals of laughter, entirely satisfying, even through clothing. "Do you have a spanner?"

"You'll have to improvise," he said.

Lenora's grin turned devilish. Her hands swept out and grabbed his wrists, pinning his arms far from his sides. He stayed where she had put him, obedient for the nonce.

She swiftly bared his chest, but when he moved, she stopped him with a touch. "If you like," he said. He hadn't thought about it in detail before now, but he could see how Lenora might be one who preferred to take charge. He was willing to let her, so long as he had his turn later. Later?

She unfastened his trousers, a delicate maneuver. Mil winced, and then held still, thinking of cold empty space.

When she licked gently around the crown of his erection, realization struck. The aliens didn't know what to expect. The two of them could have danced on their toes, and it would not have made a speck of difference to—

Never mind.

The square root of fifty-seven is seven point five-four…nine-eight. And its sine is point eight-three-eight-seven, and its cosine is point five-four-four-six…no, not good enough at all. Eighty-nine squared is seven thousand, nine hundred and twenty-one, which has a cosine of point nine-nine-nine-eight. No, that's far too rhythmic. How about three, lovely three, prime three, the square root of three is one point seven-three-two-one…

Good-bye, higher brain functions, he thought. *Will she respect me in the morning...will she shoot me in the morning?* And then he could no longer think at all, the hot, tight suction of her mouth so painfully sweet that he thought he would scream with the pain or the sweetness; then he was coming in hard bursts that seemed to burn all the way up his spine.

When he could see again, he realized that Lenora was laughing, but coughing at the same time. He couldn't think why. That wasn't usual.

Lenora rubbed her face with the tail of his shirt. He couldn't see what she was doing, but she was *still* laughing. Drowsily, he asked, "What's so funny?"

She collapsed against him, her soft cheek landing on his chest, warm puffs of her breath stroking his bare skin. He gathered her closer. At last she said, with one final throat-clearing, "Sorry. I miscalculated."

Surely she hadn't heard him spouting mathematics— no, she couldn't have. "What do you mean?"

The question made her laugh again, breaking up her sentence. "Not...your fault...never heard of anything like..."

"*What?*"

"It...it...missed...my throat. It...came out...my nose." Lenora shrieked with merriment, slapping his leg in her enthusiasm.

No. Mil covered his face with his hand. Every millisecond had been recorded indelibly by an alien space station. On top of that, he might have hurt his...well, his closest friend. "Damn it! I'm so sincerely sorry. I promise I'll make it up to you."

"It's all right. Really. Very memorable." Delicately, she scraped her nail across his nipple and grinned.

He shuddered deliciously and stroked her cropped hair. He raised his voice. "We demonstrated! Now open the door!"

Nothing happened.

Lenora wriggled upward until her face was nestled against his neck. "Really, I haven't had that much fun in years."

"Don't be sarcastic. *The door isn't opening.*"

"You worry too much."

Mil took a deep breath and sat up, pulling her with him. He yelled, "Let us out! Now!"

A strangely accented voice boomed, "We have allotted precisely three segments for the human mating ritual. Only a portion of one segment has been stored. Please provide further demonstrations of the human mating ritual. You will be released when the specified time has passed."

Silence. Then Lenora snickered. "You said you would make it up to me. Get to work."

He unfastened the collar of her jacket. "This time, I promise I won't miscalculate."

SWEET AND SPICY

Kat Watson

In my hazy sleep-drunk state, I wonder if I should open my eyes or pretend I'm still asleep.

Maggie shifts against me, wiggling one of her legs between mine. My muscles ache and protest, bringing memories of the night before. The biting. The licking. The coming. The love.

As I wake up a little more, I keep my eyes closed and fight the smile that wants to spread across my face. Her body is in front of me, lush curves of her breasts against mine, and the smooth skin of her hips kisses my own. Soft, even breaths escape her mouth and warm my cheek. Blankets surround us, keeping our bodies cocooned in our private haven inside of her bedroom, her house.

"I want to play a game," she whispers at my ear, clearly able to see right though my feigned state of sleep.

"I'm going to put my hand between your legs and we'll see how long I can spank you with my other hand until you're wet."

I recognize the statement as similar to something I read once and smile.

She slides her slim arms underneath mine, pressing our bodies tightly together. The tips of her fingers play in the hair at the nape of my neck as she kisses me intently, with certainty and passion and confidence. The kind of confidence I wish I could wear. She scrapes her teeth lightly against my neck as her fingers wrap around my hair, tugging once before she pulls away slightly. The air that gets sucked into the blankets when she moves to sit up combines with her words swirling in my brain and makes me shiver. I open my eyes.

"Please."

I'm begging with my eyes, with everything I have, praying and hoping she isn't teasing me, as she's prone to doing. She answers with a smile, relieving my fears.

We're both naked, having exhausted ourselves together the night before. We demand so much of each other and drain ourselves of everything. There's never an ounce of pleasure or effort left in either of us, having given and taken so fiercely.

With her help—touching and guiding and teasing me on the way—I'm quickly bent over her lap. She moves her fingertips to play over the flesh of my pussy before she begins, stroking and pinching my lips, and I think this game won't last very long; surely she can tell I'm already wet from her words, her body, everything about her. I worry that I'm going to be too wet too fast, bringing an end to our game before it really begins.

Still, she proceeds, and her fingers rest against my pussy. She moves her fingertips in tight circles against my clit. I want to protest at how unfair it is, how she's not even following her own rules, but when the sting begins as her first spank lands, I'm flying, lost in the air above us.

She shifts and moves her other hand beneath me. At first, I think it's so she can support me and hold me in place, but it becomes clear that it's so that her fingers can glide in and out of me. She fucks me as deep as she can from the angle she's at, making me squirm and moan. *Unfair,* my brain chants again, against my body's sheer hope that she'll continue even though she's already made me wet. Swollen and achy. Full of need for her.

"Already?" she says with a half chuckle.

My heart sinks, thinking our game is surely over. I slide into feelings of shame at my own inability to better control the way I respond to her. My body automatically begins to pull away, an instinctual need to curl into myself taking over, but her hands steady me. Ground me. Hold me in place, in every sense.

I'm surprised by the even sharper sting of her wet fingers against the swell of my ass, and the sensation makes me gasp. Her continued attention is only part of the shock; the swirling mix of pleasure and pain make up the rest. My eyes close so I can focus on the sensations.

She takes turns landing her palms and fingers against my ass in sharp spanks. Sometimes she smacks directly on the round swell, which makes me squirm, thankful for her attention. Sometimes, it's a sting in the areas with less padding, making it hurt more, but still I am thankful. I love them both, love the distinct way it feels if she's using the tips of her fingers to make it sting, or if she's used her entire hand to impact against my body, making the burn deep and hot.

I lose count of the number of spanks she's given, grateful she hasn't required me to keep track so I can focus only on the pleasure and heat building. The fingers she has inside of me wiggle and play, provoking more wetness and sounds, from the source and from my mouth.

She continues this torture, which really isn't, until I'm writhing. We're moving in time with each other, her hands synchronized and rhythmically bringing me higher. She's spanking and fucking and flicking and pinching, and dear god, did she somehow grow more hands? I can't keep track of her movements as she pushes and pushes, and I'm suddenly on the brink of my orgasm. I try hard to shift my focus and hold it at bay, needing more of her.

My head is heavy, neck resting against her legs, and I'm kind of nuzzling her as she loves and gives to me. Without thinking, I bite her calf—not hard, just a nip. Just a thank-you. Just a *please, don't fucking stop*.

She doesn't stop, but she does laugh very lightly,

and it's a much-needed reassurance. She knows me well enough to know these nonverbal cues. Her palm lands even harder and I bite back another loud moan. Now she's in the moment, and I know if I look up into her face, I'll find concentration mixed with passion. This is when Maggie is her most gorgeous, although she's always beautiful. It's a shame I can't see her, can't watch her deepest in her element.

She strikes harder against my skin. I imagine the pink blossom, imagine the way my skin swells infinitesimally in its attempt to reach out for her. Small noises of exertion come from her, mixed with soft moans and needy breaths. Her knees part farther, her body seeking contact with mine, and I gladly shift to provide it. Her pussy is wet against my outer thigh. The very first lift of her hips and she exhales in a gorgeous, erotic sigh, and I'm conflicted about focusing on pleasuring her or the pleasure she's bringing me.

She moves her hand, fingertips again reaching to my clit, and lands several quick, stinging slaps directly on top of it. They make the throb swell, and everything intensifies. I'm moments away from coming, whether from the hand she's spanking me with or the one that's fucking me, it doesn't matter.

The spanking stops, both of her hands preoccupied with bringing me only pleasure now, and my whole body starts to tighten. *Now, now, now,* my brain repeats, and I let go.

As if I had a choice.

I come hard, harder than I can remember ever coming in my life. Loud, foreign noises leave my mouth, and I am powerless. Boneless. Bodiless. I can hear her, too, her wetness slipping and sliding, and her muscles tighten beneath me as she gasps, coming against me.

Once I can think again, I realize I'm panting, my body desperate for the air it was deprived of when I began to crest into my orgasm. For a brief moment, I'm embarrassed at the way I lost all control over myself. Usually, even when I come, it's controlled and quiet. This time, it was wild abandon and reckless passion. Loud, both of us, our voices, our bodies together. There was nothing at all controlled about it, and I smile wide.

I think about how my whole body will be sore later, especially my ass, but it will be a good sore. The kind of sore that will make me smile even wider. I know Maggie will take every opportunity to remind me, remind us both, of our morning. She'll press me against the counter in the kitchen, her hands wrapping around my waist and sliding down to pull against hot, pink skin. When we're out in public and we sit at a table for dinner, she'll smirk at me, knowing.

When my breathing has slowed to match hers, I curl up on her lap a bit, needing her reassurance. She pulls me to her, and we're stretching and sliding against each other as we spread out our limbs. We move to the pillows, tangled and wrapped in each other and it's perfect. Just like she is. Just like we are.

WORKING UP A SWEAT

Heidi Champa

The sky filled with angry black clouds. She circled the gray path, her feet hitting the asphalt in near unison to his. She heard his heavy breathing next to her, saw his firm legs flexing with each step. They ran at the same time nearly every day, but they never really spoke. A few mumbled greetings here and there, but no real conversation. She always wanted to say something to him, even if it was just the tiniest bit of small talk. But she never had the courage to speak to her hot running partner. She told herself he was too young, too cute, too much for someone like her.

The first time she had seen him was a coincidence, a scheduling conflict pushing her workout away from its usual time. After that first run, she permanently moved her running time to coincide with his. *Someday*, she thought. Someday she would say just the right thing and they would run off into the sunset together. When the sun actually came back out, of course.

They ran in step for a few feet, but then he looked at her and smiled, pulling ahead. She pushed herself forward, regaining the edge from him. They went back and forth for nearly a lap, pushing each other along. As they rounded the last turn, she felt the large, wet raindrops falling on her face. The skies opened, pouring down rain. Not breaking stride, she looked up into the black clouds and heard the thunder in the distance.

Picking up the pace, she started running to the nearby picnic area, getting under the roof as the worst of the storm was coming. After a few moments of being exposed to the elements, the rain had soaked her completely. He was right behind her, following her to the relative safety of the pavilion. When he emerged from the rain, he was sodden, his face red with exertion. He leaned against the brick wall that closed in one side of the building.

She took in the bulk of his frame, the fact that he towered over her, even more so now that they were still. He took his water bottle from his jacket pocket and drank noisily. She stood by the old, wood picnic tables, catching her breath, staring out into the sheets of water falling from the roof. The drops, hitting the ground fat and heavy, were already making puddles, their rhythmic cadence filling the air. She always loved the smell of the rain, and as she took a series of deep breaths, her nose filled with the scent of wet earth. She stole a quick look at her running partner, his eyes already on her as she regained her composure.

He surprised her by holding out his drink, and she walked toward him, reaching for it without much hesitation. He looked into her eyes, holding her gaze as the plastic bottle slipped to the ground, his hand circling her wrist. His grip was tight, but it didn't hurt that much. The slight pinch of her skin under his grasp sent a fizzling shot of heat to her pussy. Her heart started its crazy beat all over again, the pounding almost as fast as it had been during her exercise.

His smile seemed to be the same one she had seen many times before on the track. But there was an edge to it, a flicker of desire behind his eyes that she hadn't noticed before. She knew it was now or never, or at least that was what it felt like in the moment. With a boldness she had never possessed, she took another step toward him, backing him up to the wall and pressing him into the bricks with her body. Resting her hands on his muscled chest, she eased the length of her body to his. His arms enclosed around her, and she felt their weight on the small of her back. She reached up and pulled his head to her, kissing him firmly on the lips, tasting his sweaty, salty flavor.

She felt his big hands push underneath her clammy shirt, as his tongue slid deeper into her mouth. The fabric of her wet sports bra was pushed aside, replaced by the rough softness of his thumbs sliding over her erect nipples. She reached her hand into his shorts and felt his hard cock, pulsing gently as she squeezed his length. His hands fell away as she sank to her knees in front of him, pulling his shorts down his thighs. She looked up into his eyes before taking him deep into her throat.

He ran his hands through her hair, pulling her down onto his shaft. She slowed him down, teasing him with her tongue. She swirled it over the head, feeling its velvet smoothness between her lips. Moving her hands along his muscular thighs, she felt his cock twitch and grow inside her mouth. Rewarding his patience, she pushed him all the way to the back of her throat. She felt his knees buckle slightly as she eased up and down the full length of his cock. Each time she pulled back, she let her lips slip over the sensitive ridge of the head, before sinking all the way to the base. He groaned, just as another round of thunder rang out above them. She looked up at him, licking the head of his cock, when he suddenly pulled her up to her feet, and pushed her back onto the picnic table.

He knelt in front of the table, pulling her shorts down, leaving them to dangle around one of her feet. He dragged his thick finger down her slit, feeling her warmth. He parted her lips with his thumbs, exposing her wetness, her eagerness. She looked up at him, waiting to feel his hot tongue on her, squirming at his hesitation. He stayed still, content to stare at her, drinking her in with his eyes. Lightning in the distance momentarily caught her attention, just as his tongue swept over her wet pussy.

His finger teased her cunt, gently circling it as he trapped her clit in his mouth, sucking it gently between his lips. He pushed one finger deep and then two, stretching her with his twisting thrusts. Her hips rolled with his tempo, pushing herself hard against his mouth. The wind picked up, and she felt the cool air rush over her, as he brought her closer and closer to the edge. Adding her moans to Mother Nature's voice, she bucked hard against his slowly moving fingers.

He stood up and pulled her off the table. Turning her around, he pushed her roughly forward, leaning her over the picnic table. Looking back at him, she watched as he rolled the condom over his hard cock, his face the picture of concentration. She felt his hard cock teasing her, rubbing her swollen pussy lips. She pushed back against him, desperate to have him inside her, but he stayed just far enough away to leave her wanting. Pressing his hands into her hips, he held her for a few moments more, before giving her what she wanted.

His thick cock stretched her open even farther, and she felt herself give way as he slid all the way inside her. Slowly, he eased out and in, feeling the heat of her all along his shaft, her moisture drenching him as the rain had. His fingers found her hard nipples, squeezing them roughly through her shirt. He sped up, until he was pounding her nearly off her feet, his power overwhelming her. She pressed her hands into the wood of the table, as she tried to steady herself against his relentless thrusts. She felt her thighs start to twitch, her pussy start to tighten as his hands returned to her hips to hold her steady.

Sensing that she was close, he eased his pace, thrusting slowly, methodically, deeply. Pressing her forehead into the table, she moaned through her clenched teeth, rocking back to meet him. When he reached down and stroked her clit, rubbing it between moist, rough fingers, she lost it. Screaming out into the storm, she felt all her muscles contract at once, wringing her orgasm out of her. Leaning on the table for support, she let him fuck her through her quaking.

Her juices covered him, her soft, throbbing wetness sending his cock into convulsions. The force of his climax caused him to lean forward against her, kissing and biting at her neck. He felt her tiny aftershocks, as he continued pumping into her, his broken moans going right into her ear. His final thrust hit her deep, forcing a strangled moan from her throat just barely heard over the thunder. He collapsed on top of her, his weight pressing her back down onto the table.

Both of them were breathing heavily, spent. He stood up as the rain was beginning to die down. She straightened up, pulling her shorts up from the heap on the ground. She looked up at him and pulled him in for one final kiss. As he moved away from her, he hesitated for a moment. He smiled, his deep voice hitting her ears for the first time.

"Thanks for the workout. I'll see you tomorrow."

Before she could respond to his words, he took off

down the path. As he rounded the corner, a glimmer of sun peeked out from behind the clouds, just in time to start its descent to the horizon.

COME AS YOU ARE

Andrea Dale

We're going to try something new," I said, keeping my tone conversational as if I were discussing a recipe I'd seen in a magazine, as if I weren't standing behind Connor and fastening cuffs around his wrists.

His fingers flexed, as if he wanted to fist his hands, but he knew better than to do that. His knuckles brushed the curve of his high, tight ass, and I paused for a moment to enjoy the sight of the rich green leather against his pale skin and, below, the fading red stripes he'd received from the crop not long ago.

I liked watching his ass flex when I cropped him.

"Something new," I repeated, moving to stand before him. His head was bowed, as was appropriate. I was tempted to tuck my forefinger under his chin, nudge his gaze up so I could watch his expression. But I suspected

I'd see his reaction in another way. "No fucking," I said. "No hands. Just your mouth on me, making me come."

His reaction was so swift it made me smile. His cock, half-hard already because of the cuffs, surged as if it had a mind of its own.

Connor loved to go down on me. Loved to worship my clit, my slick lips; loved to taste me and lick me and suck and nibble until my thighs clenched and I pulsed and sometimes I squirted. He loved my scent, the feel of me on his mouth, and it was something I frequently exploited, to both our delight.

But this...this would be different. Because usually afterward, we fucked—more often than not, with me on top, enjoying a few more orgasms before I allowed Connor his release. (Well, no matter what position I chose, the latter was true.)

What I wasn't going to tell him—not just yet—was that I wanted to see if he could come just from the pleasure of going down on me.

Because I wanted to see how quickly he'd figure that out on his own.

Now, his hands securely bound, I settled myself back on the settee against a mound of pillows, spread my legs and beckoned him to me. I felt like a queen, an object of worship—and, truly, that's how Connor approached me. We'd talked about it, early in our relationship, about how he wanted a woman he could devote himself to fully and completely, someone to love and cherish and, yes, worship. To him, I was to be adored, venerated, and I reveled in that, even as I respected that my dominion over him, as it were, came with responsibility.

That's what love is all about, isn't it?

So he approached me on his knees, subservient and obsequious, and I tilted my hips toward his eager mouth.

Slow, at first. I'd had to teach him that. Even if a woman was already aroused, she didn't want to be pounced upon and wildly devoured—she wanted to be savored, wanted the pleasure to build.

Oh, certainly sometimes I wanted to come faster than others, and I could instruct Connor to ramp things up quickly. The operating phrase being "ramp things up."

Now, he first inhaled the scent of my arousal, his eyes fluttering closed as he savored it. Then he leaned farther forward to place a gentle kiss before his tongue swirled through my lips and around my clit with a gentle reverence.

I was torn, wanting to let my head drop back and just revel in the sensations, but also wanting to watch. I loved seeing his face buried in my crotch.

"*Very* good, Connor," I murmured as he licked every inch of me with long, slow strokes. "Such a talented tongue." I could feel the blood pooling in my groin, the delicious heaviness as my arousal built.

"I said something new, didn't I?" I went on, my toes crimping the sheet on the settee as I tensed. "I said no fucking, no hands. But we've done that before."

Connor didn't respond. He knew what his task was, knew the punishment for slacking.

"I didn't mean just what you're doing to me—oh, *god*, just there." I was getting close. I hadn't timed this as well as I would have liked. Connor was just so talented! "I mean I won't be fucking you, either. Or using my hand on you. Or you using your hand on yourself."

I thought I heard a faint, querulous noise.

"It's going to go like this," I said. "When I come, you may come. In fact, when I come, you are *required* to come."

His tongue stuttered just then, a brief startled pause as the weight of my words sank into his sub-spaced brain.

I rested a hand on his head, reminding him of his duty.

My clit throbbed gently; I was on the edge. A part of me wanted something inside of me—Connor's fingers, a dildo—but I'd said no hands, and that was the fun of it for both of us. Connor was well able to make me come, hard, just from using his mouth.

"I'm getting close, Connor. Are you? I know you're hard—you always get deliciously hard when you lick me, like a good boy. Are your balls tight? Are you getting close, too? I'll be very disappointed in you if you don't come when I tell you to, you know. We'll have to figure out a suitable punishment." My words were coming in gasps now. "Orgasm restriction, maybe, or maybe I'll tie you up and make you come over and over again until you can't stand it."

The mental images of Connor begging, his cock red and swollen—in either scenario—were enough to tip me over that wonderful edge. My groin flooded with warmth as my clit pulsed. My hips involuntarily raised off the bed, and I ground myself into Connor's face.

Lost in the throes of my own orgasm, for a few moments I wasn't precisely aware of Connor. When I was able to open my eyes and focus, he drew back and sat up, his chest heaving.

The sheet I'd draped over the settee glistened with his ejaculate.

"Oh, Connor, well done." I stroked his chiseled face with my fingertips. "You've passed this first test so well…"

POSSESSIVE TENSE

Raziel Moore

Fuck...fuck. You b-bastard," she said, her breath broken, the panted words sounding bitten off of something inside.

"Mmm. Yes. That's me." Still hard, still buried in her, the trailing shudders of Nica's orgasm milked my cock for its last drops. No matter what she said, she'd come hard enough to hurt both of us. "Yes. Fuck me is right."

"Oh, god, I never..."

"I know," I mocked, "you've never done that before. You could never do that. It shouldn't feel good. 'Good girls don't.' Sane, healthy women would never..." She squirmed under me, pinioned, our sweat slick between us.

"But you're not a good girl, are you? You *could*. And you *did*." Her skin was so soft, so hot against mine. I licked her neck up to her ear; the bite mark there would be hard to hide. She shuddered at the sting of saliva on broken skin, and I felt it all the way down, her insides fluttering around me in reaction. The noise she made was halfway between moan and sob.

"What...what are you doing to me?" Her eyes were so pretty with the welling of tears, the dilation of climax, the tremor of fear and uncertainty.

"Nica. You know. I'm making you mine. Making you my whore."

That sound. That little whimper she made, like a trapped animal, like a wanton slut. It made me twitch; made me stiffen again and push inside her.

"Uh-uh... I'm not a..."

"Not a whore? Darling. Weren't those your very words? When you were begging me to fuck you? To make you come? You said it. And didn't I hear and give you what you wanted?" My mouth hovered close to her ear, as if telling a secret.

"No...yes."

"Didn't you come, again, just like I said you would? You can again, too. You *will* again, whenever I want. And you'll love it—you will want it with all that you are."

"Please." If she kept sounding like that, so delicious, so vulnerable and needy, I wouldn't be responsible. I'd start again. But then, she *was* a little right, I knew. So I relented just a bit; I would exact my price for that later.

"No. You're not *a* whore. *A* whore doesn't care who gives them what they need. I could give *a* whore to a colleague or client, a friend or a bum off the street, and you wouldn't care, and I wouldn't care, as long as your cunt or your ass was full and your body shaking with pleasure." I accented every few words with little thrusts. She whined quietly in protest; but her bucking hips and arching back contradicted her sounds. The flood of our fluids, slurps and sluices, spread the pungent stain of us on the sheets. My voice turned harsh, accusing.

"But no, you're under my skin. You're *my* whore. You fucked yourself into me as sure as I fucked myself into you, you amazing, delectable little slut. You didn't even know it. *I* didn't even know it until it was too late. And I am far, far too selfish. Too territorial with what I truly want. *You*, I will not share; not give away to anyone. I'm keeping you. You're mine." I punctuated my possessiveness with harder and harder jabs.

"Oh, god." It could have been anguish in her voice. It could have been relief. Both would've been correct. Fuck. I wanted her again. Right fucking now. And look, there she was, under me, ready and waiting.

"Now. Once more, my sweet." Being just *a* whore might have been the easier path for her, I thought. Easier for us both, perhaps. But it was too late now. I was just as lost as she. I knew it with the ache of my need. I repositioned us, reaching for the bed-table drawer. "I promise, you're going to like this, too, by the end."

"No-o…" But her voice and wet eyes lied. I felt her squeeze me inside, trying to devour me whole.

That's my girl.

NECESSITIES FOR A PERFECT MARRIAGE

Ashley Lister

Nikki screamed as she pulled open the washing machine door. The bundle of towels spilled out. Swirls of pink and crimson patterned the formerly bland cream fabric. She had never seen a more chilling sight in the goriest of horror movies. The wedding present from Josh's favorite aunt, a set of expensive cream towels from the exclusive department store Sampsons, was now ruined.

This couldn't be happening in the first month of their marriage. She had taken an extra week off work after the honeymoon to settle into married life and organize the home so it was ready for two newly wedded professionals to use as a sanctuary, haven and love-nest.

But this disaster looked set to destroy everything.

If Josh found out she had ruined the gift from his

favorite aunt he would be hurt. He might suspect she had some Freudian motive for ruining the gift. At best he would think her incompetent. At worst, it would sow the first seed of imperfection in their otherwise idyllic relationship.

She shook her head. Set her jaw. Checked her watch.

There was time to avoid disaster if she acted quickly.

She threw the towels into the rubbish. Thinking fast, she stepped out of her panties and then smoothed her skirt down over her hips. Taking two bottles of his favorite imported beer from the fridge, she snatched her purse and car keys and headed out of the house. Her heart raced as she rushed through the end-of-day traffic. She parked in the underground lot near Josh's office just as he was walking toward his BMW.

Her window was already rolled down. She leaned out and called, "Hi handsome!"

His grin combined delight and confusion. "Nikki? What are you doing here?"

She held up a bottle of beer and winked. "I've got a couple of things in this car you might fancy after a long day in the office. Fancy a ride?"

He glanced toward his own car for a beat. Then he was by her side, hunkered down by the door. Their faces were so close Nikki could have kissed him without moving more than a millimeter.

"What's going on?"

"We've been married for nearly three weeks," she

reminded him. "I'm making sure our love life doesn't turn stale."

"And you're doing that by turning up at my office with beer?"

She pressed her lips close to his ear. Her voice dropped to a seductive whisper. "Get into the car. You can see what else I've got for you."

He needed no further prompting.

As soon as he was in the passenger seat, Nikki pressed the bottle of beer into his hand. She took a quick glance through the windshield, assuring herself that their location was discreet, and then she lowered her head over his lap.

"Nikki?"

She said nothing. Instead, she stroked the shape of his hardness through his suit pants. He was already aroused. The length of his erection sat fat and desirable beneath the fabric. She guessed the suggestiveness of her whisper had charmed him to a state of semihardness. As she pulled his zipper slowly down the electric atmosphere inside the car became more charged.

"Nikki?"

"Drink your beer," she urged. "There's something I've got to do."

She exposed the thick pink flesh of his erection. He was already perfumed with the scent of arousal. She traced a tongue against his hardness and then sucked gently on the swollen purple dome.

Josh stiffened in his seat. "This is too intense. I can't

hold back much longer."

"Hold it as long as you can." She breathed the words warmly against his erection. He twitched and pulsed beneath every syllable. "Let me taste your cock until I'm swallowing every drop that you shoot into my mouth."

Josh groaned.

Nikki wrapped her lips around him and worked her mouth up and down his length. The end of his erection pressed against the back of her throat. She sucked greedily, anxious to please him with as much intensity as the moment would allow. When he finally exploded she was rewarded with the rich taste of his warm, pulsing ejaculate as it swathed her tongue.

She grinned at him as she swallowed. Never allowing their eye contact to break, she licked her lips theatrically. "Fasten your seat belt. I'm taking you home for an encore."

"What about my car?"

"You've just had a beer. Your car will be safe here overnight. I'll bring you back to work in the morning and you can drive it home tomorrow night."

He nodded. "Are we going anywhere else first?"

"One stop in the town center, and then I'm taking you home to ravish you again." She said nothing more until she was parking outside the town center's most prestigious department store.

"Sampsons?" Josh raised an eyebrow. "What do you need from Sampsons?"

She took his and hand guided it to her knee. Urging

his fingers upward, beneath the hem of her skirt, she allowed him to trace the moist flesh of her labia. "I don't have any lingerie sexy enough for the man I want to excite," she whispered. "I need to buy something that will drive him crazy with desire."

His cheeks flushed. Although he had only just climaxed she could see a promising bulge at the front of his pants.

"Do you want me to come with you?"

She giggled. "You're going to *come* with me as soon as we get home. Let me make this purchase alone so I can surprise you." Passing him the second bottle of beer she added, "Drink this. I'll be back as quick as I can."

And then she was out of the car. Smoothing her skirt back into place, hurrying into the shop, she tried not to think of the ache in her loins that his touch had inspired. She went briskly to bathroom accessories and bought a new set of towels identical to the wedding present. They weren't cheap. Nikki was devastated to think she had blown a week's wages on purchasing the replacements. As soon as they were packed for her, Nikki rushed off to the lingerie department. She bought a single black thong.

She hid her purchases in the trunk then returned to the driver's seat.

"It looks like you bought a few things."

"Necessities for a perfect marriage," she said honestly. Her hand slipped to his lap. Her fingers discovered he was already hard and ready for her. She lowered her voice and lazily stroked him with her palm. "But the first thing I'll be unpacking when I get home is something more important than my purchases."

She snatched her hand away before he could respond, and drove them home. As soon as they were parked outside the house Nikki said, "I'm going to change into my new lingerie. I'll see you in the bedroom." Unable to resist, she pressed her mouth against his. They enjoyed a long and lingering kiss. Her fingers fell to his groin as their tongues intertwined. His hand slipped slowly up her thigh, stroking smoldering fire against her pussy lips.

She pulled herself from him before the contact could prove too tempting.

In the bathroom she pushed the new bundles of towels onto their shelves. Then she stripped and stepped into the thong.

"Wow!" Josh marveled.

He was naked and waiting for her on the bed as she stepped out of the en suite.

"Do you like my new lingerie?"

He grinned. "You'll have to bring it closer so I can get a good look before I make up my mind."

She couldn't decide if it was the thrill of the successful deception, the taste of him that still lingered on her lips or simply the excitement of being near Josh. Whatever the reason, she was dripping with desire when he plunged into her. Her labia parted easily as his length slipped into her sex. She was in the throes of orgasm before he had managed to thrust three times. Because he had already climaxed, Josh's stamina seemed invigorated. When she climaxed for the final time of that session, it felt like she was collapsing into a bed of soft and luxuriant towels.

She drifted into a content and satisfied doze.

"Nikki?"

She was alone in the bedroom. Josh's voice came from the en suite.

"Do you remember those towels my aunt gave us?"

She blushed. "I remember them. What about them?"

"I don't think they were as good a quality as Auntie claimed. The damned things aren't drying me properly and they're leaving fibers all over my body. I can't believe she's tried passing off inferior-quality towels as top of the range gear."

Nikki forced a false chuckle. "Leave it with me. I'll put them through the wash again tomorrow. Maybe that will help."

He stepped into the bedroom, his body still glistening with a shiny memory of the shower's spray. "It's only a bale of towels," he grinned. "If they don't come right with another wash, we'll go out and buy some quality ones from Sampsons."

ONE SLEEP

Maria See

You are in San Francisco on a business trip. You arrived today. We're having dinner and I'm looking at you from across the table like it's the only thing in the way of my devouring you.

I will not see you again until... We're here to talk about *until*.

Your stay will last four nights. Each night you will sleep naked and will not lock any additional locks on your door aside from the one that requires the room's key card to open.

I ask you if you want me to be me, or someone else, a stranger, perhaps with a hood on to help you forget that I *am* me. "I want *you* to rape me," you tell me. You give me a copy of the key card. I won't do it tonight. It's too likely that with our arrangement fresh in your mind you will sleep lightly, too likely that you'd easily awake if I enter in the middle of the night. I will not do it on the third night, because, should the second night go by without a visit from me, you will assume I'll come on the third night, and for very good reason: if I did not show on night three, you will know to expect me on night four. This is also why I will not do it on night four: you will know I am coming; I will be out of options. I will do it tomorrow. Tomorrow night I will arrive at your hotel at approximately 3:00 a.m. I know from meeting you in your room prior to coming to the restaurant that the halls are carpeted and that your room is nowhere near an elevator, so I worry little that you will hear me coming. I will quietly insert and remove the key card and open the door to your room. You won't hear me enter, or you will hear me enter and you will pretend you do not. I'll bet that you will be on your stomach, your usual sleeping position. I will slide the covers off of you and have a knife to your neck before you fully wake.

CRAWLING THROUGH TEMPTATION

Elise Hepner

W e're almost there." His scratchy, low drawl carried through the craggy tunnel.

A bead of water dripped along her nose and she shivered. The quiet buried deep down into her being was only interrupted by the minute shuffling through the small, dripping cave passage. Who'd have thought a first-year anniversary could be so romantic? There could have been sarcasm there—but there wasn't. For two people who'd met on an online caving site this was perfection. Or their end destination would be, once Max got his gorgeous, well-toned ass out of her headlamp. Beneath the stink of sulpher and earthier, muddy things, Lela breathed in the thread of her lover's spicy cologne.

She'd follow Max to the end of the earth. Literally. Beneath her fleece underwear her nipples pebbled as she took another shuffling pace on her hands and knees. Barely enough room to breathe. Each movement constricted as she took in air through small sips, tasting the depth of ozone.

Almost there. What surprises did Max have in store for them?

A shake of her head sent her beam skittering across the darkness. A slip of her tongue across her lips. Eagerness for whatever grand finale awaited them pumped adrenaline through her veins that skittered goose bumps along her upper arms. Her stomach tightened. Only one lifeline—a primal directive drawing them closer to their conclusion—and the sexy sway of her boyfriend's ass.

No way back. Only forward now.

These caves held secrets. Half the fun was not knowing whether they'd ever come out again or if they'd be swallowed whole by a place that came before time and man. Her hands fisted in her thick rubber gloves. Her pulse thrummed inside her head. Max grunted in front of her and their passage grew narrower. She ducked her head. He wouldn't leave her behind. She needed to concentrate on the one-two step of clawing through the mud—ankles and wrists thick with it. It'd be all over her fingers except for her gloves.

Like the sensual, fun finger painting they'd done on each other's bodies two nights ago.

Anticipation. It was a twisting, twining mind fuck and a half. She loved every damn second. Every hand forward pressed her jeans tight against her naked pussy with the roll of her hips. While darkness snaked around her ankles, she crawled deeper, anxious for her final reward.

"Here."

Gruff excitement in his voice pushed her harder. She tightened her tingling lips as the cave's narrow back pressed against her spine in a caress that directly translated into her brain as sheer terror. Not wanting to get stuck there. Max was gone. He must have stood and doused his headlamp. All ready for her to follow next. The sense of pure, complete darkness—not seeing even a hand an inch away from her face—was a spike of lust.

At her back the space widened. Almost there. Her beam illuminated an entrance big enough for three people to stand on each other's shoulders and still make it through without much fuss. A small sigh. A pump of triumph making her palms tingle as Max's hand shot down cutting through the light to help her up. Even through the thick rubber and muck, his contact was a conductor for her smile. But before she'd gained her footing, his hand brushed by her hair, dousing the light from her helmet.

Inescapable darkness engulfed them plunging in from all sides. They were small, meaningless. His large, rough, gloveless fingers tugged through her tied-back hair. A shudder dipped her sore back. His other hand dug through the layers of her clothing to find the scant line of skin above her hip, tracing with the barest touch that made everything come to a standstill. How she wanted his bruising mouth. A lifeline in all the dark.

Damp, small swallows through her mouth. A shift of air against her exposed flesh. Before she could react his large hands gripped her hips, manhandled her and slammed her against the rock face. A less than subtle pain swiped up her cheek—but Max knew she liked that.

His satisfied laugh made her mute.

Rough palms forced off her pack, frisking over her curves, while she was blind. His body heat anchored her while her fingers gripped the rocks. Tremors shook her knees. A loud yank of her zipper. He might as well have ripped her pants in half with the force of his grip. Not one breath passed her lips as he forced the whole bundle of her sticky, muddy clothing to her ankles. Trapped. Exposed. A beat.

Not a sound but the soft ping of water and her galloping heart.

She shifted, nipples scraping against the rocks. A current of pleasure tightened her pussy muscles. Her bare ass was caught between the frigid cold and Max's heat less than an inch away. But so far it might as well have been a chasm. A shock of sound jerked through her body before the enveloping pain of his hand making contact with her asscheek. Warmth spread through her tired, aching muscles even as she clenched for another.

Another.

Pain unfurled through her limbs.

Another.

The warmth of her soft moan lingered against her face.

"Again," she breathed.

"Like you make the rules."

Beneath the shock of sensation her heightened pleasure climbed through the darkness.

Please, let it never stop. Arms and legs braced for the zing. Every fiber pulsating as his next smack jostled her breasts making her cry out from the rough friction. Cool air taunted her wet, tight cunt. His rough palm bruised her when his latest smack ended with his tight grip cupped along her stung flesh.

She lived for these primal explorations—seconds before release—on the cusp of the unknown.

TICKTOCK

Rita Winchester

He always yells *ticktock* when he comes home on lunch break. Christopher will burst through the door, yanking his tie loose and calling out to me as he bolts past. I work from home; I'm always here up to my eyebrows in paperwork on any given day.

I see the blur of gray suit as he rushes past and his footfalls echo on our steps. He's heading toward the bedroom. Once in a great while, when the traffic is heavy and delays hold him up, he comes home yelling his magic words and then just attacks me in the living room.

Not today.

I shove my pile of papers away and stand, smoothing my yoga pants like I'm wearing a skirt. My eyes shoot to the small dining room mirror and I see my hair, in two blonde braids, has actually fared pretty well today.

No makeup but for lipstick, but hey, it's just the way he likes me. Undone.

"Ticktock, Georgie," he yells again, and I scurry.

I hit the stairs at a good clip, heart pounding. My head is a little swimmy and my stomach abuzz. I always worry, will I get him off? Will I get off? Do we have time? But these questions and worries are all part of the excitement of lunchtime at home.

On the landing, I hear him a split second before he grabs me and hauls me into the bedroom. He's taken off the tie and the jacket. His pants are simply undone and his cock stands out poker straight, begging to be touched or stroked or, yes, I realize as he kisses me once before putting pressure on my shoulders so I kneel...*sucked*. His cock needs to be sucked.

He slides the smooth tip of his cock along my lower lip and then drags it across my upper. A slip-slide of moisture flows out of me and I shiver. "Go on, Georgie. Give it just a taste," he says.

I do. I lick with only the tip of my tongue so that he grabs my braids like reins and tugs just enough. He's being a gentleman. Knowing he's restraining himself is enough fodder to prompt more moisture between my thighs.

He knows I love this. He knows it gets me off. It is, in fact, the fastest way to get me wet.

"Pop that first button for Daddy," he chuckles. It's our joke, he knows the whole *daddy* thing does nothing for me.

"Yes, Daddy," I whisper, smiling around his cock as he slips into my mouth deeper and I feel that slight tremor of my gag reflex. A single tear escapes my eye from my efforts and Christopher thumbs it away.

"Just a few seconds more," he says, eyes growing dark after glancing at the bedside alarm clock. He takes my braids more firmly, using them for real this time. Pulling my mouth onto his cock at the speed and tempo he desires. When I gag again, he pulls free of me and gives me his hand so I can stand.

I'm only standing for so long, because Christopher is a big guy and in three big stagger-steps he's walked me back to the bed. With tented fingers, he pushes me back onto the mattress, as easy as if he's felling a tree made of feathers.

"Hips up." His voice has gone down to an urgent whisper and that is more serious than his big, booming, hurry-up-woman voice. This voice makes my nipples spike as if they're made of iron instead of warm, pink flesh.

I shoot my hips up and he peels off my pants. I'm bare underneath. I had nowhere to be today. Just home slogging through tax forms. And here I am now, bare assed and splayed on our big navy-blue bedspread. "Spread 'em."

He tosses me a wink and takes a moment to torture me as he folds—yes, *folds*—my yoga pants and sets them on the settee by the door.

I spread my legs as he turns, his big blue eyes eating up the sight of me. My belly bare because my top's shoved up some, my hip bones jutting up just a bit, the bare swell of my mound and I can only assume the flushed sweetness of my pussy. I let my thighs fall open just a bit more to make him come to me.

It works.

Christopher's making that *ticktock* noise of his that somehow works to amp up my arousal. We can fuck any time we want. A couple with no kids, the sky's the limit. But god, the lunch-hour fucks are the best. Hours plump with excitement and need. We only have so much time to satisfy each other, and that is what makes it all the better.

He's coming at me and I arch up, but he *ticks* and *tocks* at me, pressing my hips flat with his big hands. He slides his warm bulk along me but doesn't try to enter me. His erection presses, urgent and bold, between my legs but only manages to ride the swollen knot of my clitoris. That is enough to make me dance and twist under him, but Christopher pins me flat.

"Stop being so fidgety, Georgie," he laughs, burying his face in the crux of my neck. He drops gentle, heated kisses along the length of my neck and the flare of my shoulder like we have all the fucking time in the world. I fear I might go insane.

"Hurry," I sigh, moving up to try and force more contact between his cock and my clit. He's onto me, and he pulls back just enough.

"No hurry." He kisses my cheeks, my nose, my eyelids, my lips. When he sticks the tip of his moist tongue in my mouth, I try to fight dirty and suck it like it's his dick. Again, he chuckles and sucks my tongue in return. My plan has failed because he seems calm, cool and collected and I have turned into a raving lunatic. The pressure of him sucking my tongue shooting straight from mouth to breast to cunt.

"Oh, my dear god, Christopher, stick it in me!" I demand, and when he grins I have the sudden, sparkling urge to hit him.

He rocks his hips from side to side and I feel the brush and nudge of that hard shaft over the places I need it most. *Over,* not in. What is wrong with him?

My eyes go to the clock and I see our time is ticking away, running fast like salt water through a plastic sieve at the shore. "Hurry!" I hiss.

"No hurry," he says again.

His mouth drags sensually down between my breasts. When he hits my rib cage my skin gallops and shimmies because it almost—but not quite—tickles. I stop complaining when he hits my navel because I know where he's going. When he reaches my pussy, I almost give it up immediately. I've become such a slut for him and his rushed lunchtime fornication at this point. My nether lips are so flushed and sensitive that when he nips them gently, I surge up like he's burning me. He settles his mouth on me, sealing his lips over my mound. The top row of his teeth press to that tender flesh and add just enough pain to amp up my pleasure. He gets in three swirls of his tongue and I come. Christopher laughs. "Boy, you're a cheap date."

Again I have the urge to swat him, but then he's sliding that cock along my drenched hole only to slip inside of me, just enough for me to feel the pressure but not enough to fill me.

"Please, please, please!" I gasp, finally swatting him on the arm to try and prompt him.

"Very well." With a soft kiss, he drives into me. His cock stretching and filling me. I wrap my legs around him and open myself fully to his penetration. Each thrust bangs his pelvic bone to my clit and a jolt of pleasure fills me.

He's teasing me again, but he doesn't last long either. Christopher's thrusts get frantic fast and when he kisses me deeply and pulls my braids hard, making my scalp sing, he comes. It's easy to get off again after hearing his cries. Nothing does me in faster than a man coming undone.

I glance at the clock. "You'd better g—"

He cocks an eyebrow at me, smiling. "Oh, didn't I mention that I have the rest of the day off?"

"I...what? What was with all the *ticktock* then?"

He kisses my nose. "Georgie, Georgie, Georgie. Do you have *any* idea how wet that noise makes you? It turns you into a sex maniac."

This time I do hit him. But not very hard at all. After all, I have the rest of the day with him. I want him in perfect working order.

THROWING SUGAR

Jeremy Edwards

S ex was in the air the day I encountered Nina. I felt it
as soon as the sweet June morning kissed my neck,
when I emerged through my front door with my cheerful
necktie proud on my chest and the short curls of my hair
still damp from the shower.

The subway platform sizzled with the vitality of
horny humans, frisky organisms who had bundled their
hormones into workaday clothing but who nonetheless
represented pure erogenous energy. The women's thighs,
bare below flirty summer dresses, sang desire to me, and
their naked, friendly shoulders seemed to invite unseen
lovers.

And yet not all lovers were unseen that morning. On
the train, I was presented with an excellent view of a
couple standing halfway down the car from me, who

wrapped themselves into an erotic embrace as I watched with art-history-trained eyes. Their faces were blocked from my line of sight, but the woman's skirt, taut where her pelvis pressed against her guy, was beautifully framed for me by the surrounding passengers, giving the scene an aesthetic quality that enhanced its arousing essence.

I realized I wanted this, today, too—or something very much like this.

It had been four years since I'd abandoned small-town life in favor of urban society. Many of my peers who'd moved to the city around the same time were becoming blasé by now: the initial magic had faded. But I'd had the opposite experience. The city had been unexpectedly dull and dreary to me when I'd first arrived—a place weighed down by my goals and ambitions, I realized in retrospect—and only later had it flowered into something exciting, a place of fresh experiences and unanticipated thrills.

A place to keep my eyes and ears open, and my libido idling at the ready.

Out on the sidewalk, there seemed to be so many enchanting women everywhere I looked that I couldn't even glance at all of them. To be thorough I would have had to break stride, and thereby risk causing offense—and meanwhile, of course, I'd inevitably miss my chance to see another lovely individual or two. It was hopeless, wonderfully hopeless.

At the café, a bright, graceful figure with an impish smile added sugar to her coffee while I was putting milk in my own. She hummed uninhibitedly, at a volume so low that only I could hear it. I liked that.

Then, not so gracefully, she dropped some sugar packets. They fell in my direction.

"Sorry," she said pleasantly.

Perhaps it was just the fever of that day, but I sensed an opportunity.

"Are you throwing sugar at me?" I teased.

My heart raced and my cock pulsed when she responded in kind. "Of course I'm throwing sugar at you. You have a problem with that?" She smirked right at me, looking so smart and bratty—and so happy to have accidentally discovered an ad hoc bantering partner.

"I feel it only fair to warn you," I retorted with pretend stuffiness, "that flinging sugar packets in my general direction will get you nowhere."

"Aww," she pouted.

"Well...okay. Perhaps we can work something out." She laughed.

"I'm Nina," she said, as we exited.

"Philip." We both shuffled our coffees leftward so that we could shake hands.

"Which way are you walking?" she asked casually.

I explained that turning either right or left to walk around the block would get me to work with equal efficiency, as my office was directly behind the café.

"That's fascinating," she said, with a stage yawn and a wink. "But if there's more to that story, you'd better save it." She pointed at the face of her watch and raised her eyebrows at me. Then she nodded left, and together we proceeded in that direction.

"Do you drink coffee after work, too?" I asked her on the side street, in front of her workplace.

"No." She paused. "But I throw sugar."

"Now, there's a coincidence. After work, I *catch* sugar."

"Five thirty?" Nina suggested.

We acquired our evening coffees—my habitual one and the unaccustomed one that Nina ordered in my honor— and took them out into the downtown maze.

The weather was, if anything, even more admirable than it had been in the morning. And, without overtly conferring, we began walking away from the center of town, joking about office life and volleying flirtation-soaked verbal tennis balls, served with plenty of teasy spin.

"I had a feeling you were leading me to the park," I kidded as we passed through the gate. We both knew we had chosen this destination together, by unspoken consensus.

"Yes. Now you can tell everyone I took you 'parking.' Hey, you actually laughed at that!" She seemed genuinely gratified. "I'm more used to getting groans with my puns."

"No groans from me on your watch, I promise. But you may hear some *moans*, at the appropriate juncture."

"I insist on it. I'm just hoping you'll find my, uh, *juncture* to be an appropriate one."

This time I laughed so loudly that heads turned our way. Nina beamed possessively and guided me past the gawking passersby.

I wasn't usually much for outdoor sex. But there was something special about this day—and something *very* special about Nina—and it could not be denied that I yearned to fuck her standing up and as soon as possible, in some semisecluded pocket of summer evening. I was already imagining her blissful face in the barely slanting, near-solstice light; I could practically feel her mischief-tinged sweetness painting me up and down.

At a spot where several paths diverged, she stopped me, resting a possibility-charged hand on my elbow.

"I know an ideal place for...throwing sugar," she said. Her eyes momentarily lost their glint of playfulness and looked hopeful; sincere; vulnerable.

I kissed her coffee-sultry lips before letting her guide me down the rightmost branch of the path. Her fingers maintained their grip on my arm.

Nina knew the way to the little building used by park staff as a home base for summer children's programs. She also knew that these programs would not be starting until July. Though the building was locked, there was open access to a small patio behind it, which was largely shielded from the path by a vine-covered latticework wall. At the moment, this wall looked like nothing so much as a vertical bed.

And there wasn't even a bedspread to turn down.

I nibbled Nina's ear as she pulled my torso close. Her breath, like everything today, was sweet. "Perfect," she whispered, her voice belying the vigor with which she was pawing at my shirt buttons.

My hands floated under her skirt, and Nina ground her crotch against me. "I don't know what it is," she confessed with a frantic titter. "I can't remember the last time I wanted to fuck so desperately."

"I know exactly what you mean," I murmured into her neck.

"Ever since I woke up, I've been ready to crackle into flames." Her hand was on my zipper. "All day, Spark." Thus she nicknamed me, just as my cock found a temporary home in her palm.

After quickly donning a condom, I found my handholds on the waistband of her satin knickers. With sensuous slowness I escorted them down, letting the cool fabric tickle the hot flesh of her hips and thighs. When they fell to the patio, she stepped out of them, and without further ado she split her engorged pussy lips with my hard-on—wiggling on my tip so as to delight me with her softness and moisture, and herself with my stiffness.

"Share my pussy, Spark," she breathed, as she hugged me tighter to drive my cock home. Her voice was rich with complex layers of pleasure. The word *share* echoed in my mind.

As I started thrusting, I glanced down to notice the

shine of girl-come smiling up from the inside of her discarded panties. *Even her underwear is grinning,* I said to myself.

But all thought vanished when Nina began to really move our coupling forward. Her body took every bit of energy from the air and transmuted it into thrashing, primal electricity. I held on to her ass for dear life as she churned on me.

When she made me come, I came in response to the moment, the day, the summer—and Nina, Nina, Nina. I pinched an asscheek while fondling her clit, and the irresistible climax claimed her as well. She bathed me, titillating my aftershock-twitching shaft with her ecstasy, and dampening my shorts into the bargain.

"Are you throwing sugar at me?" I growled passionately, and her cunt giggled spasms of happiness in reply.

BOUND
TO SERVE

Mina Murray

Kellan will be here soon. It's time. When he demanded my secret from me last night, I thought first of lying, but he held my orgasm ransom until I told him what he wanted to know.

"What's the one fantasy you've never told anyone?" he asked.

I was on my back, spread wide before him, open to his gaze. His arm stretched out across my leg, hand gripping me right at the juncture of hip and thigh, while his elbow pinned me to the bed. I would've said it made me feel uncomfortable, but it didn't.

Kellan's other hand played between my legs, his thumb rubbing my clit, his middle finger teasing the entrance to my sex, but it was his mouth, his voice, his words that devastated me and set my senses reeling.

"I want you to tell me the one thing you're too afraid to tell anyone, even me. I want all your secrets, Angie"— I tried to thrust my hips up at him, but he pulled his fingers away—"and I won't let you come until I have them."

He'd been teasing me for what felt like hours, bringing me to the brink and then retreating. I was desperate for release, but I didn't know if I could pay the price he'd set.

"You want to come, don't you, baby?"

His fingers ghosted over my clit, and I bit my lip and nodded.

"I want—" *Oh, please, don't let him laugh at me*, I thought.

"Yes?" he asked encouragingly, increasing the pressure of his circling fingers.

"I want to serve as your table..." I was mumbling, and Kellan leaned in closer, a quizzical expression on his face.

"You want to sell me a fable?"

"No." The words tumbled out of me and I thought I would die of mortification. "I want you to use me as your coffee table."

Kellan went stone quiet. He knew how to honor a bargain, though, so he recovered quickly and stroked me just the way I needed and all of a sudden I was coming. The tides of sensation crashing over me; the shocked look on his face; the admission, out loud, of something I'd tried so hard not to acknowledge even to myself; all combined into a perfect storm of feeling and I burst into tears.

He kept stroking me until the trembling stopped, then took me in his arms and kissed me.

"That sounds hot. Let's do it."

And so here I am, on all fours and naked except for some fuck-me shoes and the rope I used to tie my thighs and ankles together. I hear Kellan's key in the lock and my breath catches in my throat. Wiping all expression from my face, I let my gaze fall to the ground.

He drops his bag at the door, shrugs out of his clothes and leaves them on the floor. Clad only in boxer briefs, he wanders to the fridge and swigs directly from the carton of juice. He then proceeds to scratch his balls, and readjust his junk.

Kellan is the most fastidiously tidy and dignified man I've ever met. He has to be putting this Neanderthal show on for my benefit. He ambles over and flops down on the couch, puts his feet up in the small of my back and pops the cap off the beer he's holding. He fumbles clumsily for the remote and flicks on the TV.

To give him some credit, he's only slightly startled when the porno he thought I didn't know about starts playing. It's definitely one of the filthier titles he owns, no high-scale production values, no artfully conceived plot, just pure fucking. A blonde woman with pneumatic tits is getting drilled onscreen, and the devil's threesome she signed up for has soon turned into an unstoppable, all-out gangbang.

I feel Kellan shifting on the couch and his heels dig into my back as he wrestles down his underwear so he can tug at his cock with one hand. I glance to the left and almost moan when I see how hard he is. His hand is gliding furiously over his erection, rubbing over the shaft and twisting over the head in a circular motion while he makes these little groaning noises.

He moves his feet, places the bottle of beer squarely in the middle of my back and starts to palm his balls with his now-free hand. I manage to hold the bottle up for nearly half a minute, but I get a mad itch in my foot and that one second of inattention leads to an upended bottle and a stream of liquid trickling over my back, between my buttocks and along the seam of my sex. It's so cold I almost yelp, but I bite my lip hard and manage to stay silent.

"Aw, shit," Kellan says, then goes to the kitchen to get a cloth.

His hand is still on his cock when he comes up behind me and starts cleaning me with the cloth, polishing over the long line of my back and down between my legs and up again, as if I truly were made out of wood and he wanted to maintain my finish. His breathing is shaky, and when he leans forward I can feel the rhythm of his wanking behind me.

It's not long before he's focusing solely on my pussy, polishing my pearl. When my pleasure overtakes me, I feel like I'm going to pass out. A keening wail rises from my throat. Kellan falls forward onto me, his head resting in the small of my back, and soon his groans are joining mine. With a hoarse little cry, he spurts his seed all over my upturned ass.

Kellan is the first to speak, once he's caught his breath.

"We'll try this again tomorrow," he says, "and next time, darling, don't make a sound when you come."

NAUGAHYDE

Sommer Marsden

Seriously. What *is* this stuff?" Jeff rubs his fingers over the top of my cheap-ass, dime-store mule.

"Naugahyde," I say, pushing my shoulders back, showing off my conical boobs and my pink fuzzy sweater.

"Nauga-what?" It does not escape my notice that his finger briefly slips beneath the band of fake plasticine leather to stroke my bare skin. His touch sizzle-pops up my calf, burns a line of fire behind my knee and tickles slowly up my inner thigh. The sensation lands with a lazy, warm flex in my pussy.

Nether lips fat with blood and slick with juices are forcing me to straighten my legs and sharpen my focus. We have a costume party to get to. We have a hope-fully future-boss for me to woo. We do not have time for...dirty things.

"Naugahyde."

"Never heard of it." His hand circles my ankle like I'm made of matchsticks. It never fails to startle me how big his hands are.

He's dressed like a greaser so when he waggles his eyebrows at me, I pretend to swoon. Only I don't have to pretend so much.

"I guess nowadays we call it pleather. But back in the day…" I have chosen to dress as a '70s house-wife, picking out a very Mrs. Kravitz ensemble à la "Bewitched." "…they called it naugahyde."

His hand has meandered up my calf and is cupping the back of my thigh. Lightning stabs my skin, electricity skitters in my blood. He strokes me with a single finger and I fear I might come.

We haven't even left the house and I'm coming undone.

"I think my grandmom had a chair covered in this stuff." He says "this stuff" but is not touching my shoe. He is touching the tops of my thighs, having raised my navy-blue polyester, elastic-waisted skirt. It is a hideous skirt. It is a horrid skirt. And it is now shoved around my waist like the world's thickest belt as my boyfriend presses his face to my oversized white panties.

"Oh, fuck," I say.

"You seem nervous," he says.

I swallow hard and hear my throat click. We should be going…leaving…on the road. Instead he is eyeing up my grandmom knickers like they're from a fine department store.

"I am," I admit.

"You'll do good. You'll do *great*. You pay attention to detail," he says and pushes a finger under the leg of my panties. His fingertip skates along my outer lip and I hold my breath. His fingertip pushes into my slick folds and he touches me for real. That breath slips free of me like sinuous smoke.

"Why do you think that?" I thread my fingers into his slicked-back hair, messing it up, liking the half grin he gives me. That half grin punches me right in the gut. It puts me right on edge, the bad-boy, you'll-pay-for-that gaze he gets when I've been bad.

"Because you pay attention to detail. And you're good at what you do. You'll make him proud. The man is no dummy. You'll get the job."

"I don't know…"

"Hush up, Jill. Listen to the voice of wisdom. I mean, you've even put on the giant old-lady panties to match your hideous ensemble."

I snort, but the laughter turns to a sigh when he tugs said underpants down and parts me with his tongue.

"We have to go. We have to go." I say it like a chant.

"We will, we will…" he answers, mocking me. Covering my pussy with his hot mouth. He nudges the split of me with his tongue and my knees sag a little, threatening to dump me out of my inferior footwear and onto my now bare ass.

"You're mean," I say, not meaning it.

Jeff grabs my hand and tugs, pulling me slowly to my knees. My top half clothed, lower half bare. He presses his mouth to my mouth, pushing his tongue against mine so I taste myself. "Not mean."

I grab his now mussed hair, my fingers greasy with hair cream. I tug and he groans and my tummy flexes with that wanting sound. "Okay," I say. I'm making no sense, but neither is he, so we're even.

"Turn around, lady," he grates, and spins me on my knees. Twisting me up more in my own hosiery, my own scratchy skirt, my own giant bloomers.

I'm on my hands and knees, high-teased hair not moving. It's stiff with hairspray and poked through with two pencils. Cat's-eye glasses I don't need to see blur my vision, but not as much as the feel of his rough hands grabbing my hips. He's teasing me, pressing the tip of his cock to my cunt. And then he drives into me, scootching me forward so I have to put out a hand so catch myself.

"For a woman with fake plastic shoes you have a fine, fine ass," he says. A burble of laughter bursts out of me and I sag against the arm he loops around my middle. His thrusts are fast and short and brutal. Stealing my breath, scratching my knees, making me feel like I'll tumble over my messy clutch of clothes and yet...it's perfect. It erases all my nagging fears and worries and my internal you're-not-good-enough-for-this-job monologue.

He strokes my clit with the pad of a single finger. Such a big man being so delicate—it's mind-boggling really. But he moves that finger with the perfect amount of pressure and thrusts so very deep inside of me, driving me forward again with the bang of his hips. He doesn't withdraw any, though. This time, he keeps himself pressed flush to the back of me, rammed deep in the core of me, and he starts to simply nudge his hips side to side so his cock rubs my G-spot in the perfect way. So perfect my lips go a little numb.

His fingers dig into the meat of my hips, and I gasp. "I might fall."

"You won't fall," he says. "Don't worry. I've got you; you're golden. Jill, baby, you're always golden."

And I come. His finger on the tight bud of my clitoris, his cock filling me to the point of bursting, his words a humbling rush of syllables in my ears.

He comes a second later, laughing in that way he has. The way that makes me remember why I love him so fucking much.

When he turns me to face him a moment later, we try to fix it—the mess we've made of me. My glasses are bent, my skirt is twisted, my giant panties are snagged on one side. And worst of all, my cheap shoe has broken. He tsks.

"Oh, shit," I say. But what is one shoe in the face of an orgasm, really? I mean, let's get real, here.

"No worries. Do you know the best thing about this fake stuff?" He's forgotten the word again, I bet.

"Naugahyde?" I say, smirking.

"Right. Naugahyde. Do you know?"

"What?" I try to fix his once-impeccable DA but his hair bounces back up with irritating ease.

"A little duct tape will blend right in."

"Oooh, duct tape," I tease.

Jeff winks at me and it goes straight to my girl parts. "Later, babe. We have a party to get to."

THE PERFECT PAIR

Sophia Valenti

I'd been thinking about Jesse all day. Whenever I could steal a moment of peace at work, my mind would wander, and I'd dream about his hands massaging my feet and his tongue teasing my toes. My commute home passed by in a flash as I spent the time imagining the look that would be on his face when he finally got to hold my pretty peds in his hands. The adoration that lights up his eyes when he gazes at my bare feet stokes my lust like nothing else.

You see, feet are Jesse's fetish, but mine is being in control of Jesse. These two desires complement each other perfectly. I choose when and where he's allowed the honor of worshipping my feet, and in the end we both wind up satisfied.

Jesse had been such a good boy all week—taking

care of the house and me—so I wanted to give him a reward. The second I walked in the door that night, I told him that he'd earned a special treat. Upon hearing my words, he slid his lustful gaze slowly down my figure to rest at my feet, as I knew he would. My black peep-toe heels were high and shiny, and offered a tantalizing glimpse of my gleaming toenails, which were painted a bold red.

I sat on the opposite end of the couch, swiveling my body around so that my feet were in Jesse's lap. I extended one leg so my foot could gently caress his cock, which had already begun to swell beneath his jeans. He groaned as I worked the toe of my shoe along the length of his hardening shaft, tracing its contours until he whispered desperately, "Please, Mistress."

I stilled my foot, knowing that my tease had brought him dangerously close to orgasm and that he didn't want to come without my permission. I bit back my smile, pleased that he'd been brought to the point of begging so soon in our session.

"You're going to have to learn to control yourself, Jesse. You're such an excitable boy," I said, once again nudging his erection with my toe tip and making him groan.

"I'll try, Ma'am," Jesse whispered, eyes cast downward as he stared at his lap—and the leather pump that ruled his desire.

"Would you like to kiss my foot?"

"Very much so, Ma'am," he answered, meeting my

eyes. His hunger and desperation were written on his face, and a frisson of excitement coursed through me. To be desired so passionately is a heady experience, and it's one I've never taken for granted; this night was no different.

Jesse's hands were shaking as he held my ankle and reverently removed my shoe. I hadn't worn stockings that day, and he lifted my bare foot up to his face. He held it still, looking serene as he breathed in deeply to inhale the scent of my warm flesh, no doubt redolent with leather. When he'd gotten his fill, Jesse planted gentle kisses on the tops of my toes, each one a sweet and tender bit of foreplay. After making his way across, his lips slid down my sole, lingering at my arch, where he dared to flick his tongue. It was a teasing touch that resonated within me, almost as if he'd stroked my clit.

I slid down the couch cushions, flexing my foot and waving my toes at him. "Do it again—lick me," I murmured, nudging off my other shoe.

Jesse lavished my left foot with wet kisses as I moved my right into position, so I could stroke his erection with my toes. My dress rose high on my thighs as I squirmed; his ministrations were making my pussy feel slick and hot, and I couldn't wait much longer to feel his cock inside me.

"Take off your pants," I commanded, tracing the length of his fly with my big toe. "Take off everything."

"As you wish," he said softly, easing me aside so he could stand and strip.

Jesse's muscular body was gradually revealed to me as he tugged his T-shirt over his head and then slid his jeans down his thighs. He's so big and strong, yet he was so eager to please and serve me—a fact that made me ache even more for him.

As he stood before me, I reached toward him with my foot, touching the tip of his bobbing cock. He bit his lip as I teased his shaft with my toes and then lifted it with my foot to press it against his stomach. He rocked his hips forward, pushing against my sole as it massaged the underside of his dick. His handsome face was flushed, and his breathing was reduced to a series of erratic gasps as I brought him to the edge. When I sensed he was on the verge, I pulled back and he exhaled slowly.

Leaning back against the cushions, I raised both of my legs, offering him a good view of my feet, as well as a sliver of my pink pussy. I crooked my finger in a come-hither motion, and Jesse smiled as he positioned himself in front of me and held my ankles in one hand, while he used his other to guide himself into my slick slit. I closed my eyes as he slid into me, filling me so sweetly as he once again began to suck on my toes.

Jesse's tongue tickled me deliciously as he pumped his shaft in and out of my cunt. I wriggled a hand between my thighs, fingering my clit as he worked his cock. A warm glow simmered inside me until my pleasure burst in a body-shaking explosion. I squirmed wildly but Jesse held my ankles fast, groaning against my soles when I finally gave him permission to surrender to his lust.

Lowering my legs, Jesse took me in his arms and whispered his thanks, which was funny since I have *him* to thank for endless hours of pleasure—only proving that together, we make a perfect pair.

TAMING HIS WILD CAT

Andrea Dale

She liked to scratch, which is why he called her his little wild cat.

It was harder to scratch him when he encased her hands in mittens that looked like feline paws.

She liked to hiss, which is also why he called her his little wild cat.

It was harder to hiss with a gag in her mouth, one with whiskers sprouting from the strap. The gag went so well with the headband bearing spotted-felt cat's ears.

If she couldn't scratch or hiss, then she couldn't complain when he buckled a collar around her neck.

"Of course," he said, "I also have to bell my cat." He dangled the shiny silver clamps in front of her, and she batted at them, making the little bells chime. He laughed, then tugged on her rosy nipples until they pouted, and tightened the clamps around them.

She growled, deep in her throat, when he lubed her ass and slipped in a butt plug—one with a curling cat tail attached. He tickled her inner thighs with the end of the tail, just to watch her writhe.

He flipped the switch. The plug began to vibrate.

That's when his little wild cat arched her back and began to purr.

AT THE
CAR WASH

Lucy Felthouse

Harriet considered her outfit carefully. She needed access, and she needed it fast. Also, she had to be able to hide what she was doing; she wanted a cheap, exciting thrill, not a warrant for her arrest and a restraining order.

After some deliberation, she chose a formfitting black top that never failed to make her feel sexy, and a loose, floaty, knee-length skirt, also in black. Granted, she'd put together a dark-colored outfit that would absorb heat to wear on one of the hottest days of the year, but she'd be fine; thankfully, she had air-conditioning in the car. Plus, the very idea of what she was about to do was already making her feel all hot and bothered, so it wouldn't make much difference.

What really mattered, after all, was what *they* would

be wearing. Or, more accurately, what they *wouldn't* be wearing. Harriet had deliberately not cleaned her car for ages then chosen a day with record temperatures to take it to the hand car wash. Why?

Because she lived for danger and naughty sexual escapades. A visit to the hand car wash where several shirtless, muscular men would clean her car while she sat inside with her hand down her knickers was definitely in order. It had been on her dirty bucket list for some time and having already ticked off several other items, it was time for her to give the filthy car wash fantasy a try.

Harriet dressed carefully, then tied her hair up into a high ponytail and applied a fresh coat of makeup. She wasn't trying to impress anyone, but the more attractive she felt, the more likely she'd be to come before she got caught.

Then, grabbing her purse and car keys, she headed out to her car and got in. She started the engine and pulled on her seat belt. Just before reversing off the drive, though, she looked around, noting the position of her seat in relation to all the windows. Harriet figured that the only way they'd be able to see what she was doing—and even then they probably wouldn't believe it—was if they were looking through the passenger-side window. She was so close to the driver's-side window that the angle was all wrong.

Nodding to herself, Harriet put the car in gear, released the handbrake and maneuvred down the drive on the way to her illicit adventure. The hand car wash was only a five-minute drive away, but she was already so excited that she could barely wait to get there. As a result, she broke out in a light sweat and a wash of heat rose up her cheeks and gathered between her legs. Huffing, Harriet switched on the air-conditioning then grinned. If she was already feeling this agitated and horny, she'd probably end up coming before they'd even given her car a preliminary once-over with the jet spray. She might even manage two orgasms!

Harriet shook her head as she pulled into the hand car wash. She knew that wasn't possible, really. There'd be no time for thinking, for hesitation. And, due to the lack of any other patrons—she'd picked her arrival time carefully and it had paid off—her time was now. Right. Fucking. Now.

Beaming as the topless guy approached her car, Harriet rolled down the window and told him she just wanted the outside of the car cleaned. Truthfully, the inside could have done with it too, but there was no way she was going to fling the door open and get out having just masturbated in her car while they washed it. It was unlikely her legs would hold her up, in any case.

No, she'd stay safely ensconced in her little motor—

Her thought process was interrupted by much waving from the several men standing a couple of dozen feet away. They were ready and were beckoning her into position. All except one were shirtless, and he wore a tank top so she still had a delicious view of his arms, which were definitely worth looking at.

After rolling the window back up, she inched closer until one man held up a hand indicating she should stop. Harriet did so immediately, and simultaneously slipped a hand up her skirt, shoved her barely there thong to one side and stroked her fingers through her folds. Her pussy was already damp, and as she gazed out of the window at the half-naked men surrounding her car, she began to play. Cautiously, at first, but as the spray of the jet wash caused her car to rock and vibrate—not to mention obscuring the windows—Harriet grew braver and more enthusiastic.

Knowing the additional movement she was causing inside the car would go unnoticed, Harriet rubbed her clit vigorously, occasionally dipping down between her pussy lips for more juices to slick over her swollen nub. Part of her wanted to close her eyes, but she didn't. Instead, her gaze flicked from the windscreen, to the side mirrors and windows, to the rearview mirror in turn, checking out the flexing muscles that were alternately spraying, rubbing and buffing her car. Each and every one of them was a sight to behold, and had one pulled her out of the car and bent her over it, she wouldn't have resisted. Not even if they'd passed her round like the last cigarette.

Boy, was it hot. As Harriet's right hand continued to stroke and pinch at her clit, her left flicked the air-conditioning switch, lowering the temperature even further before she was in danger of spontaneously combusting. A fresh blast of cold air was a blessing over her heated skin, making her aware of the fact that a fresh blast of cold water was being aimed over her car. They'd almost finished washing, she'd soon have to move the car around the corner to the area where they dried and polished exteriors and cleaned the windows.

Harriet had literally seconds to go. Milliseconds, perhaps. Concentrating fully on the pleasant rock and rumble of her car, and the damp fingers manipulating her clit, Harriet bit her lip as she felt the welcome wave of orgasm wash over her. She couldn't help it—her eyes squeezed closed and she let out an involuntary squeak as her legs clamped together over her hand. Her pussy clenched forcefully, the strength of the climax taking Harriet's breath away and leaving her feeling like a mass of quivering jelly. Thank god she was sitting down.

A bang brought her back to earth with a bump. The guy in the tank top had tapped on the hood of her car, bringing her attention to the guys waving madly and indicating she should move on. Snatching her hand from her crotch and yanking her skirt down, she put the car in gear and drove around to the drying area. Her heart thudded in her chest. That had been seriously fucking close.

Not to mention seriously fucking good. A grin spread across Harriet's face as it dawned on her that she'd done it. She'd crossed another item off her dirty bucket list. A cheeky wank in a hand car wash without getting caught.

As the muscular men surrounded her car once more,

buffing and spraying various chemicals on the windows, tires, trims and paintwork, Harriet adopted a happy, relaxed expression. She'd have plenty of time to leap around and congratulate herself when she got home, but she'd just have to keep her excitement at her dirty little secret under wraps for a little longer.

Finally, when her car was shining and sparkly clean and she handed over the cash to pay, she caught the eye of one of the other guys. He was watching her with an expression akin to hunger, then when he realized she was looking back at him, his face broke into a knowing grin and he gave her a lusty wink.

Taking her change with a hasty word of thanks, Harriet rolled up the window and drove out of the hand car wash as fast as was safely possible.

Perhaps her dirty little secret hadn't been so secret after all...

Nevertheless, it had been worth it.

THE EXORCISM

Veronica Wilde

Cara? You're my five o'clock?"

The deep voice made my guts clench. That was the voice my ex-boyfriend Ben had fallen in love with. The voice he had left me for five months ago. I turned and faced the hairstylist waiting for me.

Shaggy brown hair, dark eyes, a ring in his lip. Yep, Hunter was as cute as everyone had said. I felt a stab of jealousy and attraction at the same time.

"That's me," I lied. Pretending to be just a girl looking for a haircut. Pretending I wasn't really scoping out the guy who'd lured my boyfriend away from me. I forced a smile, aware of how crazy this whole idea was. But I'd been unable to stop thinking about Ben, and I had to finally see for myself this new lover of his.

Hunter said, "The chair's over here."

I couldn't take my eyes off him in the mirror as we discussed the kind of cut I wanted. His fingers moved through my long red hair with sensual confidence. He smelled fantastic and his easy, sexy smile spelled out what Ben had found so irresistible. I was jealous, yes. But my curiosity was taking on an uncomfortably erotic edge.

Those velvety brown eyes met mine in the mirror. "Come on. The sink's back there."

I could scarcely breathe as the hot water poured through my hair, his fingers rubbing shampoo into my scalp. These were the fingers that touched my boyfriend each night. The hands that played with Ben's cock were stroking my head. My nipples filled with heat. *Stop it*, I scolded myself. *This is your rival.*

Nor did I feel exactly sexy as I settled back into the chair, wet hair dripping down my neck. I was glad now I'd given him a fake name; I didn't want him to think of Ben's ex-girlfriend as this girl with running mascara in his chair. But when his eyes met mine again in the mirror, I swallowed hard. Damn him for being so hot. Damn him for luring my boyfriend away.

I'd known Ben was bisexual when we met. It hadn't bothered me. When he ditched me for Hunter, I told myself it didn't matter if it was a man or a woman who stole him. But thinking about them together made me obsess over what Hunter had that I didn't—besides the obvious.

We didn't talk much as he cut my hair. I tried not

to look at his torso or his crotch as he leaned over me. *Think about work,* I instructed myself. But now that Ben's boyfriend was right here, I wanted to unzip his jeans and take out his cock. I wanted to see and touch every part of him.

My panties were so wet they were clinging to my pussy.

"You seem nervous, Cara," Hunter said, when he finished my blowout.

"Just in a weird mood." *My name's not Cara,* I wanted to tell him. *It's Bridget, and you may know me as the girl who was living with Ben when you guys met.*

"I hear you. My boyfriend dumped me three weeks ago, and I've been in a bad mood myself."

My heart began to hammer. Hunter put down the blow-dryer and turned the chair so I faced him. "Which means," he said, "that you and I have something in common."

Now my body went ice cold. He knew. I unwillingly lifted my eyes to his and he said, "I recognized you when you came in, Bridget."

A scarlet flush of embarrassment burned in my cheeks. He lifted my chin. "Hey," he said. "It's no big deal. I'd probably do the same thing. Listen, you were my last appointment. Let's go get a drink."

The evening had gone dark when we went to the bar across the street, snow falling past the neon sign. We took a booth in the back and ordered a pitcher of Guinness, talking about Ben. How quiet he was and how hard it was to tell what he was thinking. His hooded eyes that could look seductive and merciless at the same time. How he drove too fast, how he wasn't as good a guitar player as he thought. And finally, the way he grunted when he was thrusting really hard and fast.

Talking to Hunter, our thighs pressed together in the malty bar-dark, was like being next to a piece of Ben. We couldn't stop laughing. Images of them in bed together still flashed through my mind, two beautiful naked boys kissing and stroking each other's cock, and it was turning my panties into a swamp. My stomach jumped every time I met Hunter's dark eyes but thanks to the beer, I could relax into my desire and let it fill me. I wanted to fuck my ex-boyfriend's ex-boyfriend. So what.

"I can't believe you recognized me," I said. The whole ruse seemed so embarrassing now.

Hunter paused. "I used to catch Ben late at night on his laptop, jerking off. I thought it was just porn—but it was a picture of you. In the park."

Oh, god. That picture where I was topless and pulling my underwear down, back when we were in our public-sex phase. So Ben still looked at it, still got off to it. I swallowed, remembering how far apart my legs were spread. "You—saw that picture?" I managed.

"Yeah." He glanced at me and then away. "And after he left, I started jerking off to it too."

Heat flooded my body. "I, uh, assumed you weren't into girls," I said thickly.

He shrugged. "I used to be, in college. It's just that guys are easier. You girls make us work for it," he grinned.

I knocked my bottle against his. "Not all of us."

Our eyes met. And then we were kissing, his mouth hard and hot on mine, his tongue thrillingly aggressive. His hands were on my thighs, then sliding between them. Breathlessly, I pushed him away. Everyone was staring.

Hunter kissed me again. "My car," he muttered into my mouth.

Back across the street, through the falling snow and evening traffic, we went. The salon was closed now and only our two cars were in the back parking lot, both covered with snow. He unlocked his Civic and pulled me into the backseat. The darkness and cold closed around us, a contrast to the heat of his skin and mouth covering mine. Those agile fingers were hunting for my breasts, pushing up my sweater.

"So hot," he muttered. I felt my bra go up, my tits exposed in the car's frozen air, and then his teeth around my nipple. Oh, god. He was mauling and biting my breasts, groaning with appreciation as he sucked them.

Hunter moved on top of me, his hard-on pressing through his jeans. I slid my hands over his firm asscheeks, still slightly incredulous that this was happening. Ben's boyfriend and I were going to fuck: it was the last thing I'd envisioned. I pulled off his sweater and our jeans came off next. Finally we were naked, warm skin on warm skin.

His fingers found my pussy. I arched my back, delirium spreading through my blood as he expertly tickled my clit, rubbing his other fingers just inside my pussy. For someone who didn't normally date women, Hunter seemed to know his way around a vagina. He slid down and opened my thighs wide, and then I felt his tongue on my folds, hot, agile and eager. His fingers moved farther into my body, slowly rubbing me in sensitive, mind-blowing strokes.

My legs were shaking. Half of me wanted to come right now but the other half wanted something more. "Condom," I panted. "Please, Hunter…I really want to fuck you."

He groped in his jeans. Moments later, the hardness of his sheathed cock pushed against my slit. I moaned as his dick slowly penetrated my tightness.

"Oh, god," he breathed. "You feel so good."

Hunter pushed all the way into me, pausing before he withdrew. Over and over he tortured me like that, with lingering thrusts that drove me out of my mind. Excitement was building inside me like a hot, wet storm and I needed to come soon or I would scream.

Without warning, he pulled out of my cunt and rolled me over onto all fours. Taking my hips in hand, he began fucking me hard and fast, spearing into me with long, vigorous strokes. A wet ache was pulsing between my legs and as I reached down to rub my clit, my orgasm erupted inside me just as Hunter's body shuddered on top of mine.

He held me against him in the snowy darkness, stroking my hair. "So much for Ben," he said, with a small laugh.

I kissed him, pulling his chest against mine. "Who's Ben?"

MY ARMY BUDDY'S GIRLFRIEND

N. T. Morley

So what do you think?" asked Mitch, his arms around Haley.

I finished my latest beer. "About what?" I asked.

Mitch grinned, leaned down and whispered something in Haley's ear.

She responded to Mitch's words instantly by arching her back and thrusting her tits out through the tight white tube top.

Haley was seated at the edge of Mitch's big, cushy armchair. Mitch had his knees apart, with her pert little ass fitted between them; she was basically sitting in his lap.

She wasn't wearing very much.

Mitch brushed her cascade of chestnut-colored hair back over her narrow, bare shoulders, so it no longer obscured her firm, small tits. Her tan legs were clad only in too-short cutoffs.

With her back arched and her tits thrust out, she smiled at me. I tried not to stare.

"About *her*," said Mitch.

"What do you mean, what do I think?"

"You know what I mean," he said. "Go ahead, Walker. You can look. You been trying not to all night. Go ahead."

So I did.

I stared at her. I looked her over *close*.

I looked at the way her slim, tight, tanned body fit so easily into her snug white tube top and half-destroyed Daisy Dukes. I appreciated the way her nipples had stiffened the second I started looking at her. My gaze oozed down her legs. My eyes took a soft, slow taste of her bare feet with their red-painted toenails, then went back up to her shorts, where in addition to the top button—which had started out the evening unbuttoned—the zipper had mysteriously migrated halfway down her fly.

I'd written off the undone button to the shorts being too tight; they sure were tight. Like she'd eaten too much and needed some extra room. But Haley hadn't eaten much; she just sat there on Mitch's side of the table, letting Mitch feed her from his plate. She opened her mouth each time he gave her a forkful. It couldn't have been enough to make her feel so full she had to unbutton her pants.

She'd been drinking from Mitch's beer, too; whenever

he handed it to her, she took a deep gulp. She downed the two shots he poured for her, too. She was clearly a little high, but she hadn't drunk enough beer to be bloated.

My dick was already stiffening.

"She's submissive," said Mitch. "You know what that means?"

"Basically," I said.

"Well, then, go ahead and say it. Tell me what you think."

"She's hot," I said.

"Hot?" Mitch scoffed. "Bullshit. Come on, Walker. You can do better than that. Say something about her body."

She stuck her tits out more. She inclined her chin slightly. Her full lips parted. She panted slightly and let out a gentle, mewling moan.

I was drunk; I was horny. Hours from home to interview for a job I didn't really want, I didn't have money for a hotel. Wiped, I was about to face the four-hour drive back to Memphis, but with no girl in bed waiting for me, I had little incentive. I had almost slept in the back of the Honda, but then I remembered my Army buddy Mitch lived around here. I dug through my shit for his cell number, called and asked if I could crash. "The couch ain't that comfortable," said Mitch. "But I'll see what we can work out."

I came over and met his new girlfriend—Haley. Twenty-three years old; didn't look a day over nineteen. Gorgeous.

I'd offered to pick up a pizza on the way over. Mitch insisted we let Haley cook up some grub. She grilled burgers. She made salad. She opened our beers. She poured whisky shots whenever Mitch decided he or I needed one. She took a couple of her own.

Every time I finished a beer or Mitch decided I needed another whisky shot, Haley got one for me quickly, taking a slow wiggle past me like she wanted me to look at her body. Or like Mitch did.

"Come on," said Mitch. "Don't be a gentleman. Say something about her body."

"It's a hell of a body," I said.

"Not good enough. Say something *rude*."

"I'm not saying something rude."

"Please, Sir?" It was Haley's turn to ask.

"Uh-uh," I said.

"Then tell me this," said Mitch, patting Haley on the thigh. She obediently spread her legs. "Tell me, Walker. Would you fuck this?"

"This?" I sneered. "I don't think so," I said.

"I like it, Sir," said Haley, her face getting slightly pink.

"I can tell," I said, eyeballing her nipples and the way they stretched her tube top.

"Well, then...how about a blow job?" said Mitch. "No strings attached."

Haley added, "Yes, Sir, please? I love to suck cock."

"She does," Mitch confirmed. Then he shoved two fingers in her mouth. Haley started sucking on them obediently, her tongue swirling around with the obvious message that it was exactly what she'd do to a man's cock.

Mitch said, "Are these the world's most fuckable lips or what? Could you stick your dick in this face? Come on, Walker. Say those dirty things you been thinking about her."

I shrugged.

Mitch's fingers came out of Haley's mouth, trailing a glisten of spit.

She told me brightly, "Please, Sir? I like it. I like hearing what men really think about my body."

I finally said: "You've got one hell of a pair of tits," I said. "Not big, but they don't need to be. And it looks like your legs must spread real easy."

Haley gave a shimmy, brightening, happy.

"They do," she said, spreading them wider. "See?"

"And she gets *real* wet when I show her off," said Mitch. He reached down and shoved his hands in her shorts. It was easy with the zipper half-open like that. Haley let out a tiny moan as he felt her up.

His fingers came out and he showed me how wet they were by rubbing them together.

Then he stuck them back in her mouth—this time coated with her juices. She licked them even more eagerly than she had before.

"Think you'd like it if she did that to your cock?" Mitch asked.

I thought about it for maybe half a second.

"Yeah," I said. "I think I damn well would."

Mitch tipped Haley out of his lap and smacked her on the ass. Haley's hand went to her zipper; she wriggled out of her shorts. She pulled off her tube top.

She came to me, naked.

Her pussy was shaved and tattooed. Her clit had a bright silver ring through it; above it, in block letters, was the single word SLAVE.

She dropped to her knees before me.

I adjusted myself so she could get what she wanted.

She looked up at me as she kissed my crotch. Mitch was watching, too. Haley's lipsticked mouth gave my cock wet kisses through my jeans; as she did that, her fingers took on a life of their own—unbuckling, unbuttoning, unzipping. She reached in and drew my cock out of my jockeys.

She was hungry for it. She opened wide and took it. I haven't got the biggest cock in the world, but I'll say I'm a helping and a half. She swallowed it all in one gulp, just a few bobbing slurps into the blow job. Her snug throat opened up and took my dick all the way down.

She stayed down awhile, playing with my balls.

When she came up for air, she was gasping. She panted. Drool was everywhere. Ruined lipstick.

Haley went back down on me, slurping eagerly. She drooled; she stroked with her hand. She worked me up into a frenzy fast, like she was hungry for my cum.

Mitch watched every second, *proud*.

I held back some moans of my own. I'd never felt a

girl give head like that. Mitch never took his eyes off Haley, but he poured another shot and downed it.

She had me close.

She panted, "Please cum in my mouth, Sir?"

A gentleman couldn't say no.

She brought me off with a series of strokes—nice and deep, almost into her throat but not quite. Her hand worked my base. I exploded inside her. I came so hard I clawed at the couch.

When I was still seeing stars, Mitch raised his beer to toast us.

"Way I figure it, Walker...you get this job, you'll need a place to crash for a while. I think Haley would like having you around."

Having swallowed the last of my cum, Haley looked up at me happily.

"Yes, Sir," she told me. "I'd like that a lot."

I got the job. And "a while" turned into more than a while. But that's another story. I finally learned to say rude things about Haley's body without any trouble— no trouble at all. And Haley loved every minute of it.

And the good news is, I never had to sleep on the couch.

TWO-MAN
JOB

A. M. Hartnett

Seventy-six Windy Gate was a small triangular house that resembled a pointed hat, or that appeared as if perhaps there was a larger house under the ground that was beginning to sprout. A hedge of wild roses shielded the neat lawn from the road. At the end of the gravel driveway was a sign, painted purple and green on black, that read THISTLE STUDIO & TEAROOM and beckoned passersby to stop in for a visit.

Not today, though. A sandwich board on the opposite side of the driveway read CLOSED ON SUNDAY. No fresh scones or tea with sugar cubes for aging vacationers. No delightful view of the garden with butterflies for the little ones to chase. Tourists following road signage to the award-winning establishment could hammer on the front door all they liked, but Gracie

Hammond wouldn't be greeting them with a smile.

Sunday morning was for church, and Sunday after-noon was for getting a week's worth of sin in the few short hours she had off.

On that particular Sunday she was still in the violet pumps that matched her crochet handbag, but gone was the modest yellow dress she had gotten so many compliments on at the tea social after the service. That particular garment had been lost in the kitchen. Ruined, no doubt, when it had been ripped off of her.

Two hours of church mingling had been enough torture for Jonathan. The twenty-year-old lacked patience, but the young divorcée had tempered his urge to fuck fast and hard by pinning him beneath her, her knees on either side of his face. His hot tongue glided in and out, the slow kind of tongue-fuck she'd tutored him in from the first day they'd met, when he'd shown up to install a birdhouse in the garden.

She moaned, the sound coming out as more of a gurgle as Jonathan's cousin worked his hips in tune with the steady suction of her lips around his cock.

Gracie was still surprised Jonathan had agreed to bring Keith to the Thistle on Sunday. After she'd quizzed him about the young man she saw him with in town he'd sulked about sharing, but in the end it was just another lesson for him. If he wanted a slice of her time on Sunday, he would have to learn to play nice.

After all, she could find another like him if she wanted. For now, she'd have them both, one at a time.

Her thighs quivered as his soft tongue worked a circle around the hard flesh. One hand splayed across her ass, the ring finger exploring. The other hand crooked under his chin, fingers gliding into her pussy to the knuckle.

With Keith's calloused hand at the back of her neck, it was Gracie who was forced to rein in the need to fuck—and she wanted it *bad*. Moving her hand from his balls to the root of his cock, she grasped him and poured the pleasure Jonathan's tongue was creating into sucking Keith off.

When she couldn't stand the triple effect of Jonathan working from beneath her, when she became so wet from Jonathan's adept tongue and fingers, she pulled away.

Gracie knelt on the carpet next to Jonathan and turned her full attention on Keith. Crooking a finger at him, she beckoned.

If Jonathan had any arguments about being second, he kept them to himself as his cousin slipped on a condom, instead creeping close to her and reaching between her legs as Keith entered her from behind.

Keith's thrusts were steady, the perfect combination with a cock that was thick and curved. Her toes curled inside her pumps as each stroke brought the fat head over her G-spot.

She parted her lips as Jonathan claimed her mouth. Tongue twisted with tongue, as chaotic as his fingers rubbing her clitoris. She felt his movements as he jerked his cock one-handed.

The heat that flashed through her body was a powerful reminder of why she continued to reject any attempt to end her singlehood. She'd been married. Her husband had never made her come as hard as she was now accustomed to and expected.

Sweat spraying from his chest to her bare back, Keith came first, bruising the plumpness around her hips with digging fingertips, grunting, thrusting without breaking pace until his cock throbbed between her slick walls.

Jonathan didn't waste a second. As soon as Keith rolled away, Jonathan wrapped his dick and mounted her. Longer and slimmer than his cousin, he worked his cock in and out, long and deep. Gracie went down as though in supplication, one hand digging into the carpet while the other took up the task of rubbing her clit.

The time for patience had passed. Her orgasm was upon her almost immediately. Her whole body was slippery and rubbery and her hand was coated with the juices that smeared her pubic hair and the inside of her thighs. She suddenly couldn't breathe and didn't care, not when every part of her body was being rocked by her climax.

She heard Jonathan moan, felt his cock twitch where it was buried deep and squeezed by the hot muscles surrounding it.

When lethargy ebbed into a glorious satisfaction she stood, stretched, and looked from one to the other.

"You know, Mondays aren't nearly as busy as I'd like

them to be. I'm thinking a half day would suffice. If one or both of you could pop in at about one o'clock…"

As they exchanged looks she grinned.

"I'm sure I can find some use for both of you."

SEX IN THE SHOWER

Thomas S. Roche

Naomi had always loved sex in the shower, but it wasn't till she did it with Kurt that things went totally out of control.

She'd first gotten dirty in the shower when she lived with her parents. She'd sneaked her boyfriend Darius in with her while her parents were sleeping.

She'd soaped him up; he'd soaped her up; she'd gone down on him a little and, owing to the taste of soap, finally jacked him off instead.

He'd climaxed without losing his balance and without making a sound. Not one that could be heard over the sound of the shower, at least. There was a soft, low murmur of pleasure from Darius's lips, but it got lost in the sound of the cascading water, and no one had heard it but Naomi.

Naomi and Darius waited till her parents weren't home to try it again. Darius and she weren't really "configured" to actually fuck in the shower, though. He had a very large cock and he was very tall. When she positioned herself for bent-over sex-from-behind in the shower, the angle of penetration made his cock seem to hit all the wrong spots. Naomi had to call it off.

They tried using lube. Naomi had needed it from the start with Darius, especially since she'd been a virgin. She'd gotten it free in packets from the Wallace River College, along with a pamphlet on the importance of its use—which she'd already picked up from the sex books the conservatives had been unable to ban in the college library. After she and Darius went all the way, Naomi quickly became a huge proponent of lube; the two packets it had taken the first seven times or so turned into just one as she got used to the process and became more economical. But she still relied on that one packet to make intercourse feel glorious, no matter how aroused she was. Unfortunately, the water tended to wash the lube away. It wasn't until Naomi discovered the potential for creative use of an ear syringe that she was able to get herself good and wet enough up inside to really take it from behind and have it feel really good. She couldn't cum—she was pretty sure she'd *never* be able to cum—but Darius could, and it felt awfully good in the meantime.

She would have done it every day if she or Darius had been living alone, but living with her parents made that impossible.

After she transferred to Moore State, the communal dorm showers were not conducive to that kind of adventure. In the first place, they were shrouded by nothing more than stall doors with curtains. In the second place, they just didn't *smell* very sexy.

In fact, they smelled like ass, and not in a good way.

Darius was out of the picture by then, and Naomi bought a cheap waterproof vibrator by mail. It was underpowered and overloud, and after one furtive try at four in the morning when she was sure no one else on her hall was up, she threw the damned thing away. After that, when she wanted to wank she waited till her roommate was gone.

It wasn't until years later that she met Kurt, who was considerably shorter than Darius and had a cock that pointed down. Naomi wasn't sure why it did or what it meant, but the first thought she had when she reached into Kurt's pants was that his cock would hit all the right spots if he fucked her from behind. Trying out her hypothesis just a few minutes later, she found considerable supporting data. His cock didn't *just* point down; it pointed down and slightly to the right, which meant depending on how she jiggled her bum, his cockhead hit her G-spot at a varying angle as the lower part of his shaft, which widened slightly down its length, tugged with each deep penetration at her labia—just enough to tug them against her clit. If it had done this along the whole length of his shaft, it would have been way too much stimulation; as it was, the sensation hit her clit in a rhythmic pattern, matched to his fucking and paired with the deep, gentle stroke of his angled cock-head against her G-spot. Naomi came hard on his cock, a very first time for her on a first date—it usually took weeks for her to get warmed up to a new guy.

They had three more "dates" in rapid succession: that very Friday, the next day—Saturday—and then the next Tuesday. Getting fucked from behind by Kurt's cock turned out to be her new favorite thing, not counting the rest of him, of which she found herself equally fond. She told him this on Tuesday—well before you're "supposed" to say such things in a new relationship, right? But she cushioned the revelation by saying if she had to choose between bent-over sex with Kurt and everything else about him, she'd be hard-pressed to decide.

"I think you'd be shown the door," she joked. "Everything but your cock."

Kurt liked that.

That got Naomi thinking all about shower sex again. She still felt splendidly sexy in the shower much of the time—she just didn't do much about it. She remembered how Darius's cock, nice as it was, hadn't quite hit the necessary spots to really blow her mind in the shower... but Kurt's probably would.

That got her wondering whether she *wanted* her mind blown in the shower—wouldn't she slip and fall?

She decided to risk it.

Kurt had never had sex in the shower—not "all the way" kind of sex—but it sounded good to him. Naomi kept her shower clean, and it smelled sexy—like lilacs and hyacinth. It gave him a hard-on just smelling it. Sex in the shower sounded *more* than good to him. So when Naomi coaxed him in and soaped him up and rinsed him off and knelt and sucked and stroked him, Kurt was an instant fan of shower sex. He came on her tits and she lathered it up before washing it away, which was hot in its own way.

And Naomi, for her part, felt a thrill as she knelt with the warmth of the cascading water on her back and the warmth of Kurt's cum on her breasts. She kissed his balls and smelled his clean body and felt a visceral, bodily sexual response to knowing that Kurt was the kind of guy whose knees didn't buckle when he came.

She couldn't *wait* for their next shower.

It happened the next weekend, late on Sunday, after a long morning cuddle and a teasing half a blow job. Kurt wanted more, but Naomi coaxed him out of bed with a purring, "But we're both so dirty…we should get clean."

Naomi's arousal was palpable as she soaped Kurt up and rubbed him down. She rinsed him good before she sucked him again; even with the faint lingering bitter sting of soap on her tongue, she could taste his leaking precum from the tip. She stroked and sucked and kissed him slowly, never letting Kurt get too far too fast, no matter how loudly he moaned. She drooled all she wanted and felt the water rinsing it away.

When she paused and looked up from Kurt's crotch

and said with a smile, "You up for fucking me?" Kurt didn't say a word—he just took hold of her shoulders. He guided her up, turned her around, bent her over.

"Hell, yes," he said as he slid up to her entrance.

This time, Naomi didn't need the ear syringe—but she'd slicked herself up with lube just to be sure. The water had probably washed most of it away by then—but it didn't matter; Kurt fit her perfectly.

His cock slid into Naomi easily from behind, and he fucked her gently with the soothing warm water pouring all over them.

This time his cock didn't just hit the right spots; it hit them harder than ever.

But Naomi had been right to worry. She came so hard she almost slipped and fell. Luckily, Kurt kept his balance and steadied her. She didn't have to stifle her moans of pleasure, and there were plenty of them—loud and emphatic.

She gave him a key to her place just a couple of days later. Their shower sex became a regular thing—every weekend morning, usually, and sometimes even on weekdays. Naomi fell quickly and hopelessly in love.

And that was *before* the day she came home to find out that while she'd been at work, Kurt had celebrated their three-month anniversary by installing grab-rails, nonslip appliqués—and, most importantly, a shower massager.

No question about it, Naomi decided.

This was a match made in the shower.

DEEP THROAT, DEEP LOVE

Kristina Lloyd

We were in Valentino's Bar, first date, third martini. It was going well so I told him how, as a kid, I used to fantasize about getting tied up by cowboys outside a saloon bar.

In return, he told me when he was a kid, maybe slightly older, he used to think bondage involved two people tying themselves together. He'd thought it was like marriage but naughtier and more fun. If you did bondage with someone, it meant you loved them.

"Kids," I said. "So sweet."

"Yeah," he said. "Not really."

A new year was starting, and we didn't want to fall in love. When the snowdrops were pushing through, we brought a little light bondage into the bedroom, still shy like the flowers. His marriage had recently ended.

He hadn't come into his own yet. He kept twirling the emptiness on his finger where his wedding ring used to be. I was worried I might be his rebound.

By the time the crocuses arrived, splashing yellow and purple across hard, blank ground, we'd moved on to more dangerous territory. He would hit me, twist my nipples, tie my wrists to my ankles and fuck me. Sometimes I would cry afterward and so would he but for different reasons. My tears were a glorious release after zoning out in that taut, trapped place of being subjected to pain. His tears were the pain of loss and fear.

When the daffodils grew tall and bright, trumpeting spring, he grew tall and bright too. His finger no longer had the pale, sickly waist of his invisible ring. Then the tulips came along, tender spears turning to heavy-headed blooms, their throats bared in offer of vulnerability. He began to care less about what I wanted in bed and more about what he wanted, which actually was what I wanted anyway. I like feeling used.

Paradoxically, he got off on me getting off, and the more he seemed to get off, irrespective of me, the more I got off. It was an unvicious circle, even when he was vicious.

Now he was sitting naked on the edge of my bed and I was on my knees between his open thighs, sucking him. I had some bondage tape in my toy box, that stuff that sticks to itself and doesn't leave you gummed up with adhesive. He reached for it, dislodging his cock from my mouth, then said, "Hands on my thighs."

I followed his order. The tape made a ragged squeak as he pulled it from the roll. He wrapped it tight around his thigh and my arm, bent to tear off the strip with his teeth, then repeated the action on the other side. I was left kneeling between his spread, muscular legs, my arms bound to his thighs.

"Now carry on," he said. "All I want is your mouth, no hands."

I continued, missing the use of my hands when I needed a backup or a breather. It made me work harder for him, made me keep going when my jaw ached or I felt a little choked. I flooded him with liquid spilling from my mouth. He sat there like a king on his throne, relishing his might.

In recollection, I think of that line from one of Shakespeare's sonnets: *Being your slave, what should I do but tend upon the hours and times of your desire?*

But at the time there was no poetry save that of cock, spit and grunting, and the desire to take him fully in my throat. I think that's a kind of poetry too, a space of being absorbed in a moment that language can weave patterns around but never hold.

I went far, far down. At the final push, my throat opened like a tiny gate and I held him inside me. With my gag reflex subdued, I was also subdued, at ease and wide open to him, connected and silenced. I sucked back along his length, feeling calmed, slurped on his end, then went down again.

He didn't sound at all calm. My nose nuzzled his

pubes and he said stuff like, "Ohhh jesusfuckingoh... yes, oh there, ohgodmy, ohh, ohhhh..."

His incoherence affected me as strongly as a tongue on my clit. When he came, he was so deep inside my mouth I didn't even taste him. I drew back, coughed, and blinked tears from my eyes. "I think I've got come up my nose," I said.

He laughed. I expected him to free my hands but instead he leaned to tug a tissue from a box, doubled it and pinched it to my nose. He made me blow like a child. "Better?"

I nodded. He cupped my head to his groin, stroking my hair, my arms still taped to his thighs. After a while, he said, "Remember Valentino's when I told you what I used to think bondage was?"

"Uh-huh."

I looked up at him as he swept my hair from my face.

"I think I was right," he said.

HOARDER

Bella Dean

Cleeeeeeeean!" I bellowed it. I was angry, but that was because I was hot. It was hotter than fuck, and I hate heat.

"I am cleaning," Mark said.

I stood in the center of his workroom and stared. There was...*stuff* as far as the eye could see. Nails in baby-food jars, loops of rope, screws, hammers, sandpaper. There was a crab bushel full of electrical wire and it appeared to be severed at both ends. Both. Ends. What the fuck was that for?

"This is not clean," I whispered. "This is an episode of one of those shows about people who hoard," I growled. But I pressed my ass to his workbench and tried to catch my breath. It might be insanely cluttered, but at least it was cool. No wonder this was his man lair.

I fanned myself and looked around some more. Men's magazines, cigar boxes full of god knew what. Jars, hinges and three clocks. Three.

"Everything here has a purpose, either presently or in the future," Mark chuckled, opening his mini-fridge. He popped a wheat beer and took a hefty swig.

"Oh, really?" I snapped.

"Really." He handed me the beer and watched me swallow three big swigs. He was amused. Even more so when I stifled a tiny burp. Thank goodness it was tiny. Sometimes beer makes me sound like a trucker after a truck-stop diner.

"Don't fuck with me," I said. "It's hot."

"Hey, you're the genius who declared the hottest day of the summer as cleaning day. Not like...*weekly* cleaning, but trucks-full-of-stuff-to-the-dump cleaning." He finished off the cold beer.

"This room is a trip to the dump!" I knew deep down it was the heat and not him, but I couldn't quite seem to zip my lip.

"Well, this room is staying as is." He crossed his arms.

The cold beer and the cool room made my poor over-heated body's wires cross. My nipples spiked and goose bumps rose up on my skin.

He touched me and I bristled.

"Everything has a purpose, my ass," I said.

"Pick something," he said, leaning against the wall as if he hadn't a care in the world. Which only served to anger me more.

"Pick something?"

He circled the hard point of my nipple with his fingertip. I jumped, surprised by the unexpected move. But once the surprise passed, the aftermath of that touch seared through the core of me, settling wetly in my pussy. He played dirty.

"Did I stutter?"

"The cord," I said, cocking my hips and raising my voice. I'd show him to mess with my head like that. I was mad, not turned on. Touching me had just...confused things.

"What cord?" His eyes danced around his little den of solitude.

I barked laughter and threw my hands up in the air. "See! You don't even know what cord. The cord in the crab bushel? It appears to be severed on *both* ends. So what the hell use you could have for *that* I'd love to know."

"Ah, this cord?" He snagged an orange length of said cord. He waggled it at me.

"Yep." I crossed my arms. He should just admit defeat now and help me empty this insanely full room.

The cord slithered from his grip to coil at my feet. "Damn," he said, squatting to gather it up.

I started making a mental list of all the shit I'd clear out of this room. That was what I *started* doing. Until I noticed he'd looped the orange cord around my ankles, binding ankle to ankle with enough give for me to move a bit but tight enough to keep me from getting my ankles free of the loops he'd tied.

"What the fuck, Mark?" I breathed, realization already starting to dawn. "This isn't a Boy Scout exhibition. Untie me."

"Oh, I'm no Boy Scout," my husband said and tugged the tie on my shorts.

"Don't do that," I said, but there was no steel in my voice. It was all breathy and...expectant.

"This?" He tugged once more to get a final bit of stubborn bow to pull free. "How about this?" He pushed my shorts down to my bound ankles.

Now I was standing in his cluttered mind fuck of a workroom in my pale-yellow panties. "Pull them back up."

"What's that? Make sure to pull these down?" He pulled my panties down lazily. Watching me with his big brown eyes as he did. Waiting to see what I'd do. What I'd say.

"Mark—"

"Shh..." He kissed me once above each knee. My legs erupted in goose bumps this time. Now I was aroused, still a bit overheated *and* in a cool dungeon-like workroom. My body was the definition of chaos. A fine example was the tickle of fluid I felt slipping from my pussy.

"Mark..." I began, but I forgot what I was going to say. I shifted as best as I could with my ankles bound and my husband's big hands on my thighs.

"See, I think you are getting way too worked up over this cleaning thing, Eva." He kissed my inner thigh, slipped a single finger into my cunt, scrambled my brain with his ministrations.

"I…"

"This is a *work*room. It's supposed to be cluttered and stuffed full of…stuff."

"I…" That seemed to be all I could say. The clearest thought I could form. Pitiful.

His tongue slid, slow and eager, over my clitoris and my knees dipped like I was curtseying. So he walked me back, shuffling forward on his knees until my ass hit his workbench and I was braced.

"I am not touching anything in this workroom but you. It's all useful. Take this cord for example…" But he broke off his own sentence and latched his searing mouth over my pussy and sucked mightily. The pressure from that suction worked deep inside of me. My clit ached for him to lick me. My heart pounded, bringing fresh blood to my cheeks that had nothing at all to do with the ninety-something-degree temperature.

"I…"

"Need to say a new word," he laughed and then gave me what I needed. Broad, slick drags of his tongue over that small knot of an organ. So much pleasure concentrated into one tiny place.

For some reason I had forgotten my hands were not bound, only my ankles, and I held them clutched together between my breasts. But I finally realized I could move them and I clutched the workbench with one hand and my husband with the other. He never let up with his tongue, delivering slippery circles and bold prods with the rigid tip of his tongue until he grunted once and stood, undoing his shorts.

He turned me so my belly brushed the lip of his table and my legs were spread as wide as his nifty orange cord would allow. He took my hand and put it under my stomach and said, "Use this if you need it. But you might not. You're wet as a waterfall, Eva."

He nipped my shoulder with his sharp white teeth and then forced three fingers into my pussy, thrusting into me until I let my head fall forward in surrender. I was going to come if he kept doing that.

"Please," I said.

"Oh, a new word," Mark chuckled.

I smiled, my ire long forgotten. I pushed my ass up and back as he slid the tip of his cock between my legs. I pushed back more eagerly when he penetrated me just a bit and then stilled.

"I'm not cleaning out this room."

"Fine, fine, fine," I chanted, nodding my head like a maniacal marionette.

"Any other room you want is fine," he whispered, sliding in another inch but stilling again.

"Yes, okay, great!" I yelped.

Laughing softly at my expense, he gripped my hips up tight and rammed into me. My belly hit the workbench and I rattled jars and tools and bungee cords. My fingers flew over my clit, I didn't really need it, but the extra pressure felt too good to deny.

"This won't take long," he groaned. "Something about seeing you all trussed up does it for me."

I sighed, pinching my clit hard between my fingertips as Mark surged forward and when he grunted, taking my earlobe in his teeth and my breast in his hand, I started to rub again and I came. As soon as I came, he lost his battle and groaned out his release against my neck.

"Did you hear me?" Mark panted, stroking my breast gently so the nipple went erect again.

"I heard you."

"And?"

"If this is the payoff, you can hoard all you want." I was blushing. It felt good.

"Let me recuperate, and I'll let you pick another item. We'll see what we can do with that." Then he bent to untie me.

TV REPAIRS

Sophia Valenti

There you go," Joe said, and in nearly the same instant, the television flickered on. A peppy blonde was onscreen swearing that "you at home" could make a gourmet meal with everyday ingredients found in a typical kitchen. I couldn't pay attention to her delectable spread, however, because my eyes were currently feasting on the sliver of fuchsia satin that was peeking out of the waistband of Joe's jeans.

Joe was on his hands and knees, with his head buried behind the set, as he explained that a couple of cables had popped loose. I blinked my eyes, wondering if I was dreaming. Nope—still there. Those were undeniably panties. No man's underwear could be that shiny and sleek and pink.

Joe's a strong, six-foot-two guy who plays rugby on

the weekends. His well-muscled frame is the epitome of masculinity, and was the number-one reason I couldn't take my eyes off of him when we'd met a few weeks ago. But the fact that he had this kinky secret—this softer, sensual side—thrilled me in an indecent way.

He and I had only been on a couple of dates, when I was on the phone complaining about my television woes. Joe immediately offered to come to my aid. I hadn't been surprised that he fixed my problem so quickly, but what did surprise me was this delicious, pink revelation.

I'd promised Joe pizza and beer for his efforts, but I was suddenly hungry for something else—for the sight of this big, handsome man wearing nothing but those delicate panties. I wanted to run my tongue along his cock, tracing his satin-covered erection, and make him groan with abandon.

Joe carefully backed out from behind the set, standing up with a lopsided grin. His dark blond hair was mussed, and he looked sexier than ever to me. I couldn't hold myself back.

"Thanks," I whispered, throwing my arms around his neck and raising myself up on tiptoes to bring my lips to his. I gave him a long, lingering kiss, filled with lustful promises that I planned to deliver on. I slid my hands down his back, cupping his muscular ass as I deepened our lip-lock, this time teasing him with my tongue, flicking against him and opening him to me as I moaned softly into his mouth.

I ran my hands back and forth across his ass as I imagined what that sleek satin would feel like under my fingers, and I was desperate to experience it for real. I reached for his waistband, but he stopped me with a gentle hand.

"You don't have to thank me *that* way," he said, his stubble-covered cheeks blushing red.

"But I want to," I purred, noting the self-conscious way he licked his upper lip. His nervousness was heart-meltingly adorable.

"It's just—"

"It's okay." I rose up higher on my toes so I could whisper in his ear. "I saw them. They're pretty—and I want to see more."

I felt Joe stiffen in my arms, and for a moment, I wondered if I'd pushed him too far, too fast. I pulled back to look into his green eyes, which were wide with wonder.

"I mean that," I said, caressing his cheek.

Closing his eyes, Joe turned toward my hand, nuzzling it for a moment before he pulled me close for another kiss, but this time he was in charge. His arms gripped me tightly as he claimed me with his mouth. His tongue teased mine only briefly before diving deeper and taking my breath away.

We parted and looked at each other for a beat. I could read his eyes and saw that he believed me, and that he wanted nothing more than to share this part of himself with me. I took Joe's hand in mine, whispering huskily, "Come," as I led him down the hallway and into my bedroom.

Joe immediately brought his hands to my blouse, working the tiny shell buttons through their holes with a deftness that surprised me. He pushed the shirt off my shoulders, and as the garment fell to the floor, his eyes fell to my bra-covered breasts. He cupped them gently, his thumbs trailing over the edges of the French lace in silent admiration.

"It would look so sweet on you," I whispered as he caressed my bra. "I know a shop. They have the most beautiful things, in all sorts of sizes."

Joe looked up at me, his gaze filled with hope and arousal.

"I'll take you shopping," I continued, running my fingers down the front of his shirt and over his denim-covered bulge, which had grown considerably larger. "I can't wait to dress you up like my own perfect doll."

"You'd do that for me?" he asked in an incredulous whisper.

"Uh-huh. But not now. Now I want to see you—in your pretty panties."

This time, when I reached for his jeans, Joe didn't stop me. I popped open the button and slowly lowered his zipper, the denim parting to reveal the front panel of those fuchsia panties, stuffed full of hard cock. A wave of arousal washed over me at the sight, and I hurriedly stripped him out of his masculine clothes and urged him onto the bed.

After wriggling out of my skirt and kicking off my heels, I parted his legs and crawled up between his spread thighs. I traced my fingers along the lines of tense muscle, kissing my way up to his crotch. Leaning forward, I planted a soft kiss right on the front of his panties, making him rear up and groan. I grabbed his hips, holding him tight to the mattress and keeping him where I wanted him as I ran my tongue up and down his satin-covered bulge. Joe's breathing was ragged, and he tangled his fingers in my hair as he struggled to keep his composure.

I dragged my tongue back and forth, until the front of Joe's panties was dark and clinging to his formidable shaft. I could see every contour of his cock, and the image was making my own panties damp as my pussy dripped with longing. I was done teasing him; I yanked down the front of Joe's underwear, leaving the lingerie banded around his thighs as I took his dick in my mouth. I fingered the sides of his sleek panties as my lips rose and fell on his shaft, bringing him close to the edge, but stopping before he could reach his peak.

I backed away, and Joe was staring at me with half-lidded eyes that roamed along my body. I knew he was admiring my lingerie as much as he was admiring me. That made me smile, and I didn't try to hide it as I strad-dled his hips. Rocking back and forth, I gently teased his cock with the soaked crotch of my panties. The lace was smooth and slick with my honey, and Joe bucked up toward me to increase the pressure. The sexy friction of the lace rubbing against my clit had me teetering on the edge of orgasm in no time.

I rose and yanked aside the panties as I grabbed the base of Joe's shaft. Holding him steady, I lowered my sex down onto him, his cock filling me completely. I could feel his bunched up panties beneath my ass, and I reached behind myself, stroking his balls through the rumpled satin as I began to ride his dick. I knew each time I moved, the lace was dragging along the length of his dick. That same lace was continuing to tease my sensitive clit as I ground my crotch against his.

The sinful stroking of the lace—combined with the snug, wet heat of my cunt—was rapidly working Joe into a lather. He reached up to palm my bra-covered tits as his hips jerked up off the mattress. The sudden pressure was too much for me, and I cried out as I felt my climax break. My pussy spasmed around his shaft as he jammed his hips up one last time, before he shivered through his own release.

I collapsed on Joe's chest, and we both laughed at our sudden, frenzied coupling before eventually growing quiet.

"You're the only one," he finally murmured. "The only woman who's been okay with it." I could hear years of disappointment and hurt melting away as he spoke.

I turned his chin toward me, so I could look into those bottomless green eyes. "You don't have to hide. Just be yourself. That's the guy I want."

He kissed the top of my head affectionately, and when I drifted off to sleep, I dreamt of satin and lace—and Joe.

TRIPTYCH

Kat Watson

My day had been utter shit. From spilling coffee all over myself during my walk to the office to getting yelled at about something out of my control, it was nothing but frustration. I walked through the front door of my apartment, kicked off my shoes and exhaled deeply for the first time in nine hours. Just after I finished pouring myself a full glass of red, I heard the front door and smiled.

"Hello?"

"Hey," I called back. "In the kitchen. Want a glass of wine?"

"God, yes," Olivia said, walking around the corner.

I handed her a glass and she leaned in, her soft lips melting against mine. When she pulled back, I laughed at the way our lipstick blended together; the contrast of my light pink with her deeper red had turned into an interesting swirl on her mouth.

"How was your day?" she asked, eyes fixed on my lips. I wondered if she wanted another kiss or was having the same thoughts about our makeup.

"Long. Yours?"

"Eh. It was fine." She shrugged then walked behind me to rub my shoulders. "You're all tense, baby. Come on, I'm getting the table."

"No! You just got home from work."

"No arguing." She'd already unfolded the massage table we kept in the dining room. "Strip and get up, facedown."

I did, knowing what was ahead of me. Liv had magic hands, and though I felt bad that she'd just finished a day of the same kind of labor, I looked forward to the excellent massage.

The oil was warm as her hands kneaded my over-worked muscles. The one drawback of getting a massage from her was that her sweeping touches not only relaxed me, but stirred my need. I was glad it was the end of the week and hoped that meant we'd have time to indulge in each other. It'd been far too long since we'd been able to reconnect slowly and lovingly; the rush of life swept us up, stealing our precious time together.

"Turn over, sweetness."

At her day job, she used a sheet for modesty, but with me it wasn't necessary. My body was as much hers as mine, so I rolled and waited. My eyes closed again after we exchanged a brief glance and I smiled to see that she was also undressed.

Her skin slid against mine, the oil making it glide easily. My muscles released under her touch. When she climbed onto the table, her knees surrounded my hips. My lips turned up again, and my eyes opened.

"Hi," she said softly. "Relaxed?"

"Mm-hm," I hummed, brain and body jelly.

She scooted down and began a feathery-light trail of touches up the outside of my thighs. "Good. Let me make you feel even better."

Kissing me softly, she let the passion build slowly. Her hands roamed, stopping to tease the small hoops through my nipples, eventually settling between my thighs. Soft fingers slid over the top of my pussy, dipping to glide inside, bringing me closer to the edge of my orgasm. When my legs began to shake, she pulled away, kissing down my stomach then across my thighs. The softness of her mouth skimmed my pussy, and the breath left my body. She pushed her fingers inside, sliding her lips and tongue against my clit.

"Turn around," I said.

Humming against my skin, she did as I'd asked, bringing her knees to my ears and allowing me to mirror her actions. Using my fingers to spread her, I pushed my tongue inside as far as I could. I focused on her, the taste and smell and sensation, until she won, distracting me until I could only feel.

I was so distracted by her that I didn't notice Jason

had come home. When I heard his low groan, I turned to look at him, smiling, as his clothes hit the floor. Olivia never slowed her movements. My eyes closed again as my whole body tightened against hers. My back arched as she persisted, fingers fucking me as her tongue lapped back and forth over my clit. As I came, I felt Jason's hands squeeze my legs, calluses scratching, his presence reminding me of his love.

While I came down, I thought about when I first fell in love with Liv. We'd been friends forever and I tried to deny my feelings for her for almost as long. She confessed her feelings for me, leading me to a long talk with Jason. He reminded me that he loved me no matter what—we were already committed to each other in every way. I couldn't figure out how to make the pieces fit and work if we added Olivia, though. They gave me time and gentle nudges, and now we functioned as a family of three. I was luckier than most and didn't have to give up any facet of who I was or compromise what I wanted from life—the love of a man *and* a woman.

I didn't have time to sink deeply into those thoughts; Olivia crawled off me, the slight breeze against my over-heated body making me shiver. A hand from each of them curled into mine, helping me up, and we walked to the bedroom.

Standing back, I let go and they climbed on the bed. Liv hadn't been sure she could ever be with Jason without me, but as I watched him love her, it was so clear that it was always meant to be this way.

"Get over here," Jason playfully said over his shoulder.

"What if I'm enjoying the view?" I teased.

The muscles in his back and ass flexed and Olivia's breath hitched, a slow moan coming from her. I imagined them—his hands pinching and pulling her nipples, his mouth kissing, licking and nipping.

"I think you'd enjoy it better if you were part of the view."

His voice was muffled against her skin and a sting of jealousy coursed through me. He was right. I wanted in, on, above, below, penetrated and loved: everything.

I sat on the bed behind Olivia. Kissing the side of her neck, I kept my eyes on Jason as I touched her body. His wink was a fresh reminder that he was there for us both, and I laughed as he pulled our legs down farther on the bed. If ever there was a man that could handle two women, it was Jason. Skilled didn't even begin to cover it.

Grateful that Olivia was smaller than me, I adjusted to her weight on me with little effort and I watched as Jason aligned his body with hers. My mouth pressed against the skin of her neck, fingertips reaching to touch him as well. As his body entered hers, one of his hands moved to my thighs, spreading and stroking.

He pushed into Liv slowly, his fingers entering me at the same pace.

"More," I breathed, desperate. "Harder."

"Such a sweet, greedy girl," Jason said. "Patience."

My whispered curse caused Liv to giggle, until he actually thrust harder. Feeling them move made me tingle, her skin shifting and sliding more against mine the harder he pushed.

Jason mumbled then withdrew from both of us, sitting back and shaking his head. Before I could figure out what was wrong, he picked Olivia up and turned her over. His fingers resumed stroking me to orgasm, his thick cock buried deep inside of her again.

The bliss I'd soaked in earlier amplified as my curves fit to hers. She gave little pants and gasps between the jarring impact of Jason's body behind hers. God, I knew that feeling so well.

Olivia had loved me softly, tenderly wiping away the stress of the day. Jason was hard and fast, taking his frustration and turning it into extreme pleasure. My body tightened around his fingers as Liv's teeth pulled at my lower lip.

From the way Jason's hand was positioned, I knew he was touching us both—bringing us to the tenuous precipice of orgasm.

"You gonna come, baby?" I asked.

Her answer was a drawn out, "Yes," of hot air against my skin.

Watching her eyes close, I knew she was deep in the throes of her pleasure, and I wanted that too. I pushed against Jason's hand, seeking and finding more friction. Olivia's mouth was at my nipple, tongue lapping and teeth pulling the ring there as my orgasm began. My head fell back, eyes tightly closed, and I let out an unintelligible noise of pleasure.

In my postorgasmic haze, Olivia kissed me slowly before she got up, likely headed to the bathroom. Jason's body covered mine in her absence and once she'd returned, the three of us tangled together, lucky me in the middle.

"I love it when you guys get started without me," Jason confessed.

We laughed together, much like we'd loved together. We conquered hardships together and it wasn't always idyllic and perfect, but it was perfect for us.

SEASONAL
AFFECTED
DISORDER

Gina Marie

The air smells clean and sharp like minerals, tastes like new snow eaten from a mitten. I can hear cars up on the road above the river, but we are alone down here in the alders and scrub. Wet ferns are brushing my fingertips. I touch them back, wanting. Always wanting. My breath is coming out in little puffs while he fingers my zipper and reaches down the back of my jeans to squeeze my ass. The breeze is cool, but the sun is warm on my face and heats a little triangle on my chest that is exposed when my boy pulls off my jacket and reaches up inside my silk thermal shirt to pinch a hard nipple. The moss is bright green. The leaves are gold, bronze and yellow. A little snow has dusted the distant hills. It could be autumn, or maybe it's winter or early spring. I don't care. It's not raining. I am outside and the river is singing as it curls around the bend and froths and pools against basalt boulders.

We were driving along scouting for wild mushrooms, singing along to the radio, drinking whiskey and eating pork rinds when he suddenly pulled over and said simply, "Here." Of course, I knew exactly what he meant by this and followed him greedily into the ravine.

There is a shotgun blast in the distance. It excites me for some reason. Bear season? Deer season? I imagine myself playing a game where I am running naked through the woods. Running away from hunters. Playing hide-and-seek for real, following the deer trails high into the mountains, bleeding a little onto the snow to throw them off.

"You are an animal," my boy says, licking at my earlobe and unzipping my jeans, his warm fingers probing deep inside. "A very, very good, naughty animal." I hear a fish jump in one of the slack pools nearby. I can see the ring of ripples out of the corner of my mind and their glossy, smooth humps excite me. "What kind?" I ask, taking his balls in my hand through his faded denim and holding them tight in my fist. "What kind of animal am I?" He bites at my neck. "A fucking beast of an animal," he says, "A horny little fucking beast. An excitable little fainting goat."

The word *goat*—fuck! That makes me horny. Like the sound of a fish jumping and the smell of snow-chilled air and yellow leaves and river currents. Like *everything* makes me horny. My pants are now around my ankles and my silk thermal leggings are halfway down my ass. A sunbeam is warming the edge of my thigh, but my nipples are as hard as rock hammers. He is kissing me gently while talking dirty about excitable, fainting, fucking beastly, horny goats and rubbing my clit. Steam is puffing from my mouth. I hear another car winding around the curve slowly, then stopping, tires crunching. A cold breeze flutters the leaves and ruffles the water. A second shotgun blast echoes through the trees and a couple of ducks take off from the shore of the river. His face is between my legs. I am arched against the base of an ancient moss-covered oak. There are oak galls scattered everywhere. He fingers my quivering insides while sucking on my clit, sucking hard, finding the place that makes me melt, makes me scream. Head back, legs spread, I come hard, screaming like a talon-gutted rabbit, thighs quivering. My boy lifts his face from my wet crotch, his lips and the tip of his nose shiny with my juice. "You are a very good animal," he says again. "Good for eating." Then he chops me up and makes a stew out of me right there against that tree.

He pulls my face down by my ponytail, pushing my hungry lips over his bone, then spins me around and takes me from behind. His cock is wet from my mouth, slippery with my juice, hot and hungry and hard. My face is pressed against the damp moss of the tree trunk. A squirrel crouches on a fir branch and chatters. My boy's strong hands are gripping my hips while he pumps wildly into me. In my mind, I am running naked through the woods. I am a very good animal. I am a very bad animal. In my mind, we are crashing through the trees, scratched and bleeding from the branches and thorns, daring to be chased, wanting to be caught until we end up here, against this old oak. He is moaning as he pumps me fiercely. Little bits of moss are clinging to my lips and it turns me on. His hands, his hot cock, the river, the sunbeam on my neck, the smell of his skin, it all turns me on. He convulses hard with orgasm, pulsing against me, groaning low and soft like water on spawning gravel. The poor oak shudders and a couple of galls fall to the ground. This makes me want it all over again, of course, the galls falling like that.

We rearrange our fabric and head up the hill. My crotch is sloshing with every step. From the road, I look down toward the river and spot the tall oak. I can see a patch of matted ferns where we were very bad animals. Somebody had a nice view. This, of course, makes me wet all over again. I look over at him and boy is he grinning, having just realized the same thing. The sun angling through branches makes me want to spin. What time of year is it, anyway?

THE SCRIBE

Tabitha Rayne

I've just hitched up my skirt. I'm kneeling and the hem is up at my buttocks, almost exposing them, but not quite. The familiar tingling anticipation sweeps over my flesh as I part my thighs, just a little, and lift one of the implements laid out before me. I always start with the smallest—the finest.

I hold my breath and close my eyes, letting my head fall back, jaw slack, in the pose that signifies the beginning of my ritual.

I run the tip of the long, fine shaft up the inside of my thigh, swirling and sweeping as I go, imagining the pattern it makes on my skin. My hand is shaking and the hairs on the back of my neck bristle in delight. If you really concentrate on your body, you can feel which nerve endings are connected. For example, if you arouse or tickle the tiny fine hairs just at the corner of your mouth, it sends a tingling sensation to the inside of your elbow—if you follow the line and sweep just there, you can trace a path all the way to the heavenly dip and peak of your sex. I defy you not to try it now. Go on, let your hand reach to the side of your mouth, go on...

The door. I hear the door open. My thighs clamp shut in shame and I'm shuffling my skirt back down when he strolls into the room.

"What's going on here then?" He sounds like he's being jokey but I'm so humiliated and ashamed at being caught that I can't read his expression. I have a flash-back to the same scene when I was small, only it had been my mother who'd walked in then.

"What the hell do you think you're doing?" she'd screamed in an explosion of fury, and I'd stared at my stained skin and cried.

"Nothing," I stammer, gathering my pens and brushes to my bosom and scrambling to stand.

"Come on." He stoops low and I surrender back onto my heels. "Show me."

He stares at me with those eyes. Those artist's eyes that scrutinize, study, absorb and analyze. He knows my body intimately, inside and out. I've posed for him a hundred times and lain down for him a thousand.

He eases the pens from my grip and lays them on the floor. His fingertips are cold as he gathers my skirt and pulls it up to my resisting fists that are balled into my lap.

"Please, let me see."

I watch the curling ink come into view as I relax my hands. Hard black scribbles both adorn and sear my flesh.

"What's this?" he asks with curiosity, not anger, and I feel I might tell him.

"It's mine."

"Your what?"

"My arousal," I say. He slides his palms onto my thighs, tugging the fabric up farther, and sighs. I tremble, thinking he's going to chastise me for marking myself so viciously.

"It's beautiful," he says, and shuffles backward so he's on all fours staring at my work. He leans in and parts my knees, inhaling my dampening want. He reaches out and picks up one of my pens. A Rotring thick-nib fountain pen. One of my favorites. "May I?" he asks tentatively, and I am wide-eyed at his request.

"Of course," I whisper, quivering. I lean back on my palms and spread my thighs wide. He is intense as he makes the first mark. A long sweeping scroll from knee to groin. I shudder as he stops short of my thickening pussy lips. I hold my breath and indulge in the sensation of the ink drying. That's it. That's the nirvana I'm after. It's such a subtle, tiny triumph; you have to be in a very special place to perceive it. It's like being licked by a tiny angel. He does the same on the other leg, slower this time so it dries while he's still applying it, raising goose bumps in its wake and shooting a nerve tentacle of pleasure to the peak of my clitoris. The rising carries on its journey and I fill my chest with breath to meet it at the tip of my nipple before it retreats back to my pussy. He's on to a brush now. He swirls my Japanese sable bamboo onto the wet charcoal block, round and round until it's good and swollen with moisture. He bids me to unfurl my knees and lie back like a Vitruvian man.

He paints the soles of my feet, between my toes then over the arch and ankles. My whole being is centered in the tip of the cool fibers as he continues, swirling and caressing every dip and curve of my body. My stomach flutters as he makes his way over first one knee then the other, writing, drawing. I feel letters being teased onto me, then shapes and waves. I am losing myself in this slow careful ecstasy. At last the brush swoops over my mons, intertwining with my own curling fibers. My pussy is slick with desire now, and I wish he would dip into me. I open my legs as wide as I can and tense my buttocks, forcing my entrance high. He obliges and sinks his face onto me, inhaling and breathing me in. He parts my thighs farther with his forearms while a finger from each hand opens my plump, ripe lips. He waits for a second or two, just watching my pussy twitch and contract in anticipation. I reach down and grab his hair, pulling him onto me, my bud, my cunt. He flattens his tongue down the whole length of my sex and I groan as he expertly points and darts into me then back to my clit, where he swirls and laps and paints all the patterns he has made on my legs. Just as my inner muscles begin to convulse in that tell-tale peaking, he stops and lifts his face away.

"You like to feel the ink drying, don't you," he says, then blows gently onto me, ruffling my pelt. It is sublime. He crawls up over my body keeping my legs thrust apart with his own meaty thighs. I can see him bulging through his trousers. I know he wants me, I know I've turned him on. He pulls at his zipper and his cock falls out heavily, full with want and desire. A thick, feral musk fills the room as our scents meet. I reach down to pleasure him, but he grabs and pins me by the wrists over my head with one of his hands. With the other, he grabs his shaft and guides it to my opening. He lets go and just hovers there, pressing lightly until my pussy can bear the teasing no longer and I lift my hips to urge him inside. He releases his tension and sinks into my hot clutching depths and I can hear us both groaning in the distance as I become that point, that tiny point where everything begins. It is minuscule and expansive at the same time and he stretches me beyond myself as he thrusts his solid dick in and out, faster and stronger until I feel raw with his ramming. He slides three of his artist's rough fingers into my mouth and mimics getting head until they are soaked with my saliva. He grabs my breast on the way back down and squeezes, causing me to squeal in pleasure as the shock waves travel to the desperate nub between my lips. With his fat cock buried deep inside me, he starts thrumming my clit with his three fingers, bringing me off in a flurry of heat and moisture. I breathe through each wave as they build and build until my pussy is spasming and my clit is peaking, and I'm thrashing about underneath him begging him to go on, to fuck me, to give me everything. And he does. The surge comes from deep within his balls and out through his shaft into me, spurting heat and wet and I clench around him not wanting to let him go.

He collapses on top of me and we pant softly together, our hearts almost meeting through the boundary of our chests. Eventually he flops off to the side and closes his eyes, falling into a gentle twitching doze.

I sit up to look at the mess that has been made of my thighs and the cloying shame of defiling myself threatens to spoil my bliss—until I see what he has drawn. On each thigh in the most exquisite design, two birds hold a delicate banner containing the most beautiful script. My breath is taken from me as I read the simple words: *I love you.*

COME TO THE LIGHT

Maria See

It was the fourth time we'd had sex. Each time before, when we were done, she rushed to cover her breasts with the blankets as I reached over to turn on the night-stand lamp and to get my after-sex cigarette and the ashtray. I'd finish my cigarette and head to the bathroom. When I returned, her men's tank top was back on.

The first time we were together, I begged for her breasts to come out and play. Her luscious, hot-as-hell DDDs. It was obvious that she was not going to free them on her own, but her protest was weak, a "No," that whispered, *Keep working me and I'll give in. I want to give in.*

She didn't like her breasts because they "weren't butch," she said. Because they presented her curvy female body to everyone she met.

Oh, but they *were* butch. Sade just didn't think the words *butch* and *breasts* belonged together. *I*, however, thought they were a match made in heaven.

It's no secret that I'm a breast woman. But butch breasts are a special type. Breasts belonging to a butch— to a butch who is my lover—always feel like they are a present just for me, one normally wrapped and hidden from the world, its ribbon only mine to pull. Butch breasts are rarely displayed in the manner that I often display my breasts, my cleavage a focal part of my outfit. No, butch breasts only take special outings. They only make an appearance when it's deserved, or when their need for touch cannot be silenced. Either situation is one I'd take any day.

But like I said, Sade didn't share in this adoration of mine. At that time, my mouth, my hands and my skin had all only known her breasts in darkness.

I wanted her to *see* my mouth on her breasts. I wanted her breasts to turn *her* on.

I reached for the light again. It was not because we were done.

She grabbed the comforter.

I turned on the light and opened the nightstand drawer. I removed a blindfold from the drawer and handed it to her.

"Put it on me," I told her.

"Put it on me but leave the light on."

I paused for a moment, and there was silence.

"I know *you* see your breasts," I continued. "You

see them in the shower, and when you dress. It's me who you want to hide the vision of them from. So do that. But no blankets and the light will stay on."

She gave no verbal response. She took a deep breath and placed the blindfold on me. I felt for the covers and threw them from the bed.

I straddled her, my knees at her sides and my tongue slowly, lightly licking each areola, my lips closing around each nipple, my teeth biting them with an application of pressure the purpose of which was not pain, but, instead, to hold them in place while the tip of my tongue nimbly circled their extremities.

I had intended to make a show of it for her, but I don't know if I succeeded; I may have become distracted and selfish. I moved my lower body to the right, my right leg then between her legs, my left leg on the outside of her right leg. I placed my dripping pussy on her right thigh and started to ride.

"Is this okay?" I asked, removing my mouth from her nipple as I moaned, as my juices ran down the sides of her leg. "Do you like watching me?"

She didn't say anything. She started to moan, too.

NIGHT HEAT

Vida Bailey

The storm wakes me. The heavy weather has finally broken and brought with it fresh relief. I slide out of bed and sit behind the curtains. The window seat surrounds me, a little box of moonlight and flickering lightning. Thunder rolls the pouring rain from the clouds and I can see it spitting and bouncing on the street, when the moonlight allows. I grow cold, nipples stiff, shoulders shivery. But I don't go back to bed. The street is deserted, all cats and foxes sheltering from the storm. The room lies dark behind the thick curtains. This is the witching hour.

I hear the sheets move at the stir of a body. The bed creaks, feet pad close. The curtains pull aside, open to the dark and the warmth of the room. Of him—bed and sleep heated. I know that smell well; so many nights

I've lain beside his sleeping figure and inhaled the air he exudes in sleep. Heat and sweat and sweetness, redolent of the weight of dreams. He slips in beside me, letting the dark into my little light hidey-hole. The rain has stopped. The moonlight shines on him and silvers his naked body, rendering his brown flesh pale.

He kneels beside me.

"I'm watching the moon."

"It's beautiful. You're cold."

It's true, I am. I've become ridiculously chilled. A cold white thing, apart from the sleeping, cozied, night-time world. He watches with me for a while. I don't lean into his warm body; I don't want to imprint my cold-ness under his skin. I think about pressing my white, icy, moonlit hand to his warm, dark chest, and watching his skin pale as I leach all the heat and color out of him. But he is sitting close enough that I can feel his body heat still.

"Come back to bed."

I reach up to put my arms around his neck, as if I'm a little girl, as if he could lift me, scoop up my roly-poly, wobbly body and carry me back to bed. I rest my face against his chest and breathe him in. I feel filled with the cool moonlight. I shine. He stands and takes my hand, leads me out of the light, through the curtains. He slips back into the warm space that waits for him and pulls me with him. I follow, and there's room for me in the burrow. I am moon chilled, he is earth warm. I don't bleed him dry when he kisses me. Instead the heat spreads deep inside me; warm liquid, honeyed light runs through me from the touch of his tongue on mine, everywhere his lips touch. His hot mouth on my cold nipples plunges me into the current; his fingers push inside me and prove I am not frozen through. I am melted; I haven't sucked the warmth from him, he has thawed me.

I try to reach for his cock, but he holds himself out of reach.

"Soon."

He whispers into my belly, burns kisses onto my thighs and pushes them apart. The feather cover is a cave, his hot breath fills it and I welcome back the darkness. I see red night as his hands spread me open and hold me still, as his tongue splits me, slicks me, slides from my wet center to my clit, once, twice and then fastens on. He sucks my clit into his mouth and licks, firm strokes, and he moans onto my tender skin. His voice vibrates deep into me, and I jerk, moving toward and away from it, overloaded. His fingers find me again, pressing into me, pushing against my inner wall, up against where his tongue is licking. The burn starts to spread; I'm going to scream, I'm going to drown. My hands are in his hair, one foot has found its way to his shoulder. Sweat beads my skin and I'm starting to twist, when he tears himself off me and his body covers mine. Before I can cry the loss of his mouth, his cock is hard against my clit, the length of him crushing, rubbing, and he's in me in one, long, agonizing stroke. All my swollen, throbbing flesh welcomes the almost-pain of it.

He fucks me deep and slow and hard, and I hang on, pinned down, aflame. He licks the sweat from my face, bends his mouth to my nipple and grinds my clit with his thumb. The chill is forgotten. I am a hot thing, one that lights for him. He glides in and out of me, pants his desire into my ear. His tongue swipes at the seashell whorls there, hot breath pushing into me, raising torrid shivers on my neck. It's the trigger. My cunt clenches around his length, pelvis spasming against him, the sensation so strong part of me tries to escape. But his hips pin me still, his cock wrings every last tremor from me. And then his teeth find my shoulder, and he's pounding against me, shooting inside me with a groan. My pulse beats in the bruise he leaves, heart and cunt and blood all throb. The air is still clear and new, but the chill moonlight is long banished here in the heated dark. He has reached deep inside me and I am warm from the inside out.

FOR THE MOMENT

Kiki DeLovely

I looked up just as she parted her lips with the tip of her tongue, meeting another pair of lips. Even through the crimson darkness I could tell it was hard, deep, hot. My ultimate butch-on-butch fantasy coming to life. I had felt them moving on top of me—knew it was inevitable and was quite pleased it was happening so soon—sensed its fruition just in time to catch that first glimpse of my own personal goddess-sent, ambrosia-dripping dream. As the intensity of the kiss mounted, their fingers—working individually, then in tandem, then separately again—increased the intensity with which they fucked my cunt. They stretched me wider as the two pairs of lips worked each other over and two pairs of hands heightened my already sensitive sense of touch. Surprised by each new movement, varying changes in tempo, one pressing harder here, the other lighter there, switching my entire body into high alert with their notable differences, their shared passions—growing even more fervent as we built upon the blaze.

I gasped, sunk my teeth into flesh, screamed out, grasped for whatever was within reach, as one twisted her fist into my cunt and the other worked her hand into my ass. Realizing I had again been squeezing my eyes closed, so completely absorbed in the all-but-overwhelming sensation, I consciously engaged my field of vision to take in these beautiful butches—admiring the definition of their muscles, lines cut sharply across their unique strengths, intention set deeply in each of their faces.

They crawled up closer to me, shoving a tongue into my mouth, followed by a slight moan, teeth biting down, and then lips rubbing urgently against me—I grabbed a fistful of each one's hair and pushed them together for my own amusement and arousal, undoubtedly heightening their own in the process—and just as it got really heated, I jerked the two apart, leaving passion and wanting to fill the space between them. Feeling like some sort of sick puppet mistress, I continued the process until they had had enough and decided to take control again, easily overpowering me as one followed the other's lead. They pinned me down and fucked me hard and fast, deep and slow, into my own unique bliss and back again, practically to the point of exhaustion, until I was screaming out yet utterly unable to form a single word.

I may have been the one among the three of us who spoke the most words leading up to that point, but it was only nonverbal vocalizations coming out of me thereafter. And those two handsome creatures needed no words between them whatsoever—working perfectly in synchronicity—T.J. surprisingly bowing to Harlan's dominance, allowing Harlan to fuck her, me (not so surprisingly) loving every second, luxuriating in the immensity of it all. We had only this one night after all. One night before T.J. left town in the morning. One night to make the best of all this tension between the three of us.

From the very first second when they enveloped me as we stood next to the bed—lips on my face, neck, chest; teeth on my back, digging into my shoulder; four hands wandering across my body, exploring the heat—there was not a second of hesitation while we all wondered just where exactly this would lead. As I felt those four hands navigating the landscape of my curves, my skin completely enraptured by their touch, my mind paused for just a moment in deep appreciation and I thought to myself, *How the hell did I get this lucky?* And therein ceased all other outside thought.

Harlan and I were new lovers living in a small town and with my old lover flying in from the Bay, it was clear we had to take advantage of this opportunity. It's not every day that a femme like myself has the chance at such a hot threesome, given the size of our incredibly small queer community. So we had T.J. meet us out at a bar, and though there were few words between them other than the obligatory introductions, I could tell the night was going to smile upon us. The three of us made our way silently and swiftly over to my place where I led them each by the hand into my bedroom. It took no time at all for the ravaging to begin.

I had never before been so filled in my life, had never been able to take so much. But then again, I had never been offered quite so much either. My nipples ached, my pussy was sore, I could only imagine what my body would feel like in a couple days, and still I wanted more. Between T.J. and Harlan, they had had me in every position imaginable—and some I definitely hadn't ever been creative enough to dream up—generously giving of cocks, fingers, fists, tongues and teeth. Those two hot butches took everything out of me and then went back for more. And then went back for each other.

Much later, at a point well into morning hours, the three of us found ourselves spooning—Harlan grinding against my ass, me pushing up against T.J., who then reached back and slipped a hand down the front of Harlan's boxers. I followed suit, working my hand between her cock and clit while T.J. grabbed ahold of her cock firmly. We stayed like that, bodies enfolded and pressing perfectly into each other, fitting together with ease, fucking with a motion of fluidity until rays of light peeked through the curtains and sleep began to blanket us.

And just before sleep had fully embraced us, with each on either side of me, I recalled how their movements conjured a feeling of vertigo. As though I was swallowed up by the ocean, waves gently pounding against me, shifting my body to and fro of their inadvertent volition. I vocalized this oceanesque feeling to them as they both began to curl up around me, intertwining limbs, the three of us giggling, a sweet closeness shared as we drifted off, dizzyingly satiated. For the moment.

OBEY
ALL SIGNS

Andrea Dale

*D**uring your driving test, the examiner will note how you obey the rules of the road and traffic signs and/ or signals,"* Chuck quoted from the DMV handbook.

I stared, dumbfounded, at the road sign, then at my husband. "Are you serious?"

"You want to pass the test, don't you?" His voice was stern, his expression implacable.

My rational brain panicked, while at the same time my body betrayed me, my panties flooding with moisture and my nipples springing to attention so suddenly that the seat belt, rubbing against one, was excruciating.

I'd grown up in the city, never needing a car until we'd married and moved to California, where public transportation was a joke. Chuck was coaching me.

I'd been doing fine so far—not running through yellow lights, looking both ways at intersections, remembering my turn signal when I changed lanes.

"It's not a verb, like *Stop*," I protested. "It's a noun, like *Railroad Crossing.*"

"Do you think arguing with the driving examiner is going to help you pass?" Chuck asked.

Of course not. More importantly, arguing with Chuck always got me into more trouble. In deliciously perverse ways.

Like right now. He'd had me drive his convertible to a fairly remote road and instructed me to pull over just before the caution sign that said, simply, Hump.

And he wanted me to obey that sign.

Knowing I had a hang-up about public sex.

Weak thighs and a fluttering stomach joined my growing symptoms of arousal. That explained why he'd had me wear a pencil skirt with a thigh-high slit: not to turn on the faceless examiner I hadn't yet met, but for Chuck himself. And for me, because I could hike it over my hips.

I did that now.

"Give me your panties," Chuck said.

Cheeks flaming, I couldn't keep from glancing around to make sure no other cars had crept up while I wasn't looking. Wriggling out of my underwear in the confined space took a little doing, but eventually I managed.

There was a wicked glint in Chuck's dark eyes. "Sopping," he said, approval in his voice, before he hung them over the rearview mirror, filling the air with my musk.

He told me to spread my legs, stroke myself until I was close, ease off, do it again. I hated that, hated being denied, loved that he could make me hold back even thought I hated it. Truth was, I didn't come very close. I was constantly aware of where we were, outside, public, with the chance of anyone driving down that road at any moment.

Then, finally, he opened his pants, freeing his fat cock, and I clambered over to straddle him, sinking down with a delighted shudder. He unbuttoned the top of my shirt so he could reach in, tweak my nipples.

I posted, ground down, "humped." I didn't whimper like I usually did, out of desire and frustration and lust. No, I practically held my breath, listening. And then, ohgodohgod, I heard the whine of an engine, a motor-cycle, growing louder.

Closer.

"Someone's coming," I whispered frantically. No idea why I felt the need to whisper. Just panic.

"Well, then," Chuck said, "you'd better come pretty fast, because you don't get to stop until you do."

I couldn't, but I had to, and the frantic terror of being caught wove together with frustrated need, the need to come, building higher and higher until I was sure the bike was just around the corner and something snapped inside of me and I came, shrieking and shuddering in a red wash of hot sunlight.

At the same time, I felt Chuck's cock swell, and his hips slammed up, prolonging my orgasm with his own.

"Get back in your seat," Chuck hissed, and somehow I managed to, with my skirt pulled down again, as the motorcycle approached behind us. I could feel Chuck's come trickling out of me as I tried, and probably failed, to look nonchalant.

The motorcyclist slowed down, way down, and for a moment of sheer dread I wondered if this were a further plan of Chuck's—not that my orgasm-addled brain could figure out what traffic law could be interpreted to mean sucking off a stranger. Then I realized he was looking at my flushed cheeks, my half-open shirt...and my panties dangling in full view from the mirror.

And as he gunned the motor to speed away, that realization sent my traitorous body into another shaking orgasm.

GIRLS SLEEP
WITH GIRLS

Giselle Renarde

On our way to Gina's parents' cottage, we decided to pay my boyfriend Dylan's grandmother a quick visit. She was a tad traditional, he warned, but the four of us—Gina, her boyfriend Ali, plus Dylan and I—had all been crammed in the car so long we couldn't refuse a stretch. Anyway, his grandmother lived all alone, only distant neighbors looking in on her. It was a bit of a sad situation, really.

Dylan's grandmother greeted Gina, Dylan and me with a friendly smile, tea and cookies. Ali "the foreigner" got tea and cookies, but no smile. Classy.

As we stared out the front window in silence, the skies opened up. It poured like I'd never seen. Rain turned to hail and the steel sky turned charcoal.

"Do you think we could stay overnight?" Dylan

asked his grandmother. "We hate to impose, but it's not safe to drive."

"Of course! Stay!" Grandma replied. She glared noticeably at Ali before eying all four of us. "There are two spare bedrooms. Girls sleep with girls. Boys sleep with boys. That way there's no monkey business."

We all tried not to laugh as Dylan agreed to the sleeping arrangements.

"She might even be cute if she wasn't so racist," Gina said after the matron showed us to our room. For night-wear, we could have rushed to the car in the rain for our luggage, but I had no qualms about sleeping naked. Tossing my clothes on the floor, I slipped my bare skin under the lovely, crisp sheets.

When Gina crept into bed, her warmth spread across my skin like a wave. I'd never noticed her floral perfume before.

"Girls sleep with girls," Gina said, imitating Dylan's grandmother. "She thinks girls can't get up to no good?"

As if to challenge that belief, Gina's hand roamed to my thigh. Her fingertips felt like silk against my skin. I couldn't pretend to be surprised; it was somehow implied this would happen on holiday. The way she looked at me, I'd always known.

When I turned away from her, she didn't take it as a rebuke. She only moved in closer. Her cheek was on my hair. Her breath was on my neck. It was nearly as hot as her hand as she traced a path up my thigh. She raked my pubic hair. I set my leg against hers, opening up. The moment her finger touched my clit, I jumped. She wrapped an arm around me, holding me in place. We didn't speak as she stroked my wet slit. Even as I stifled my reaction, she kept rubbing.

Gina cupped my breast, and I felt the pressure in my clit. Every part of my body seemed connected by live wires, and connected to Gina skin to skin. I was so wet, wetter than the storm outside. Even my thighs were drenched in juice, and I wondered if Gina was equally aroused, but her front was pressed so close to my back I couldn't reach to feel. Her fingers slid around my slippery pussy lips, like she couldn't get a good hold anymore. Too damn wet. So she inched down my body, rolling me onto my back, one arm still lodged between my shoulders and the mattress.

Her breath on my nipples forced them to grow harder than I'd ever seen them. They were like dark pebbles on the rounded mountains of my breasts. When she licked them, I nearly lost it. When she sucked them, I had to cover my face with a pillow. The wet heat of her mouth made me wild, forcing me to buck my hips at her hand as it circled my pussy. Then she slipped a finger inside my slit and, god, my thighs just started trembling. I was losing control, but I didn't care about the squeaks of the bedsprings as long as I wasn't shouting Gina's name to the rafters. The last thing I wanted was for this pleasure to be interrupted.

Gina forced more fingers inside my pussy, and the

pressure stretched my borders in every direction. I wanted to watch her face as she did all this, watch her mouth on my tits and her fingers invading my cunt, but there was no way I was taking that pillow off my face. I was getting close, and I didn't want anyone to hear me. Anyway, there was a strange comfort in the recycled warmth of my own breath, the shallow feeling in my lungs as I gasped for air through cotton.

She fucked me with her fingers. Hard. Sometimes it hurt a little, her nails, but I was so turned on I didn't care. I rode her hand, thrusting my hips, making her fill me again and again. It wasn't like a cock. A cock couldn't fuck me this fast, couldn't slam up against me this hard. My head was buzzing. I was biting the pillow. Gina was biting my tits. God, she didn't stop. My pussy was making all kinds of wet squelching noises as she rammed me with her fingers and I was shaking all over, loving the raw passion, and I knew she knew.

When I felt an orgasm coming on, I clenched my teeth. I didn't want to make a sound. Dylan's grandmother might hear. Every muscle in my body tightened. Gina must have felt the pressure against her fingers, because she pulled out and stroked me so swiftly I thought she'd start a fire in my clit. A noise rose up through my body until it squealed from my throat. The pillow caught it, but not completely, and I heard Gina chuckling against my breast as she kept at my clit.

Before long, I couldn't stand any more. I tried to close my thighs, but she pushed them apart and slapped my pussy with her wet hand. Nobody had ever done that to me before. The sound of it, the sensation of being spanked on my hot pussy lips, made my clit pulse. She did it a few more times, then clenched her whole hand against my mound and squeezed. My clit jumped in there, like a baby chick pecking its way out of an egg. Still, she held me like that, clutching my cunt, until my breath regulated and I pulled the pillow off my face.

Her smile was warm, satisfied, with a hint of a Cheshire grin. We breathed together for a long time, smiling, trying hard not to laugh. And when the night went quiet again, she said, "I wonder what the boys are up to."

THE DEALMAKERS

A. M. Hartnett

Jesse seethed as she scanned the nearly empty parking garage. Her ride, a bubbly working mother named Gail, had promised to wait the fifteen minutes it would take Jessie to send off that one last crucial email. She had finished in ten, yet by the time she had stepped off the elevator and into the garage there was no Gail. Only two cars remained. It was as though at six o'clock all eight floors of the T&E building just vanished in some apocalyptic sci-fi moment.

Slipping her hand into her pocket, Jessie rubbed the now useless transit pass that normally got her home at the end of the day. She'd thought she was doing a good thing by giving up her car to take public transit. The change worked out beautifully: sitting for twenty minutes with her iPod and a book was by far preferable to the crunch of gridlock. Then the buses and ferries went on strike and she was stuck begging rides to and from her apartment on the opposite side of the harbor.

She was digging for her cell phone and trying to remember the radio jingle to her favorite cab company when her attention was drawn to the echoing shudder of the elevator doors opening into the garage.

It was like someone had flipped a switch and turned the heat up in the parking garage. Marcus Latham, head of sales, strode out of the elevator with his gaze on the phone in his hand.

Though they'd been working in the same office for three months, it was only recently that their paths had crossed in the break room. There was an instant mutual attraction between them, and Jessie had enjoyed more than a few masturbatory sessions with Marcus in mind. Neither had made a move, but the constant flirtations had fostered an unspoken agreement between them that sooner or later their professional relationship would turn the corner into something much more personal.

Marcus looked up and his stride faltered for just a moment. Then, tucking his phone into his jacket pocket, he grinned.

"Don't tell me you've been camping out here during the strike. The penthouse suite between P-Ten-A and P-Ten-D?"

"I have more class than that, Marcus. If I was going to become a cave dweller I'd at least squat in the Marriott garage. I'm sure I can find someone in the bar willing to bring me an Irish coffee before bed in exchange for sexual favors."

He tilted his head to one side and regarded her through lashes so thick she envied him. "I'm sure you could."

His words were spoken so slyly and loaded with implications that Jessie's cheeks went hot. She enjoyed the silence that followed, enjoyed the way his stare remained upon her and the way the heat followed the trail his gaze blazed down her body.

She sucked a deep breath through her nose and dropped her phone back into her purse. "Save me cab fare and offer me a lift across the bridge?"

"What do I get in return? Navigating bridge traffic is a lot more involved than making an Irish whiskey."

Jessie had no desire to play coy. She returned his grin with one of her own. "I'm sure we can think of something. You can always let me stay with you, and we can improvise."

He raised a brow and his low chuckle surrounded her. "I'll bet you can. You're a very creative girl."

The sensual quiet coupled with his penetrating stare. Jessie could feel the electricity skittering down her body as he drew closer.

She stepped back until she was pressed against a pillar. The concrete against her back was cold through her thin jacket but the closer he got, the less she felt it.

He stopped in front of her and placed his hands on her waist, and with his touch the heat running through her blood became so intense she felt uncomfortable.

His gaze fell upon her lips as he pressed against her, angling perfectly into her body. His cock was hard and pressed through their clothes. When he kissed her it knocked the wind right out of her.

She grabbed on to his arms to keep from falling, but she needn't worry. Marcus's big hands clamped down, and he slipped his leg between her thighs.

"Oh, Jesus Christ," she said as she stood on her toes and then slid along the hard muscle against her crotch. She could feel the heat of his body through the lacy band covering her pussy. Every last nerve in her body felt it, like a flash fire running along the insides of her thighs, under her arms and across her back. She ran her hands along his arms, tracing slopes of hard muscle and hot skin.

He leaned in and flicked his tongue against hers. "I can't wait to get you alone."

"We are alone." She pushed against his thigh and laughed against his mouth, then tilted her head back as he mouthed along her chin.

If he'd reached down and caught the hem of her skirt, drawn it up to her waist and told her he wanted to take her right there, she would have wrapped her legs around his waist and let him ride her into oblivion.

A shiver ran through her as he kissed the slope just beneath her ear. Jessie felt the scrape of his teeth an instant before he pinched the skin. Her whole body surged.

He released her so suddenly she lost her footing. She threw her arms around his neck and dug her fingernails into the back of his neck.

Marcus hissed, but he didn't hesitate: he reached between her legs and pulled aside her panties. A low sound rumbled in his chest as he ran his middle finger along her wet slit.

He nuzzled against her cheek and chuckled as she slipped her fingers into his hair and took two thick handfuls. "If you're impatient I can help you out."

"Do it."

She twisted his head until his mouth angled over hers. She sucked his tongue deep into her mouth as his fingers pumped into her cunt. He had thick fingers, rough and knobby, and with every thrust the joint passed over her G-spot and sent a pulse throughout her abdomen.

She broke the kiss with a moan as he crooked his thumb over her clit and began to rub the puffy hood surrounding it. Her blood pumped faster and faster and the sound gushed in her head.

"You're as hard as I am," he said, his voice little more than a rasp that ran along her spine. He flexed his fingers. "Imagine how good it'll feel to have my cock right here."

"Are you always such a tease?"

"Who's teasing?" His tongue darted at the corner of her mouth and he smiled as he withdrew his finger. "You know, I'll bet there are cameras all over this place. Some poor bastard is getting quite a show."

Jessie's moan choked at the back of her throat as her whole body was seized by an agonizing throb. She arched her back as he curled his fingers back inside her pussy.

"Give it to him."

With a low chuckle, Marcus went down on one knee. Her sling-back clattered to the ground as he slung her leg over his shoulder. His smile widened as he tilted his head back.

Delicious anticipation skittered along her cunt as his tongue sliced along his upper lip. Jessie pressed her heel between his shoulder blades and Marcus went forward.

She swore again and sucked in a deep breath as his tongue wriggled over the tip of her clit. Hanging her head down, she watched the swipe of his pink tongue, watched the steady roll of his shoulder as he worked his arm like a piston and pumped his fingers into her.

Her whole body became a cord pulled taut as he sucked her clit. She pushed against the pillar with her shoulders and clamped down on the back of his head, grinding her pussy against his mouth.

Every thrust of his fingers, every swipe of his tongue worked in unison and sent her spiraling. She started to buckle as glorious heat pulsed through her.

The cord snapped. The back of her head smacked the concrete but she didn't feel the dull pain, not while the pressure behind her eyes swelled and reddened. Her slick inner walls squeezed down on his fingers and she lurched forward. His mouth kept working and her climax just kept crashing against her.

"Stop. Oh, fuck, stop," she begged, barely able to force the words out, and pushed him away.

Marcus grinned and licked his lips clean as he looked up at her. "How's that for improvisation?"

Jessie sucked in a deep breath. "Looks like I'm not the only creative one here. Take me home, Marcus."

AMONG
THE TREES

Heidi Champa

My knees sank into the mud, but I had long forgotten about the rain. I could only focus on his cock, moving in and out of my mouth. I had to lean my head back to take it all inside, the fat head hitting the back of my throat, making me gag just a little. One of his strong hands was around the back of my neck, the other twined in my hair, fucking my mouth roughly. I was completely wet; my clothes right down to my pussy. I had somehow managed to convince him to let me stay out of the mud for a while, but soon enough, I found myself on my knees, the cold mud squishing onto my skin. I seemed to sink deeper into the ground with each thrust of his hard cock. My hands were still tied behind my back, as they had been since we left the house.

Abruptly, he pulled out of my mouth; rainwater

running in before I had the chance to close my lips. He yanked me up to my feet, his eyes burning into mine. I could feel the mud running down my legs into my shoes; my favorite sneakers now ruined. The rainstorm was an unexpected turn of events. But I loved it. He turned me so my back was against him and pulled my shirt open, letting the rain hit my bare chest. His hands were so hot and the water was so cold. His thumbs rubbed my nipples until they ached, the teasing interrupted by sharp pinches, just to remind me who was in charge. My tied hands were rubbing against his cock, which was starting to get hard. His mouth bit my neck, another jolt of delicious pain to go with the overwhelming pleasure.

Suddenly, I was back on the ground, my body hitting with a sloppy thud. I felt his knee on my back, nudging me over until I couldn't stop myself from falling forward. I couldn't see him, but I heard him kneel down behind me. It was amazing how quiet it was, despite the rain pounding in puddles around us. My shorts were lowering down my thighs, new beads of water splashed onto my bare cheeks. It ran in ripples down between my legs, causing me to shiver. His hand cracked down on my ass, the sound ringing out into the stillness. Pain shot through me and I gasped, my mouth hovering right above the mud.

Two more slaps came right after, pushing me to the brink. He stopped and let the cold rain hit me, let it cool my newly hot flesh. Before I could fully recover, two fingers entered my pussy. I squeezed my cunt around him, wanting so desperately to rock back into him, to push myself back on his fingers like mad. But I knew better than to test him like that. I just let him fuck me, maddeningly slow as the rain started to speed up. He slapped my ass again, the dull, throbbing pain crowding out the pleasure of his fingers for just a few moments. He curled and swirled his digits inside me, making me cry out into the mud. I wanted him so badly, but I wasn't sure if he would oblige me or not.

In the next moment, his fingers were gone from me and I heard his zipper open. I felt so empty, and I waited impatiently for something to happen. My hips seemed unable to resist rocking toward him just an inch or two. For my trouble and effort, I got another slap on the ass. I started to yell out, but it died in my throat as he entered me. Lurching me forward in the mud, he grabbed the rope holding my hands for leverage and fucked me so hard, so good. I tightened my fingers around the ropes, trying to feel his skin, but I couldn't. So I just took it; took his cock over and over again.

To torture me, he stopped thrusting and just left his cock inside me, his stillness driving me crazy. I had to fight every urge in my body to move myself forward away from him. I was afraid if I did that, he might leave my cunt altogether. My body started to shake, the pressure mounting inside me. He laid one hand on the center of my back to stop my shuddering. In that moment, despite my predicament, I felt so safe. Even the cold rain and the ropes around my wrists seemed to disappear.

After long, long seconds, he pulled his cock almost all the way out of my cunt. I fought the panic that rose up in my throat; tried to hold back my fear of losing him. But he returned to his powerful, deep strokes. This time, I knew he wouldn't stop until he was good and ready.

The needy, desperate ache bloomed deep inside my cunt, and as the rain ran down over my eyes, I felt my pussy squeeze him violently. Two more quick, hard slaps hit my ass and the unexpected pain broke me. I couldn't hold it back anymore.

My orgasm shook through me, my screams sent out into the woods. He didn't slow down at all, pounding me through my pleasure. Grabbing my hips with thick fingers, he pushed into me violently before groaning out his own release into the air.

I could barely breathe, my body feeling wounded and wonderful. Once he got his strength back, he pulled me up, helping me to my feet. I could only imagine how I looked; caked with mud and half-naked. I didn't care, and neither did he. The rain finally began to stop as he untied me and cleaned me up before the ride home. He too was splashed with mud, but he looked clean compared to me.

Before we drove away, I took one final look into the woods, the last of the raindrops clinging to the leaves and branches, making everything clean again.

LAST CALL

Sophia Valenti

H ey, Melissa. The usual?"

Melissa nodded with a barely there smile as she slid onto the stool in front of my bar. She's always the proverbial ray of sunshine, so I was surprised to find her looking less than her usual perky self. I was also surprised to see her slinking in near closing time. She's an 8:00 p.m. drinker—one who sips something fruity before heading out for a night of dancing with her giggly friends. She wasn't giggly tonight, though. If anything, she looked a touch nervous and a whole lot introspective.

Melissa is one of my favorite regulars—and my secret crush. She's a girly-girl, all perfumed and cotton-candy pink, from the tips of her perfectly pedicured toes to the sugar-scented gloss that covers her full lips—lips that I always have a tough time tearing my eyes away from. This night was no exception, but I worked hard to kick my inner pervert to the curb. It's bad business to fuck the customers—trust me, I know. Besides, Melissa wasn't into chicks. That giant rock appeared on her finger a few months ago, and I'd heard her chatting about her wedding plans with some dude whose name escaped me. In fact, if I was remembering correctly, her "big day" was coming up fast. I wondered if that was the problem—even wondered if the wedding was off. It wouldn't be the first time a glum customer entered my place to recount a tale of lost love.

After sliding a cosmo in front of her, I leaned against the worn wood of the bar, one of my fingers finding a favorite divot. I traced the rough edge of the chipped countertop as I casually queried, "Wedding bell blues?"

Melissa cocked her head, offering me a half smile. There were those lips again. Pink and slick and making me long to part them with my tongue.

"Yes and no," she answered softly, her gaze falling to her drink as she swirled her stirrer.

"How do you mean?"

She took a ladylike sip from her glass before continuing. Her gloss left an imprint on the rim, the ghost of her lips taunting me. "Alexander is great— that's my fiancé." She took a deep breath that she let out as a cranberry-scented sigh.

"That sounds like the 'yes' part. What about the 'no'?"

"He said he doesn't want me to have any regrets."

"About what?"

"Things I haven't done—or *people* I haven't done." She looked up at me, her hazel eyes glinting with bits of gold and burning with sensuality. Was I reading her right? Was Melissa coming on to me?

I nervously licked my upper lip as I mulled my response.

Melissa's eyes momentarily fell to my mouth, as if imagining a more wicked use for my tongue. Her lustful face revealed a passion that I hadn't realized she had inside her. Look at that. Deep down, my pink lady was a red-hot seductress.

"Alex told me to have one last fling before the wedding. He even named some guys he knows I like— but I don't want any of them."

"Then who *do* you want?" My words came out more breathy and desperate sounding than I'd intended.

"You. I want you, Cat." She appeared to be steeling herself for a rejection that would never come.

At that late hour, we were the only two souls in the place. But even if the bar were packed, I don't think I would have been able to resist her. I leaned forward, indulging my long-held dream. Her sticky gloss smeared against my lips as I kissed her, flicking my tongue against hers as she moaned into my mouth.

Threading my fingers in her silky brown hair, I lost myself in her scent and taste. *So much for not screwing the customers.* I knew this was going to be a one-time thing, but I didn't care. She was soft and sweet and smelled so damn good. I wanted her, even if all we had was a single night—even if, come morning, I had to return her to Alexander the Great.

Breaking our kiss, I locked the front door and flipped the OPEN sign to CLOSED, then I led Melissa upstairs to my apartment. It's small but cozy—and most importantly, it has a queen-size bed. We tumbled onto the mattress together, still kissing madly as we stripped each other naked. She was as beautiful as I'd ever imagined— all sensual curves, her full breasts topped with petal-pink nipples.

Knowing this was the first and last time for us, I memorized the sight of her exquisite nakedness, letting my hands roam her body as I learned all of her secrets— how she cried out desperately when her neck was kissed and how she groaned with longing when two fingers were shoved into her slick sex. Melissa bucked her hips toward me as I curled those digits inside her, their rhythmic movement and pressure making her gasp and squirm as she climaxed against my hand. Her velvety walls clutched and released my fingers, echoing the waves of her pleasure.

After that, Melissa took control, swiveling her body around so that her pussy hovered above my lips while she ducked between my parted thighs. As her tongue swirled around my clit, I sighed against her juicy flesh and then took my first taste of her, sliding my tongue along her slit. Minutes stretched to hours as we gave in to our lust and drank our fill of each other.

I couldn't think of any better way for us to toast her single life good-bye.

I'D RATHER
GO BLIND

Tenille Brown

He gave her a choice.

"You can be blind or deaf," he said.

Tonight, she wouldn't have it all; he wouldn't allow it. She had been spoiled for far too long.

So, quickly, and without question, she gave him her answer.

"I'd rather go blind."

The words came from trembling lips and she looked him in the eye as she said it.

"Fine then," he said, and put the earplugs down on the table.

He turned her around and covered her eyes with the black silk scarf. He tied the ends around her head taking care not to tangle or pull her soft, black curls.

She couldn't see a thing when he was done.

"Get up on all fours, on the table."

His voice came from directly behind her, and with his assistance, she did as she was told.

She hadn't even gotten a glimpse of his tool. She wouldn't know what he would be using to tame her.

Ironically, as she waited in the seconds that turned to torturous minutes, she closed her eyes anyway anticipating him drawing back his powerful, dark arm. Then he landed his first blow.

It saturated her, sending desire streaming down the inside of her thighs. He had pulled a plug, pressed a button and she had sprung a leak instantly.

He was using a paddle. She guessed that easily.

But, was it her, or was the sound of him spanking her amplified times a million? For the first time she wondered if the neighbors could hear. If he had drawn their attention and their ears were pinned against the wall waiting for the next strike.

Slap! Slap!

Every strike that followed paled in comparison to the first. Blows number two and three, she barely had time to draw a breath between. And then there were the ones that came tumbling after.

He seemed to seek out particular places on her rear on which to land his blows, but of course she wouldn't know where until they were already there and she was feeling the burning sting. Her ears were ringing from the sound and her cunt was singing from the pleasure.

Now she was leaning back on her haunches, expecting

him to aim center, but he came from the left instead. He came down on her hard with the paddle, but not as hard as she had expected, and not nearly as hard as she had hoped.

There he was again with his delivery, right away, this time on her right cheek, which she had unwittingly jutted out a little farther than her left. He had come at her from the side and landed a perfect and sound smack that echoed in their massive playroom.

She was perspiring behind the silk scarf that temporarily blinded her. His pace was unpredictable. He struck her in five-second increments, then ten, then thirty.

She was shaking.

It hurt more this time. It had never hurt this much. The pain had never been this strong or sweet. She reached out for an edge that she couldn't see, something to steady herself, something to hold on to when she felt she couldn't take anymore.

"You have to be blind, but you don't have to be silent," he reminded her, and with that she released a grunt in a voice that didn't sound at all like her own.

It was followed by a whimper and then a series of sobs and screams.

Strike!

He seemed nowhere near stopping and she wasn't sure she wanted him to, because now she was so wet she couldn't stand it.

The spanking continued for ten minutes more, until she begged him to let her come.

"Please," she pleaded, tears at the corners of her eyes.

"All right," he said, but not before he landed one last, heavy-handed blow to the center of her high, tight and unexpectant ass.

Smack!

She erupted and shortly after her legs gave in. She landed clumsily on the table in a heap of exhaustion, pain and sweat.

The last touch he offered was his palm, massaging her tenderly on her sore cheeks.

"You may take off your scarf," he offered softly.

But she couldn't. He helped her, loosening the ends and letting the scarf float to the floor at their feet.

"Look and see," was his next direction.

He handed her a hand mirror and she angled it so that she could get a glimpse of the purple and blue decoration he had made of her formerly cocoa ass and upper thigh.

"Beautiful," she whispered.

"Beautiful indeed," he agreed.

RUBBER CHICKEN

Thomas S. Roche

M elinda put her hand under the table and began massaging my cock.

As she stroked, she put her full, bee-stung lips up to my ear. Against my earlobe I could feel the stickiness of the lipstick she'd caked on when she'd excused herself to go to the ladies' room, after the dinner but before the speeches.

"Do you want me to stop?" she whispered. Her breath was warm; it goose-bumped the flesh on the back of my neck. It made my cock swell still harder against her hand, pushing into her grasp through my tuxedo slacks.

I did and I didn't. It was one of those things. Having been relegated to a tertiary table with people I didn't even know from the Kansas City office—they were nice enough, but a little bland—we were tucked more or less in the back corner of the banquet hall. We were quite a ways away from the podium or—for that matter—anyone important to my career or social life.

After the dessert dishes were cleared, the droning speeches had started in earnest, and now—only fifteen minutes into the program—I knew we could look forward to an hour and forty-five minutes more of this crap.

But if I were to rise and depart, I might draw the notice of my boss—who was three tables over. Even reading, in fact—I'd cleverly stashed a slim paperback book in the breast pocket of my tuxedo—might draw unwanted attention. The most I'd been able to get away with so far was checking my email incessantly on my phone—which is certainly rude, but far from unusual. And frankly, my emails aren't that interesting.

This, on the other hand, was an inspired bit of audacious misbehavior on the part of my guest, Melinda. We hadn't even slept together; in fact, I barely knew her. In fact, we'd only met in person a few hours ago, when the limo I'd sent for her dropped her off at the hotel bar.

Melinda was a playmate from online. The things she'd done on webcam for me would have likely scandalized the entire convention of sales executives, with plenty of scandal to spare. But we hadn't been to bed together; not yet. I was only in town for the banquet. I hadn't been sure I'd have time to see her, a fact I'd been honest about. When I told her about the banquet, she told me about this slutty little cocktail dress she had—formal, but slutty. She told me about it and sent me a JPG of the catalog where she'd found it. The rest is history.

She was wearing it when I first laid eyes on her, and she was wearing it now—which was perturbing to me because I wanted it off her, and on the floor of my hotel room. Or maybe I just wanted it yanked up and pulled down while I pinned her and caressed her tits and pulled her hair and fucked her and spanked her and showed her what happens to bad sluts who meet men for the first time wearing dresses like that.

For now, though, I just enjoyed the view: the dress was red and *very* low cut, which made it look both graceful and provocative because Melinda is stacked. The top halves of her tits were exposed, the nipples lightly tenting the material; with my arm around her, my fingertips grazed the side of one bulbous breast and the charge running between my hand and her flesh was electric. With my leg up against her as she leaned against me, I could feel the hem of her dress riding up; one stocking's lace top was visible, as was the place where it hitched to her garter. I could feel the texture of the lace and the ripple of the rubber beneath it as I rubbed my thigh surreptitiously against hers.

She wasn't wearing underwear—that much I'd found out already, with my grabby hands in the shadows of the hotel bar, before I even got her drunk or stoned. She was bare shaved under the dress, her garter belt framing what would have been perfect even if it hadn't been pierced and haloed by a stylish tattoo that said TAKE ME.

Melinda leaned hard against me, tipsy with table wine and probably still feeling soft-focus from the joint we'd sneaked in the hotel's rooftop garden before they began seating for the banquet. How the hell else is a man with any taste supposed to choke down rubber chicken? Between sucks at the doobie and kisses to her neck, I'd apologized to her that the food on our first "date" would almost certainly be so wretched.

She'd said, "I don't give a damn. I've only got one thing I really want to eat tonight. You'd better hope I can wait till the banquet's over. I'm not sure I can."

She couldn't, it turned out, because there was her hand, stroking my cock through my pants beneath the tablecloth. Had the lights not been so low, or the tablecloth so long, it would have been risky in the extreme. As it was, it was still very risky...but just risky enough.

She was an expert at it, from what I could tell. Her forearm moved rhythmically without her shoulder or upper arm displaying the slightest hint of what her hand was doing. She was so damned good at giving a surreptitious hand job, in fact, that I didn't even stop her when she glanced around furtively and, finding the coast clear, unzipped my pants.

I glanced around, too—the room was dark, the tablecloth long, and no one was watching. Why not?

Her long slim fingers reached in, tugged the waist-band of my underwear, pulled out my cock. She wrapped her fingers around my hard shaft and began to stroke. She caressed me gently at first, growing stronger and more insistent as she put her lips against my ear and made soft purring noises. She breathed harder and more sensuously as she got more and more aroused.

"Fuck," she whispered. "Oh, fuck, I wish I could suck it right now…"

She could have…all we would have had to do was leave. But this was more fun, I decided, so I let her do as she wished, breathing and purring her dirty talk all over my ear as she brought me closer and closer.

"Run my lips all up and down the shaft," she whispered. "Slide my tongue all over your big fat head…" She thumbed it gently. And I realized her fingers were greasy—no wonder she'd refused to let me add a dash of balsamic to the olive oil, or to let the waiter clear the plate. As her hand caressed me more insistently, she murmured, "Take your balls in my mouth…rub your cock all over my face…oh, fuck, I wanna open my mouth wide and take your whole dick down my throat… Would you like that? You want me to deep-throat? You want me to open up wide"—she parted her lips and mouthed my ear suggestively—"and take it all down past the back of my throat? I've got no gag reflex at all, you know…all that dirty training you made me do for you with your dildo—"

A vivid image came to me—Melinda opening wide

on webcam, finally choking the dildo I'd sent her down until the flange at the base pressed tight against her lips. It was a dildo molded directly from my cock; an old girlfriend and I had made it on a lark, but she'd broken up with me before she used it, so I had sent it to Melinda...leading her through deep-throat training on a toy guaranteed to adapt her skills for exactly the purpose she described.

The image was too much for me, as was her soft, sensuous voice saying such dirty things, and her warm breath on my neck. She'd slipped a cloth napkin down there to catch things and further disguise what she was doing.

She jacked me off. I came. I tried to keep it cool; it wasn't easy. I had to bite my lip. She let out a soft, low, happy murmur, gently biting at my neck as I came.

Applause rippled through the banquet hall. The droner on stage was finished. He left the stage, to be replaced by the MC, introducing the next professional boredom-jockey.

"Did you like that?" Melinda asked, her voice slightly louder. "Did you like how I jacked you off, Sir?" It was safe, under the cover of the applause, but it still felt filthily illicit to be hearing it out loud, instead of in a whisper.

"It'll do," I said sternly, but my smirk gave me away.

Melinda wiped me up with the napkin, tucked my cock away and zipped up my pants. She took a very discrete lick of her hand and made a *yummy* noise.

She put her lips back to my ear and said happily, "You taste a lot better than the rubber chicken."

We didn't stay much longer after that. My boss can go fuck herself.

SUGAR UPSETS
MY VAGINA

Kristina Lloyd

PVC, latex, leather and leashes: not my cup of tea, but the people here like it, and I like that they have somewhere to go. I'm a little spaced out. I'm drinking bottled Czech beer and earlier, we smoked some weed that made my scalp prickle. The friends I came with are away somewhere, up to no good. I don't mind that. I'm watching this sex carnival from the margins.

The room is color saturated and molten, light sliding over costumes that gleam like liquid. A woman with orange hair in a beetle-black catsuit is giving head to a guy reclining in an elaborate leather chair raised on chrome scaffolding. His wide-spread legs are hooked over padded arms. His eyes are closed. The chair makes me think of my last gynecological exam. I asked her not to use K-Y because it gives me a yeast infection. She opened a drawer packed with little sachets. "It's the glycerin," I said. "Sugar upsets my vagina." I meant the PH balance, but she understood.

She checked a couple of sachets. "Sorry, they don't list ingredients."

"Well, I'm sure I'll be okay without."

When she pushed the speculum into me she apologized for being rough.

"No, it's fine," I said, then I worried I might have sounded too eager.

It wasn't erotic though, of course. And strangely, neither is this club. It's fun, warm and friendly, but I'm not feeling the lust, not yet.

I look away from the couple and my attention is caught. Several feet from me stands a guy in a big, black coat and heavy boots. His dark hair is shaved and he has that mean, handsome look I'm nuts about. He's staring at something and nothing, head up, strong jawline. He has an aura of quiet authority. The coat looks expensive. Cashmere, maybe. Square shoulders, broad lapels, buttons fastened, hands in his pockets. He's wearing an armband bearing a militaristic-looking symbol.

I take a swig of beer and move from the shadows. Above the music, I ask, "Are you dom or security?"

He smiles down at me. He has plump lips and good teeth. "Security."

"You're the sexiest person in here."

He laughs and looks away, back to something and nothing.

"Time do you finish?" I ask.

"Four." He grins again as if he finds my interest amusing.

"Time is it now?"

He checks his wristwatch, making it peek from under his sleeve with a swift punch of the air. He has a great watch: chunky, silver, macho. "Twenty past one." Hand back in his pocket.

"Jeez," I say. "That's so unfair."

He smiles again but he's not looking at me anymore.

We stand there for a while watching a woman getting flogged. Her flogger, a guy in a rubber vest crisscrossed with studded leather, swirls the baton with that practiced wrist-flick that never fails to look camp. On impact, strands of leather fan across the woman's buttocks. They're playing by the rules of the club and I'm not. But I imagine she and I share the same goals. We want someone who'll make us feel tiny, vulnerable, nervous and safe. Right now, I don't know if she's feeling it but I am.

Then Security moves away, a glacier carving a path through the crowds. I put the bottle to my lips and drink, acting as if I haven't noticed.

The woman's arse grows pinker.

Three hours later, I'm walking home alone, hugging my coat to my body, heels ringing on the pavement. Behind me, drunken voices fade into the distance. People cross roads at strange angles because they can. There's no traffic at this hour. There's an urge to trespass. Even the gulls fly low over the central white lines.

"Hey! Hey!" calls a voice. I turn and he's running to catch up, smiling. How do you run in a coat so big? He falls into step alongside me, hands in his pockets, breath making fast, icy clouds. "Do you want to take me home?" His eyebrows lift and his grin is playful. He's chancing it, and I respect that.

I laugh. "I'm heading for the taxi rank. My feet are killing me."

He asks where I live and when I tell him, he says, "That's not far. Hang on."

He stoops for me, tells me to grab his neck and then he scoops me off my feet and into his arms. I cling to him, laughing hard. He grunts, hitches me higher and starts walking fast, chest puffed out.

"Crikey, how much do you weigh?" he says.

"Fuck off," I reply.

Twenty minutes later, his coat is hung up in my hallway, his boots are by the door and his cock is in my mouth. His groans suggest this is beyond belief. I like them, the ones who sound as if they've never had it so good before. I'm on my knees by the bed and he's standing with his feet apart. He's like a colossal, hairy statue. He wraps his hands in my hair and draws me onto him, holding me steady as he fucks into my throat, picking up speed.

He pulls out and tells me to get onto the bed on all fours. When I clamber up, he whacks my arse once, a perfect, stinging hit.

On the way home, I'd asked, "Are you dom now you're not security?"

"No," he'd said. "But I fuck hard."

He rubbers up and slides into me, prizing my easy flesh open with his thickness. His hands grip my hips as he starts to drive, slowly at first then faster, faster. I moisten my fingers and rock my clit till I come. I feel weak, but he slams on and I complain I need a break.

"No, you do it," he says. "Fuck back at me."

I grip the headboard and do my best, banging backward onto his cock. However hard I try, I can't match the power and depth of his thrusts. "You do it, please," I wheedle. "You're better at it than I am."

He laughs quietly, withdraws and flips me over because by that point I'm extremely pliant and flippable. He pushes my legs back and fucks me as if his life depends on it. He's making huffy, spittly noises and he claws my tits, practically using them to gain purchase. Sweat from his forehead sprinkles my face. I wish I could lick him. Inside me, he's enormous, relentless, ferocious, and I'm loving every second because, as I said to the lady, sugar upsets my vagina. I need it nasty and brutal, and this guy's got it in spades. I swear, he's more aggressive than some men I've been with who identify as dom. When he comes, it sounds as if his lungs are being ripped out by a gigantic fist.

Later, we lie in silence until he says, "I like it here." I'm not sure if he means in my flat or in the postorgasmic languor we're sharing. He holds me close and prints a kiss by my ear. It's almost dawn. We're sleepy. I start to drift off, happy to feel the slab of his chest beneath me and his strong arms around me. Our bodies soften, and I listen to his breathing grow low and slow.

The circle is complete. Because even though I like it rough and I go home with strangers, I adore those confident enough to hold me tight and soothe me, those rare creatures who afterward can give me that sweet sense of security.

CLEMENT

Sommer Marsden

He lets me run through the rain. I feel his eyes on me, soft and approving like a hand stroking my skin.

I dart between raindrops, at least that's my attempt, but the deluge is insistent and so I end up driving my body through silver sheets of water that slip from the gun-metal sky.

He wants to be fucking, but he's patient and kind with me, letting me have my moment. Tempting lightning, inciting thunder, feeling the cold air on my skin like the kiss of a benevolent frost god.

I've come from dark and tight and brittle times. I've come from a man who smothered and hid me and silenced me with his disapproving looks. Once or twice with irritated hands.

I've come from bad.

Guy has brought me good. He's brought me quick-
silver thunderstorms and light laughter. He cuts me tall,
orange tiger lilies and short, squat bouquets of wild-
flowers he plucks from his back garden.

He let me live in his house a week after we met at a
party. He let me deny him my physical company while
daily offering me a comforting hug, a listening ear, an
accepting heart. Until I healed.

Above me thunder booms and I slide on the slick-
ening grass. We are close and I reach up to touch his
nose and he reaches out to touch my breast. Speckled
with warm rain, a pregnant drop hanging from the tip
of my nipple. He smiles and I kiss him, fast and full on
the lips before darting away again.

Out here in his yard, shielded by six-foot fences and
dogwoods mixed with bamboo mixed with fruit trees,
I am an invisible nymph. His own personal lawn art.
The girl who will kneel in cool mud to suck his cock the
moment I let the joy that now lives in me burst free.

A fork of lightning tongues the sky, and he says softly,
"Bernadette."

He's only worried about me being electrocuted, that
much I know.

I hold up a finger and remember the first time he kissed
me. The warm curl of his tongue over mine, the velve-
teen crush of his lips to my lips. The way he'd pushed
me back softly, somehow restraining and cradling me at
the same time. The way he'd dragged his cock along my
soaking wet split and then slipped into me a patient inch

at a time until I was gasping his name and urging him faster with clutching fingers.

I remember him being so…good. He is so good. And the lightning shoots a message to my heart about how much I love him.

Another flash in the fattening sky, and he says again, "Bernadette."

"Coming," I say, and run toward where he stands under the deck on the patio. I don't slow, simply leap against him, all long limbs and flying hair and a distinct absence of grace. But that's okay. I am the ugly duckling who is more brilliant and beautiful for having met this man.

"Coming?" he says, catching me up in his arms.

My momentum carries us down to the chaise lounge and I'm yanking at his belt, straddling him, putting him in me so I can sink down and be full of him. My body flushed and swollen and slick with need. I start to move and his hands come up to touch me. Thick fingers stroke my nipples, touch the freckles spattered across my chest like a fawn-colored constellation.

"I love fucking you," I say.

"I love *you*," he says.

"I love you too. Good weather, bad weather, rain, sun, shine."

"You like to fuck more in inclement weather," he says.

I grin, lean over him to kiss him, grinding my hips until that first sunshine-yellow burst of pleasure sounds inside of me and I am coming, his fingers digging into my flesh. His teeth nip at my lower lip and make my orgasm that much brighter, that much sweeter.

"True," I say. "Maybe it's the danger. Inclement weather turns me on. *Almost* as much as a clement man."

"Is that what I am?" Guy asks, his eyes going suddenly serious.

"You are that and so much more," I say, my throat going a little tight as I watch him surrender, his body growing rigid with his release. He's panting under me, his skin hot and wet beneath my fingertips. "You're everything," I say.

And I mean it.

HEART ON THE DANCE FLOOR

Stella Harris

They're lucky no one looks twice at two girls standing close together, whispering and giggling. People just accept a higher level of intimacy between female friends and Danielle intends to take full advantage.

They move together, not quite dancing, not quite on the beat, but just swaying, their bodies brushing against each other. Danielle guides their movements, repeatedly getting so close that Jen takes a step back. Danielle herds Jen, one step at a time, until her back is against the wall in the darkest corner of the club.

The flashing colored lights swing their way a couple of times a minute, but when the frantic illumination moves on they are plunged into near darkness once more.

Danielle has never been more grateful for Jen's preference for short skirts. She's such a petite thing, she can get away with it.

"Dani, what are you doing?" Jen asks, pretending to be scandalized as Danielle slides a hand between her thighs, fingers playing against the soft, tender flesh. Jen bites her lip and glares, but the effect is wasted when she's bending her knees and thrusting her hips at the same time, trying to guide Danielle's hand to where she wants it. Jen likes to act coy, but she's got an exhibitionist streak a mile wide.

Danielle's fingers creep higher as she angles her body just so, making sure no one in the club can see exactly what they're up to. It's only another inch before her fingers reach the crux of Jen's legs. She's glad their heights complement each so perfectly.

Danielle knows exactly what Jen likes; she also knows exactly what works, even when those things are not the same. Jen claims to hate being teased, and yet nothing gets her hot faster than a touch that's not quite enough. Not quite where she wants it. Jen will moan and beg and demand. Danielle thinks Jen just likes the sound of her own voice, that she likes to put on a performance. But she can't do that now, not here. No, now she needs to be content with the softest utterances, speaking with her body.

But Danielle knows her, knows what makes her tick and what makes her purr. She doesn't need direction.

When Danielle's fingers finally slide across Jen's panties she finds them already soaked through. Jen always gets wet fast and Danielle loves that. Loves that her mind and her body are both so unapologetic about their desires. The wetness of the fabric makes her panties a nearly insignificant barrier; they cling to her every curve and fold as Danielle's fingers gently explore.

In some ways, these first touches are her favorite. She loves exploring every inch of Jen's body at a leisurely pace. Sure, she loves getting her off too, making her scream and come—but she loves these moments before she's working toward a goal the most.

"Dani, goddammit." Jen whispers into Danielle's ear, biting down on the lobe to make her point.

"Take it easy, sugar. I've got you," Danielle whispers in response, but all the same she tilts her head, saving herself from a more vicious bite.

She'd love to draw this out all night, but eventually someone will notice them, or more likely one of their friends will come looking for them. And while they wouldn't be surprised to find them like this she'd just as soon keep this their secret. So she works her hand in the side of Jen's panties, tugging until she has enough room to move the way she wants to.

Even though she knew how wet Jen was, she still gasps when her fingers slide into Jen's slippery wet heat. She feels too good to be real.

Jen's head falls back to rest against the wall behind her just as the club lights point their way. Jen's long, exposed neck is illuminated with all the colors of the rainbow, making the sight of her throat moving as she swallows surreal.

Jen has gone weak in the knees; she'd crumble to the floor completely if it weren't for Danielle's body pressing her into the wall. Danielle knows Jen can't usually come standing up, but she's determined to make Jen come apart, right here, right now.

Danielle uses her foot to kick Jen's legs apart, granting her more access. This wider stance allows her to easily sink her fingers deep into Jen, filling her up as she presses forward just so, making Jen shudder.

She picks up her rhythm, fingers sliding and exploring, circling Jen's swollen clit before dipping deep inside of her and then pulling out to start again. She rests her free arm on the wall beside Jen, leans in close to whisper filth into her ear, just how she likes. Jen says she loves to watch dirty words spill from her pretty mouth, but right now she'll have to be content with just listening.

"You gonna come for me, baby? Right here in the middle of the club?" Jen says something in response to that, but Danielle's not sure she's using recognizable words. "God, you feel so good. I love fucking you." Jen just whimpers, beyond words and beyond thought; her arms encircle Danielle's neck, desperately holding on for the ride.

The next time Danielle's fingers sweep across Jen's clit she keeps her focus there, rubbing fast and hard, drawing insistent little circles. At the same time she bites down on Jen's neck, right below her jaw. When they're alone this never fails to draw a deep moan and although she's mostly silent now, Danielle is pressed close enough that she can feel her body shaking.

The shaking increases until her whole body's rocking back and forth in the small space allowed between the wall and Danielle's body. She's panting and murmuring, *Fuck, fuck, fuck.*

Danielle can feel Jen shaking against her fingers too, her body pulsing, and she stokes her until her breathing starts to slow, then pulls her hand away, wiping it on her jeans before tugging Jen's skirt back down.

"How're you feeling?" Danielle asks, wondering if Jen can speak yet. In answer, she just says *fuck* one more time.

"Perfect, wanna dance?" Danielle asks, eyebrow raised. Jen glares at her, takes her hand and follows her onto the dance floor.

THE NOT-SO-BLUSHING BRIDE

Lucy Felthouse

I never, not once, ever thought that it would actually happen.

Until it did.

And now I can't get it out of my mind.

I'm a chauffeur, and the majority of my work is driving wedding cars. You know, taking the bride and her wedding party to church. Then taking the newly-weds to their wedding reception and sometimes, later, on to the airport or a hotel.

So you can hardly blame me for having weddings on the brain. As a bloke, though, it's not the wedding itself that I think about. I don't get all gooey and gushy over the church, the rings, the flowers, the cake. That would be weird.

It's the bride that occupies my thoughts. Now, before

you think I'm some kind of creepy pervert, let me explain. It's not like that. I don't paw at the brides that ride in my car, flirt, or make inappropriate comments. In fact, I don't do anything that would make them uncomfortable. I am the epitome of professionalism and respectability at all times.

Until they get out of the car and go on their way, that is. It's the times that I'm left to my own devices that my mind starts to wander down its naughty path. And, given that I'm generally employed for entire days with long periods of time where I do nothing but sit around, you can hardly blame me for doing something to occupy my time.

So I entertain myself by sitting in the car. It's not as boring as you might think. I have an eReader, therefore I have plenty of reading material at my fingertips, and if I'm hungry or thirsty, I can jump into the back of the limo and grab something that the company has supplied for the wedding party. Naturally, I don't sample any alcohol—I'm not an idiot.

I don't think dirty thoughts every time I'm sitting alone in the limousine—despite the statistics, men don't think of sex constantly. A lot, yes, but not *constantly*. Usually, it depends on the bride. If I don't find her attractive, then I tend to do lots of reading in my periods of downtime. However, if she's hot, then my imagination fires on all cylinders.

Which brings me neatly back to my fantasy. You know, the one that recently came true, in spectacular style. So, here goes:

I have always wanted to fuck a bride on her way to her wedding.

Despite knowing that the majority of brides these days aren't exactly pure and innocent, I've always really fancied screwing one of them senseless in the back of my limo before dropping her off at her destination, where she'll commit herself to someone else for the rest of her life. There's no need to start psychoanalyzing it—I know it's because it's taboo, forbidden, corrupt. And therein lies the attraction. And, as I said, for a long time it was just a harmless fantasy that nobody knew about.

Then Tilly came along.

Usually, the bride is accompanied from her house—or wherever she got ready for her wedding—with at least one other person. This, naturally, has always made my fantasy completely unattainable. I could hardly see the father of the bride turning a blind eye while the hired help lifts up his little girl's dress and fucks her, could you?

Tilly bucked the trend—in more ways than one.

First, she was ready when I knocked on the door. Usually I turn up a little early in order to spur preparations on a little. I know brides are meant to be fashionably late—but often, if it weren't for me, they'd be pushing-their-luck late.

Second, she looked nothing like a bride. When Tilly answered the door, I looked past her into the hallway, about to ask where the bride was, when she pulled the door shut behind her and said, "Shall we?"

I promptly shut my mouth and held out my arm to escort her to the car. All the while, I was discreetly checking her out. I'd seen a lot of different wedding dresses in my years as chauffeur, but Tilly managed to surprise even me. For starters, I'd never seen a bride wear black before. She looked like a goth, particularly with the crazy purple stripe in her black hair, heavy makeup and platform boots.

Third, she wasn't remotely nervous. She was full of happy chatter from the moment she walked out her front door, even asking me to open the partition between the cab and the rear of the limo so we could talk on the way to the registry office. I didn't mind—it certainly made my job more pleasant and besides, she was really interesting to talk to.

Not to mention completely gorgeous. She may not have looked like a typical bride, but she was still stunning. Even as we were yakking nineteen-to-the-dozen, I was imagining what she was wearing under that slinky dress.

As it happened, though, I wasn't the only one with sex on the brain. When she first gave me directions to somewhere other than the registry office, I didn't think anything of it. I just thought perhaps her nerves were finally kicking in and she needed a little breathing space.

As I followed her next command, I asked, "Everything all right, Miss Tilly?"

"Oh, yes, Bradley. Everything is just fine."

I shrugged and carried on driving. It was only when she directed me down a quiet country lane that I finally started to think that something wasn't right. My overactive imagination began to wonder if I'd been duped—perhaps Tilly was part of a gang, and they were going to knock me out, leave me for dead and make off with the limo.

As I plotted how I was going to get out of the predicament, Tilly spoke again.

"Bradley, pull over in that lay by, then get in the back."

Something about her tone made me relax—I wasn't about to be carjacked. As the tension seeped out of me, the arousal crept in. Why did she want me to get into the back of the car? She couldn't possibly want to...

"Take off your hat and jacket. And put the screen back up so nobody can see us."

Despite my brain's misgivings, the blood rushed to my cock. It was all I could do to park the car without crashing.

As soon as I shut the door, Tilly spoke.

"Get your cock out, Bradley. We don't have long."

"But...won't we be more than fashionably late?"

"Not if you're quick. I deliberately booked the car fifteen minutes early. I've always wanted to fuck a chauffeur."

There was no arguing with that. I grappled with my belt and fly and pulled out my cock. Tilly's green eyes glinted as she passed me the condom she'd just retrieved from her cleavage. Without a word, I ripped open the packaging and rolled the rubber on. When I looked back up, Tilly was already kneeling on the floor of the limo, the top half of her body leaning on the seats and with her dress up around her back. She wore a tiny black thong.

I knew this was no time for hesitation. I'd fantasized about fucking a bride, she'd fantasized about fucking a chauffeur. It was a win-win situation.

I pulled her thong to one side, grabbed her hips and positioned my cock at her entrance. She was already wet, so when she pushed back, I slid in effortlessly. I paused, savoring the sensation.

"Bradley, we don't have much time."

I didn't need telling twice. Gripping Tilly's pert ass, I fucked her, hard and fast. The sensation of her pussy was divine; hot, wet and tight, and it wasn't long before the feel of it, coupled with the riskiness of the entire situation, pushed me to the edge.

"Tilly..." I said, warningly.

"It's okay...I am too."

Then, my orgasm hit with force. I let out a violent shout as my balls emptied into the not-exactly-blushing bride, who was clearly in the throes of her own climax. We yelled and moaned together in pleasure, before calming down then disentangling without a word. I snapped off the condom and threw it into the bin.

"You know how to get to the registry office from

here?" Tilly asked.

I nodded then clambered out of the car and back into the driver's seat. I pulled on my hat and jacket and straightened myself up before starting the engine and driving to the original destination. I didn't open the partition again until we pulled up outside the building.

"Ready?"

She nodded, and I resumed my professional persona as I helped her out of the car.

"Okay from here?"

Tilly nodded, and gave me a cheeky wink before heading inside. Just before she was swallowed into the gloom of the building's hallway, I spotted a suspicious-looking stain on the back of her dress.

I didn't say anything. It wasn't my place.

HOMECOMING

Sophia Valenti

I'd just swallowed the last sip of my margarita when I felt the vibration of my phone in my purse. I pulled it out to read the text: *Seven o'clock—and don't forget your hairbrush.*

I swallowed, my mouth suddenly feeling dry. Glancing at the time, I became filled with panic. It was twenty minutes till seven, and I was with coworkers at a bar a few blocks from the office, celebrating the closure of a very lucrative contract for our agency. There was no way I'd be able to make it back home and then to Jason's place in time. I'd been expecting to hear from him the following evening, having spent the week dreaming about the sinful pleasures he'd promised me upon his return. But he'd gone and surprised me, first by showing up early, and second by giving me an impossible task.

I offered a hasty good-bye to my staff, hoping they'd blame the liquor for my flushed cheeks. But I could feel the heat in my face, embarrassed because I was rushing off to have my bottom bared and spanked by the one man who knew my secret cravings—and didn't hesitate to fulfill all of my kinky dreams.

I grabbed a cab uptown, asking the driver to wait while I ran inside to fetch the hairbrush from the vanity in my apartment. The brush was an antique, made of sturdy mahogany. It was beautiful and the mere sight of it made my cunt clench. To any visitor, it appeared as innocuous as any of my other beauty tools, but I knew the truth—that it was a precious gift from my master and that he regularly used it to spank me until I begged him for mercy. It was an ever-present reminder of my submission to him, never letting me forget the pain and pleasure he so easily and readily bestows upon me.

The cab ride to Jason's place felt like it took an eternity, which wasn't true, but it certainly took longer than the five minutes I had to spare. And I found myself at Jason's door with my heart beating wildly and my pussy already wet—a full ten minutes past his deadline.

"You're late, my naughty girl," he hissed. Before I could apologize, he grabbed my hair firmly and pulled me toward him for a kiss. His tongue probed my mouth roughly, making me feel completely taken and possessed.

We were still standing in his hallway, kissing hotly, when he reached up and pinched my nipple through my blouse. I groaned into his mouth, feeling my face redden even more than it must have done already.

"Do you have it?" he whispered hotly in my ear.

Before presenting the brush to Jason, I looked up and down the hallway nervously, but I saw no one. I'm always worried someone will see me handing it to him, because seconds later they'll no doubt hear the sound of wood meeting flesh and guess that I'm being punished. The thought always floods me with embarrassment and never fails to turn me on.

Jason took the brush from me and grabbed my arm, pulling me inside his apartment and locking the door behind us. He already had a chair set up in the middle of the living room, and he immediately sat down and tugged me over his lap.

That hello kiss was all the romance I'd get for a while, and I knew it. Jason tugged up my skirt and yanked down my panties so that they were banded around my thighs; I felt cool air course over my hot, wet sex and my clit pulsed with need. I wished with all my might that he'd touch me there, even though I knew he wouldn't— at least not yet.

The smooth oval of wood swirled against my bare ass, a sleek tease that set my nerves on edge. My world was quite literally upside down as I lay draped across his lap, with my palms against the carpet and my hair hanging in loose curls around my blushing face.

"You already know how bad you've been," he said, matter-of-factly. "So don't expect any love taps from me tonight. You're here to be punished. Do you understand me?"

"Yes, Sir," I answered in a quavering voice. I was frightened and nervous, but I also couldn't wait for him to start. I wanted him to hurt me, to heat my ass, to bring me to the edge of climax before he'd fuck me and take me over the edge with him in a shuddering explosion of bliss.

I held my breath when I felt him lift the brush from my cheek, attempting to steel myself for what was to come, but no matter how many times he's spanked me with it, there's no preparation for its wicked intensity. The wood connected with my naked skin, sounding as loud as a thunderclap and delivering a sharp spark of pain that flooded my body. My breath escaped in a rush, and he delivered the second blow to the other cheek before the sensation from the first even had a chance to completely register. In no time I was gasping and kicking, my panties sliding down my legs as Jason delivered blow after blow with harsh precision, until my entire ass felt hot and tender, and I was on the verge of tears. But even as I gasped and begged, I could tell that my pussy was slick with juice, arousal vibrating through me in a way I couldn't deny.

Jason could no doubt hear the hitch of emotion in my voice. He's that in tune with me—to my every movement and tiny utterance; it's one of many reasons why I feel so loved by him.

Knowing I'd had enough, he dropped the brush

and brought his hand between my thighs, trailing his fingers along my wet slit. I closed my eyes, getting lost in the feeling of his finger gliding inside me. He added more until my cunt was packed full, and I rocked back against him, grinding against his muscular thigh and loving the friction of his jeans against my swollen clit. My skirt was a rumpled mess, but I didn't care. All I cared about was my desperate need to come.

"God, you're so hot," Jason muttered, his voice thick and heavy with want. "You're ass is red, and your cunt's absolutely dripping. And you're just so damn sexy when you're bad. What am I going to do with you?"

In answer to his own dreamy question, Jason eased me off his lap and positioned me on my hands and knees. Wasting no time, he stripped and slipped his cock into my pussy, and we both moaned softly. Jason rocked in and out of me, his pelvis slapping against my ass flesh and reawakening the burn of his blows. Each new wave of heat made my cunt drip that much more, encouraging him to pick up his pace. Before long, he was slamming into me wildly and reaching around my body to strum my clit. In one beautiful, overwhelming moment, I let go—let all of those feelings break and swirl around me, carrying me into a breathless state of ecstasy. Jason followed me seconds later, groaning as he shuddered and plunged into me one last time, before we collapsed together on the carpet.

Jason sat back and pulled me close to him for tender

kisses that made me feel cherished, making the moment more perfect than it already was. To be in his arms once again was like coming home, and there was no place I'd rather have been.

DRESS ME UP PRETTY

K. Lynn

Okay, you can look now."

Nathan did as he was told, opening his eyes and taking in the sight of his boyfriend. He felt his breath catch in his throat, and his fingers dug into the edge of the bed where he was sitting. Across the room, Tony stood by the door, looking like he was about to bolt with one wrong word.

He was beautiful, that was Nathan's first thought. When Tony had promised him a surprise for his birthday, he never imagined this. But there was Tony, in a red silk dress that was pulling across his chest and emphasizing hard muscles instead of the cleavage it was designed for. The fabric held no pattern, no ornate stitching or lace to make it stand out as anything special. It bunched tighter at the waist, giving the illusion of curves that Tony didn't possess, and then flared out before it stopped midthigh on his smooth legs.

"Holy fuck, you shaved, too?" Nathan asked, his breath speeding up to keep time with his racing heart rate.

Tony shifted his legs, and Nathan could see a blush rising in his cheeks. "Just the legs. It looked stupid if I didn't." He ran his hands down his thighs, trying to smooth out the nonexistent wrinkles of the material. "Is this okay? I mean, this was what you wanted, right?"

Nathan's mind was screaming yes, this was exactly right, but he tried to temper his eagerness. "You look so hot, you know that?" Tony's blushing wasn't going away, but he gave a soft smile, so Nathan figured he was okay with the compliment. "What made you change your mind?"

"You mean after asking me for five years?" Tony laughed then gave a shrug, causing his dress to inch up his thighs as he did. Nathan's fingers once again clenched at the mattress, aching to take hold of the delicate flesh. "You only turn thirty once, so I figure you deserved it."

Nathan could feel himself growing hard in his boxers. When Tony had left a note on his pillow, ordering him to strip out of his clothes, Nathan figured they were just going to have sex. Now, it seemed more like his boyfriend was watching out for Nathan's health. If he still had his jeans on, circulation to vital body parts would have been an issue.

"Come here." His voice was rough, which caused Tony's smile to grow wider.

"You like this, huh?" Tony asked, taking small steps toward the bed. Nathan wasn't sure if it was because he was trying to prolong the teasing or if the dress was hindering his movements. With each step, the material would ride up his thigh, giving a tease before falling back into place.

When Tony came close enough, Nathan placed his hands on his boyfriend's hips, pulling him in. As Tony's knees hit the edge of the mattress, bracketed by Nathan's legs, he gave a short laugh. "You've caught me, now what are you going to do with me?"

"I think it's time I unwrap my present." Nathan ran his hands down the red silk, the fabric tickling his fingers until he hit the edge where material met flesh. He dipped his fingers beneath the edge, working his way back up the smooth legs until he touched something rough at Tony's hip.

"No," Nathan said, his eyes widening as he looked up at Tony.

His boyfriend nodded, placing his hands on Nathan's shoulders. He licked his bottom lip before he answered. "Had to have the whole package, didn't I?"

Nathan pushed the dress up so that he could get a better look at what lay beneath. And there they were, a pair of red silk panties, lined along the edge with the lace he had felt before. The soft material pulled over Tony's hips, but the bulge of his cock stretched the material almost to breaking. They were definitely not designed for the something extra Tony had.

"You like?" Tony asked, trailing his hands up from Nathan's shoulders to skim along his ears and cheeks before resting there.

Nathan could see the tip of Tony's cock peeking out of the waistband of the panties, flushed pink and already leaking a bit of precome. He focused his attention on the hardened cock beneath the silky fabric, pressing his face against it to give tiny kisses. Nathan hooked his fingers around the lace waistband and pulled the panties down to Tony's thighs, watching his boyfriend's cock spring free.

He grasped the hardened cock with his right hand, rubbing his thumb down the underside to tease it into full arousal. It never took Tony long to go from willing to able when Nathan started. Nathan leaned forward, giving the tip of Tony's cock a swipe with his tongue, tasting the salty sweetness of his precome. Tony's hands tightened on Nathan's face as he opened his lips to start taking in the hardened cock. He pushed forward and pulled back little by little until he had half the length in his mouth. He had never been able to deep-throat Tony, but his boyfriend didn't mind. Nathan had a system and it worked just fine.

As his right hand pumped the base of Tony's cock, Nathan hollowed his cheeks and sucked the end, pulling the cock in and out of his mouth. He could feel Tony was getting closer to the edge, his moans increasing with each squeeze of Nathan's hand. His own cock was to the point of aching now as well, pressing against the seam of his boxers and begging for release. Nathan ran his left hand down, beneath the elastic of his underwear, and gripped himself. He began to squeeze his own cock in time with Tony's, trying to get them both off. Tony's only reaction was his increased panting, jerking his hips up each time Nathan's mouth ran along his length.

Nathan sped up his hands, bringing them closer to release, when he felt Tony still beneath his touch. That was the only warning he had before warm come flooded his mouth, and he worked hard to swallow it all down. Nathan continued to rub himself, squeezing and swallowing in sync, until his hips gave a jerk and he could feel his boxers grow sticky and wet.

He drew back, his mouth releasing Tony's spent cock, and gave it one last squeeze before letting go. Nathan withdrew his hand from his boxers, wiping it on his underwear to try and get rid of some of the mess. He looked up at Tony, whose expression was still a bit dazed, but he seemed to be coming back to his senses.

"You really get off on this, don't you?" Tony asked, his words coming in short gasps as he tried to catch his breath.

"Get off on you," Nathan corrected, moving his hands until they were once again on Tony's waist, his fingers grabbing the bunched material of his boyfriend's dress. "But it was a wonderful present, thank you."

Tony just hummed, rubbing his thumbs along

Nathan's cheeks. "Maybe if you're good, I could be convinced to do it again."

Nathan's eyes widened a little as he smiled up at him. "Something to look forward to for my next birthday?"

Tony gave a short laugh. "Or before. You never know when I might surprise you."

COMMITTEE WORK

Jeremy Edwards

Oh, am I early?" Lorraine looked around the conference room. "I was afraid I was a little late."

"No, you *are* a little late," said Dr. Melling cheerfully. "But only a little."

After being a junior colleague of Dina's for two years, Lorraine didn't know why she still had a tendency to think of her as "Dr. Melling"—especially since the department favored *professor* over *doctor* on the rare occasions that they bothered with formality. Maybe it was the warm but penetrating character of Dina's eyes, as seen through those adorably round-and-tiny glasses. Dr. Melling, always shining through these glasses, had a confidence-inspiring presence—at the same time, paradoxically, as Lorraine's lust for her inevitably made the assistant professor a self-conscious, neurotic mess.

"How are you tonight?"

"Not bad," Lorraine replied. Settling into her seat, she then added a "How about you?"—but she was conscious of having waited an instant too long to say it, thus introducing a moment of awkwardness. She was also acutely aware that she wouldn't have given a thought to such a trivial blunder around anyone besides Dina.

"Where's the rest of the committee?" She hurried now to propel the conversation forward. Meanwhile, Dr. Melling had turned her head to glance at the crisp notebook that lay slightly to her right on the table, and Lorraine found herself fascinated by a lick of hair that curled past the nape of the lovely woman's neck.

"Three people have been in touch with lame excuses. So it's going to be just us tonight."

Though she knew that her long-simmering attraction to Dina Melling had been part of why she'd volunteered for this administrative extracurricular, it had never occurred to Lorraine that they'd end up alone together upon convening. As far as she could remember—and, of course, she *would* remember—she hadn't ever been alone with Dr. Melling under any circumstances.

They proceeded with the committee work. Because of the poor attendance, decisions were made quickly: two faculty members could only generate so much deliberation. Moreover, Lorraine was too awed by the other woman's smooth competence, and too damp and giddy from her one-on-one nearness across the table, to contribute much.

"So that's that," said Dr. Melling after thirty minutes. She smiled at Lorraine. "Now I just have to get off my erogenous ass and find some more reliable faculty members to join us next time around."

Lorraine sensed her face flushing some indeterminate berry color. Had she heard Dina correctly? Her *erogenous* ass? People didn't just say that as a figure of speech, did they? Her blood went hot as she visualized Dina's trim, gently rounded bottom exposed for her, inviting contact.

"Any ideas?"

"Huh?" Lorraine, startled out of her inner movie, nearly shouted the syllable.

Dina grinned reassuringly. "Any ideas as to who might be willing to sit on this committee?"

But Lorraine wasn't interested in getting people to sit on committees. She was interested in getting Dr. Melling to sit on her face. "I'll have to think about that," she said weakly.

Moving slowly and deliberately, Dina rose from her chair and walked to Lorraine's side of the table. She stood behind her and spoke in a hypnotic alto.

"I presume you noticed, Lorraine, that I referred to my 'erogenous ass' just now."

Lorraine began shaking. Dr. Melling, awaiting her reply, steadied her, placing her hands on her shoulders.

"I wondered if I'd misheard you."

"It *was* a peculiar thing to say, wasn't it? But I had a feeling you might appreciate the sentiment."

"Yes," Lorraine whispered.

"I've observed, for a long time, that my ass is particularly erogenous around you." Dina lowered her voice further. "You make me feel like someone's tickling me with an ostrich feather."

Lorraine's pussy wept, and her heart skittered.

"I'd like your hands all over my little derriere, gorgeous," Dr. Melling specified.

From behind her, Lorraine heard the sound of Dina's side-zippered skirt being unzipped. When she stood, turning to face her senior colleague, she saw that the skirt was a mere echo on the floor.

She almost forgot to breathe as she reached for the front of Dina's black knickers.

"You have no idea how horny I am in these panties," said her colleague, squirming elegantly to emphasize her point.

Lorraine laughed—nervously, dizzily, even joyously— and grasped Dina's waistband with both hands. She breathed hard now while she watched panties descend and woman emerge.

Dr. Melling, with the silk of her fine, dark pubic hair shimmering under the fluorescent lights, set about deftly extricating herself from the underwear, her shoes, and the skirt that clung to her ankles. Her maneuvers brought her handsomely proportioned bottom into Lorraine's field of vision, and Lorraine found herself giggling again as she made a lusty grab for both cheeks. She dropped to her knees and lavished a symphony of kisses and caresses all over Dr. Melling's erogenous ass, while Dina hastened to conclude her partial disrobing—electing to retain her blouse, her thigh-highs, and of course her glasses. With Dina wriggling in her face with dignified abandon, Lorraine had never felt so turned on in her life.

She reached under and down to touch Dr. Melling's moist pussy. Dina turned her head, her mouth forming a silent moan. When their eyes met, Lorraine bravely blurted her desire: "Sit on my face. Please."

Dina's eyes glittered. "The bench," she suggested.

The padded, backless bench to which Dr. Melling ushered Lorraine was situated just far enough out from the wall to allow for a nice lewd straddle. Eager to get into position beneath such a straddle, Lorraine lost no time in tearing off her sweater, complete with bra, and folding it into a makeshift pillow. The free swing of her breasts added extra zest to her state of excitement—especially when Dina took a moment to play with them, making her nipples spark with want.

Lorraine lay down with her knees up, her feet planted on the vinyl cushion, and her clitty on fire. A heartbeat later, Dr. Melling's erogenous ass hovered above her face.

She clasped the divine, sensitive cheeks, and pulled Dina into a sitting position. She felt the sizzle between her own legs as she began to lick the sweet furrow—Dina's perfectly poised slit. Her ears went erect when she heard a sigh as crisp as the abandoned notebook: the sound of Dr. Melling melting.

While she ate the delicious woman and frantically fondled her bottom, Lorraine squeezed and relaxed her own thigh muscles, bucking her hips in a dance of arousal. She knew she couldn't make herself come in her pants this way—but she'd get as close as she could, then rip her jeans open for Dr. Melling's tongue. The prospect of that event made her lick Dina's gash with extra gusto; and when her tongue tip hit her colleague's rigid clit, the ass in her hands vibrated in ecstasy, and hot, sticky love juice bathed her face.

Dina had been clutching Lorraine's knees in her throes, but now she moved a hand to her crotch, rubbing Lorraine's fly just so. As the tension exploded and her panties became a wet heaven of rippling pleasure, Lorraine hammered her heels on the bench, wallowing in the feeling of being an impatient animal. She hadn't even waited for the tongue, couldn't even wait to bare her cunt.

Yes, things were accomplished quickly with an efficient little committee of two, thought Lorraine.

QUEEN OF PARKING-LOT BLOW JOBS

Giselle Renarde

I did it again today. I visited my girlfriend at work. *Reprobate writer seeks innocent Melanie for backseat naughtiness in underground parking lot.* Yes, I've been wicked again. Spank me, Jesus.

Before this gets too confusing, what with "blow jobs" in the title, let me clarify: I'm a woman, Melanie's a woman—we're a lesbian couple—but while I'm a woman with a pussy, my girlfriend's a woman with a cock. She's trans, hence the mention of blow jobs. So that's one mystery solved.

Melanie didn't always let me at her nether regions—in fact, there was a time not long ago when she assured me we would never have the kind of sex that involved a pussy and a cock, or a mouth and a cock, or pretty much anything else and a cock—but luckily we've matured as a couple. And with maturity comes backseat blow jobs.

I love sucking my girlfriend off, and I don't care how sleazy or sordid that sounds. The moment my tongue touches the slick satin flesh of her tip, I just flood my panties with juice. It's crazy how wet I get, right from the very start, right from the second I give the gentle curve of her cockhead a nice little lick. She gasps and bucks her hips, and that beautiful moment gets me every time, whether we're at home in bed or in the underground parking lot beneath her office tower.

Giving a blow job in a parking lot is risky, especially when your girl doesn't want the whole world to know she's got a penis. I thought I'd outgrown all this sex-in-cars stuff, but as an adult I've rediscovered the sketchy and the vulgar, and I love it. The key to really enjoying the experience is to have faith in your partner. If I didn't trust Melanie to keep an eye on the surroundings while I'm working in her lap, I'd be too panicked to give good head. And what's the point of giving a blow job if your heart's in your throat? Doesn't leave much room for cock.

It's a whole lot easier when she's wearing a skirt. That way I can just bury my face between her thighs and it's like giving head in a little tent. Today happened to be very chilly, one of the first cold and windy days of autumn, so Melanie wore businessy black slacks. Not ideal, but I can work with anything.

I didn't visit her at work with the explicit intention of letting her fuck my face. In truth, I just missed her. I just wanted to see her smile. The sex stuff just kind of happened. The plan was to go for a brisk walk. We only went down to her car because that's where she'd left her heavy jacket—a must with the wind picking up. I'm not even sure why we ended up sitting in the backseat of her little car flanked by high-rise SUVs, but once we were in there I had to suck her off.

She seemed surprised when I grabbed her crotch and stroked it. With everything tucked away, her mound always felt as smooth as mine. But I knew better. I knew there was a cock buried under layers of panties and tight, binding undergarments, and I wanted that thing in my mouth.

When I tried to unzip her fly, she laughed at me. I always struggled with her pants, because she had a bit of a belly and it pushed out on the zipper. Finally, she undid it herself. That amazed me. Every time I got away with some public sex act, I was always in disbelief. But this time, my woman fished around inside her panties and drew out a flaccid cock. It was my job to get her hard, but I was good at that.

Diving into her lap, I wrapped my mouth around her entire shaft. When my lips met her pubes, I started to suck. There's something I've always loved about her soft cock—I can get the whole damn thing in my mouth without gagging. Of course, once it's in there, it never stays soft for long, and this day was no exception. The moment I tasted the salty-sweet flesh of her shaft against my tongue, it started to grow exponentially. Before long, I couldn't keep the whole thing in my mouth.

That's when I felt her hand on the back of my head, pressing me down. There must have been someone walking by—yes, there was, because I remember hearing the clip-clop of heels on concrete—and I tried to keep my throat open, but the more I thought about it, the harder I gagged. Tears welled in my eyes. My nose started to run. My throat had never felt so full of cock, and that moment seemed to last forever.

My girl's hand was like an anvil on my head. I whimpered around her girth, but she didn't let me up. My tears and snot and saliva soaked her black pants, but there was nothing I could do about it. Finally, she let up her hold on my head and apologized about a thousand times. I didn't let her hard-on out of my mouth long enough even to tell her it was okay. The waiting had worked me into a frenzy. I wrapped a fist around her shaft and pumped it hard with my hand, sucking the top half like crazy.

I wanted her to come. Now. I wanted to hear her make those orgasm noises and to feel her muscles clench and release. I wanted to taste her jizz because—I'm not sure why, but her cream didn't taste like a man's. It was sweet like clover, not heavy, not musky. Delicious. I wanted it.

My fist pistoned up and down her shaft, and my head came with it. I devoured the cock that had grown from little to big in my mouth, creating a crazy amount of hot suction to tempt her over the edge.

When I heard her say, "Oh, god," I knew she was close, and I also knew what I could do to push her over the precipice. With my free hand, I felt around between her legs. Her balls were in there somewhere, hidden under layers of tight panties. When she gasped I knew I'd found them, and I pushed there, squeezed, applied all the pressure my fingers could manage as I consumed her cock.

It worked. I knew it would. It always did. She bucked up into my throat so hard I had to close my fist around her shaft and push down. She said my name, which was always the best part of bringing my girl to orgasm. Second best was the flood of cum against my tongue. Every time I swallowed, there was more. I downed the stuff, squirt after squirt, until the pulses slowed and eventually stopped.

I teased her tip with my tongue, and she laughed, pushing my head away from her waning erection, pulling her top down to cover her naked cock. It's the last thing she'd want anyone but the queen of parking lot blow jobs to see.

HELLUVA THING

A. M. Hartnett

Not that I'm complaining or anything, but what are you up to?"

Tabitha raised her gaze to meet Duke's, but she could hardly be expected to answer, at least not while his cock was sliding over her tongue.

She should have known it wouldn't take him long to figure out something was up. It wasn't often she brought him a home-cooked meal. It wasn't often she bought him the expensive rum. It wasn't often she put on the really slutty underwear and blew him before dessert.

"Tabs?"

She made a small sucking sound and lifted one shoulder.

Duke didn't look convinced. Blissful, yes, but skeptical. "Did you put a dent in my car when you were pulling out of your driveway?"

"Nggh-nnn," was her only possible response. She closed her eyes, grasped his shaft and closed her lips around the circumference. He pushed against the floor with a grunt. His ass came up from the cushion and his dick went deeper into her throat.

True, she was after something, but it's not like she didn't enjoy being in this position. She liked sucking him off. She liked the sounds he made. She liked feeling like the only woman alive who knew how to get him off just right.

Duke sagged against his pillow as Tabitha slid her tongue along the underside of his cock. She teased him at first, watching his expression go from calm to strained, and was contented that she had thrown off his investigative groove.

He parted his lips and a strangled sound preceded his words, "God, I love how you suck me."

Duke twined his fingers in her hair and pulled her head up until only the fat tip remained between her lips. With a smile, she ran her tongue along the groove on the underside of the head. Duke groaned and sleepily watched while she coated her lips with the cloudy dew that oozed from the tip. The salty tang popped on her taste buds as she licked every drop.

It was what could have pushed him over the edge, but she drew back. Duke clenched his teeth and growled, but he gave no argument as she stood and adjusted her garter belt and stockings.

"Come on," she said in a husky tone. "I'm ready to go off."

"Not until you tell me what you want."

Tabitha could have screamed. She could have stamped her foot and busted some shit over his head. Instead, calmly, she said, "I don't know what you're talking about," but she knew it was pointless.

They'd been friends for so long there was little point in hiding anything from him. She had known Duke since the first grade. In high school they'd developed an on-and-off fuckbuddy rapport. When his marriage went into the shitter, she'd been there for him. When hers did the same, he was waiting for her.

If they could have made it a whole week without getting into a screaming match, they'd have had a hell of a thing. For now she'd settle for a good screw and a smidge of sympathy.

Leaving him in bed, Tabitha wandered to the window seat and peered out at the quiet, suburban street. She'd make him come to her. A moment later the bedsprings creaked. She heard the snap of latex and then Duke was turning her in his arms.

She closed her eyes and breathed him in until it seemed like there was nothing else in the world but that scent, his warmth, and the heaviness filling her abdomen.

"How do you want it?" he asked in that low, growly voice that gave her the shivers.

"You know."

His fingers found her clitoris swollen and her cunt

slick. "Right now I just want to play with you. Switch places with me."

She sat on the window seat and leaned back on her hands. Excitement skittered through her belly as he nudged her thighs apart and rested her feet against his shoulders.

Grinning, Duke ran his middle finger along the cleft. When he raised his glistening fingertips to his lips and licked away her juices, she curled her toes with anticipation. She held in an elated breath as he teased her stiff clitoris with the tip of his sheathed cock.

"You're dripping, Tabitha."

She lifted her head and looked down her flushed body, and then at his. Duke was magnificent, pure sex. His biceps flexed as he gripped her leg just above her small foot, and his shoulders rolled as he positioned himself to penetrate her.

He fucked her hard and steady. Hookups that had become a regular thing in the past few years had given them a cadence that never got boring. He went balls deep, pumping to build his tempo. His balls slapped against her ass, jarring a moan out of her each time.

The sounds he made, those stuttering grunts from the back of his throat, made her crazy. Though in his clutches, she was able to rock and bump with each thrust. His fat cock rubbed her G-spot, and he bumped her clit with each pass. It all combined to send her spiraling up into that hot, liquid vortex.

Abruptly, he lifted her and in a blink they were on

the bed, Duke resuming his position and pace immediately. Her breath trapped at the back of her throat and her whole body pulsed. As hard as it was to do, she fought to keep from closing her eyes and shutting out the glorious sight of Duke before her: the scrunching of his brow and the splotching on his cheeks coincided with the way his cock throbbed between the slick inner walls that milked him.

His fingers tightened around her ankle. He arched his back and shoved deep. His euphoric tension bled into her, keeping her electric even as her body grew heavy with satisfaction. She tipped her head back and sighed as he surged.

The next few moments brought only the hush, the panting and stroking, the awareness of each other via long looks and sleepy smiles. He shook out his shoulders and released her. Tabby stretched out like a cat and fell back with a sigh, then watched his shadow in the bathroom as he cleaned himself up.

Strolling back to the bedroom, Duke dragged his feet and yawned, then flopped down on the bed. Face squashed into the bedding, he mumbled something she couldn't understand.

She rolled over, her arm draped over his back and her hand on his ass. "What did you say?"

He turned his head. "You can tell me what you want now. I'm pretty sure I'd sign over the house to you at this point."

She gave his ass a squeeze and went silent for a

moment. "I want to have a baby, Duke, and I want you to be the father."

Nuzzling into his shoulder, she bit her lip and waited for his response. First, nothing, then his eyes grew wide and he pushed up like a shot. "What? Are you fucking kidding me?"

She gave his ass another squeeze and laughed. "I'm fucking with you. Jesus, are *you* fucking kidding me? No, I lost my job and I want you to help me find a new one."

Down he went, flopping on his back with his hand covering his face. "That was a shitty thing to do."

"No, it wasn't. It was a joke. Your brains are just congealing at the end of a condom right now."

He peeked through his fingers at her. "Okay, so you want me to help you find a job. All the fanfare was for this? The food, the booze and the sex?" He tucked his hands behind his head and grinned at the ceiling. "I think that this afternoon should be a starting point to favors rendered."

Tabby narrowed her eyes at him. "Oh, really? You want a home-cooked meal every night?"

"Let me fuck you like that every day after work and *I'll* have dinner waiting for you." His gaze cut to her and his smirk widened.

Tabby basked in the little pop of jubilation at the thought of a regular and vigorous schedule with Duke. "That sounds like a deal to me."

Duke raised his hand, pinkie out.

Giggling, Tabby hooked her finger with his.

MAD GHOSTS OF LUST

Kristina Lloyd

Everything came clattering down as it would in the movies. Shampoos and shower gels got knocked for six, a bar of soap slithered to our feet, a razor scooted down the side of the tub. He fucked me from behind, water splashing between us. Struggling for balance, I bashed a tap. The temperature shot up, making us shriek. That might have got a laugh from an audience. I turned the tap down. Too cold. Up again, better. I flailed for something to hold, grabbed the shower curtain then thought again because curtains cost money and anyway it wouldn't have worked except as a metaphor for reckless passion.

So I braced myself as best I could, one hand on the slippery tiles, another on the tub edge. Steam enshrouded us carrying scents of cosmetics, visions of vanilla chiffon. Pale streaks of foam spiraled into the drain and vanished.

His hands dug into my hips. In the midst of the vapor and wetness, his cock shored me up, enormous and substantial where I was soft and hidden. They wouldn't show that in the movies. This wouldn't even make a porno because it wasn't camera friendly. Impossible to see our thrusting contact, secondary sex characteristics and my all-important twisting face.

"I'm going to be late," he hissed. "Move your foot."

The tub squeaked beneath me.

Janet Leigh's shower scene popped into my head. A layer of knowledge beneath the surface of the story tells me they stabbed melons to make the sound of her being knifed. And that she stayed in the shower for too long: she soaped herself, rinsed, then lingered for no other reason than the sensual enjoyment of water, the caressing of her wet self. Ain't that always the way? Woman gets punished for her pleasure.

I get punished for my pleasure too, but you have to flip the logic of that sentence to appreciate my meaning.

An hour before the shower, he'd trussed up my tits in a rope harness, making them balloon and flush. He'd fixed clamps to my nipples, tied my wrists to the headboard and, around my eyes, he'd wrapped a navy-blue, polka-dot scarf which my friend Maggie had given me as a thank-you gift after I'd fed her cat while she was holidaying in the Netherlands. I'd never liked that scarf. Sorry Maggie. We use it for bondage now.

He fucked me harder and harder. The pain biting my nipples soared, leveled out and soared again whenever he knocked or twisted the clamps. He dug his fingers into my blood-suffused flesh. Colors bloomed behind my eyelids and when I was there, the colors were my world. Flickering clutches of coming pulled me into myself and flung me out. Inside and outside, all at the same time.

Ecstasy escapes description; it's like trying to package steam.

In the shower, I didn't come. He did, pulling out of me, his white fluids chasing suds down the drain in separate blobs and strings. It didn't look like bliss.

He had to dash. Dinner with some clients at eight. He dried off and I stayed in the shower for too long, because I can without dying for my desires. I will do. They don't give you your sexual freedoms. You have to claim them.

When he'd gone, because I wasn't finished yet, I lay on the rumpled bed, and brought myself off with my fingers. I thought of how he'd behaved earlier, sadistic and cruel, reveling in my cries from the pinch of the clamps and the slam of his cock. Then I fell asleep for an hour or so. When I woke, my hair was in a crazy, damp tangle and my breasts were a mess of scratch marks and blotches. And he was probably eating wild turbot because he usually does when it's on expenses at Saxby's. I would too.

The point I'm making: sex isn't like it is in the movies; it isn't even like porn. Sex isn't like anything except itself.

At the time, it is most like bodies and least like bodies.

And afterward it falls back to lie in our memories, mad ghosts of lust rising up to consciousness on the train, at our desks, in our dreams.

BOOKMARKED

Alison Tyler

Gina sat in her bed and tried to read *High Window*. She'd devoured the novel many times before, but familiarity didn't stop her from rereading her favorite works. Tonight, however, the words blurred in front of her eyes. She could only see the man in the store—his name was Andrew Martin. He'd written that on the bookmark. She toyed with the slim piece of stiff blue paper. Should she call him? What would she say?

She reached for the phone. Put it down. Picked it up.

She dialed the number, then almost slammed the phone down again when she heard his voice: "Hello?"

Her first word came out as a husky whisper, "Hello," as if she were auditioning for a part as a 1-800-porn actress.

"Hello?" he said again, and she cleared her throat

and said, "I'm the girl…" but then she didn't know what to put after that. The girl who masturbated in your store. Jesus, Gina, get a grip. She was a second from disconnecting the line when he said, "Don't hang up. I've been waiting for your call."

She swallowed over the lump in her throat but didn't say a word.

"You've been on my mind all day. I can't stop thinking about you. Will you come over?"

"This isn't a booty call," she said, but she was lying. It was midnight. She was calling a stranger. She wanted him to fuck her. What other type of call would this be?

"No," he agreed. "It's not. It's different. I want to do things to you…"

She sighed, "Like what?"

"You're so nervous, so twitchy. I want to tie you down…and punish you."

"Oh, Jesus," she sighed.

"You'd like that, wouldn't you?"

Like wasn't the right word, but she didn't attempt to correct him. "Yes, I would," she said, and it sounded like a confession.

"Can I come over? Can I play with you? I'll go slow. I promise."

"No," she told him. She could hear his disappointment over the line, even though he hadn't spoken. "You can come over, but you can't go slow."

She gave him her address and then she waited, pacing through her apartment wearing only her robe. She felt as if she were in a waking dream—she could see herself in the mirror, could hear her thoughts, feel her actions, but she felt as if the whole world had been plunged under-water. Everything was slow, languid, distorted.

He knocked twenty minutes later and she let him.

"Vanilla," he said, and he smiled. "Are you trying to give me a message?"

"It's always been my favorite scent. That's all. Just a scent."

She didn't know what to do, standing there in the hallway. He looked different than he had at the store. Less scruffy, that was for sure. More adult in his button-down white shirt, dark jeans, black boots. He was taller than she'd imagined, and he looked so serious.

He lifted her face toward his, his fingers under her chin, tilting up.

"I saw you," he said. "You sat on the ladder in my back room and you put your hand down your skirt."

She still couldn't believe she'd done that. Only borderline crazy people did things like that. But he didn't appear disturbed by her actions.

"What were you thinking about?"

Nothing like this had ever happened to Gina before. She decided to be fully honest. Where she might have said, "I don't know" in the past, this time she said, "You fucking me."

He smiled, and that softened the seriousness of his expression, the look in his eyes.

"It's been a long time for me," she said. "I guess I

forgot that part of myself." That was her only expla-
nation for what she'd done, and it was the truth. She
hadn't been on a date in over a year, hadn't slept with a
man in eighteen months, since her last brief disaster of
a relationship.

"It's an important part," he said, and he pressed
against her, pushing her toward the wall. She sighed and
then bit her lip. She wanted him to fuck her. Her whole
body was aching. He seemed to sense her needs, but he
didn't give her what she wanted.

"You touched yourself in my store," he said, "in a
public place, without permission. You're going to need
to be punished for that."

Oh, god, he was speaking to her in a language she'd
only fantasized about.

"Do you understand what I'm saying?"

She nodded.

"Do you accept what I'm saying?"

"Yes," she stammered. "Yes, Andrew."

"Turn around and face the wall."

She did as he said, and she felt him lifting her
cream-colored satin robe to her hips. He stroked her
ass through her panties once, almost lovingly, before
bringing his palm back and smacking her bottom hard.
Gina groaned and arched her hips back, showing him
with her body that she wanted more.

"Good girl," he said, admiring her position. She
heard the sound of his buckle being undone, and she
glanced over her shoulder at him.

"Ten with the belt," he said. "I think that would be fair. Don't you?"

She nodded. Her hair fell in front of her eyes and she tossed her head back.

"Have you ever been whipped before?"

She shook her head this time, and then she found her voice. "No, but I've wanted it." Her voice was trembling, but she made herself say the words aloud. "God, I have wanted it bad."

He doubled the belt, made the leather snap. She sucked in her breath, faced the wall and waited. Andrew did what she'd asked him over the phone. He went fast. The ten stinging blows landed in rapid succession as they met the curves of her ass. Gina held herself in check, palms flat on the cold wall, accepting each fiery stripe. The pain burned inside of her, but it was a sweet pain. Different from anything she'd thought, anything she'd fantasized. Better. She relished every blow. When he was finished, Andrew dropped the belt and reached for her. He carried her to her bedroom and threw her down on the bed. Gina waited for the next command, but there was none forthcoming. Andrew was in motion now, pulling down her panties, undoing his button fly, climbing behind her on the mattress.

He put her on her hands and knees and took her doggie-style. She groaned out loud from the moment the head of his cock parted her pussy lips.

"I don't want you touching yourself without my permission again," he said.

She tried to reply, but she only managed to moan.

"Do you understand, Gina?"

She tried again, hearing the words in her head before she said them out loud. "Yes, Sir."

He responded by fucking her harder, gripping her long dark hair in his hand as he pounded into her body. She held herself still as he worked her, unsure of whether he'd want her to buck back against him or not. This was new to her. Outside of her fantasies, her daydreams, the stories she told herself when she came, this was new.

But it felt old. It felt as if she'd always been on the bed with this man, always had his hands on her body, always had his whispered words working through her mind.

He reached one hand under her and began to rub her clit as he fucked her. She made a low, keening sound under her breath, unable to stop herself.

"Come when I tell you," he said.

Could she? Gina felt that she was right on the edge, teetering. What if he didn't tell her fast enough? What if he didn't say that she could and she came without permission? What if...

"Come now," he said, and she thought, *Thank fucking god,* as the climax broke within her. She could not remember a time of greater pleasure. Her ass still felt hot from the hiding he'd given her with his belt, but her pussy felt liquid with the intensity of her bliss. Her arms were trembling. He held her in place with his hands on her waist as he slammed into her. She had the sense to realize he'd let her come before he reached his own orgasm, and this gentlemanly touch made her smile to herself—as if he'd held the door for her, or placed his coat over her shoulders on a chilly evening.

He came as hard as she had, and then wrapped her in his arms and settled with her on the bed. She reached to pull the sheets around them, and when she did, her book fell off the pillow.

Andrew saw she'd had the book open, spine cracked. She saw the frown on his face as he slid the bookmark between the pages and shut the novel, but he didn't say a word. Still his hands went under the covers and he traced the lines he'd left there with his belt. Bookmarked.

CUCKOLD'S NEST

D. L. King

He was young and his cock was as hard as a steel rod. No foreplay was necessary. He took off his clothes and, bang: hard and ready. Not like your sad, little caged protuberance. I can't imagine you were ever like that, were you?" She shook her head in mock sadness as she gazed at Bob. He knelt, naked, with the exception of the chastity device affixed to his cock and balls. He yawned, silently.

"Does this bore you?"

"Sorry, Ma'am." It wasn't so much that it was boring, it was that it was just stories. He needed more.

"And then today, at lunch, I seduced a UPS guy. All tan and muscles, he looked great in his uniform shorts but he looked even better out of them. Nine-inch cock, at a minimum. Straight and thick. And boy could he eat.

Someone had trained that boy well. I had three orgasms before we even got to the actual fucking. I thought about you—stuck here, cleaning the bathroom or the kitchen or whatever it was you were doing."

"Look, Barbara," Bob stood up. "I just don't think this is working anymore. It used to be great, but I need more now."

Barbara looked at him. Stepping out of character, she said, "What do you mean, baby? This is exactly what we discussed."

"Well, I think it's time for a renegotiation. I mean, it's always the same: big cock yada yada yada, muscles yada yada yada, long, blond hair yada yada yada, better in the sack—do you actually have sex with these random guys?"

"Of course I do! I wouldn't lie to you. Is that what you think? That I'm lying? That these guys don't exist?" Barbara sat down on the bed and ran her fingers over his chastity device, playing with his caged cock, running her little fingernail over the skin that was reachable through the slits and fondling his balls. "Do you want me to bring one home, fuck him in front of you?" She could already see his skin swelling, filling any available wiggle room.

Barbara arrived home with the barista from her coffee shop. Bob had to admit, he was something—shoulder-length blond hair, green eyes and tall—really tall. He wondered what the guy thought when he saw Bob, naked, in cuffs and a chastity cage.

The guy pulled Barbara to him, kissing her almost violently. Breaking the kiss, still holding Barb, he opened his eyes, made eye contact with Bob, smiled around her mouth and winked. A delicious shiver ran through Bob.

"Come here, Bob." Barista Boy's arm was around her shoulder, his fingers playing inside the neck of her blouse, underneath her bra. "I'm going to free you so you can properly appreciate everything Alex is going to do to me. You can touch yourself all you want but you'd better not come." She unlocked his chastity cage and let it fall to the carpet. "Go sit in your chair and watch what a real man does with your wife."

Bob's cock was already lengthening and thickening as he made his way to the hard-backed wooden chair in the corner. It got appreciably larger as he watched Alex undress his wife.

Alex tweaked her swollen nipples before hooking his thumbs into the waist of her panties, pulling them past her hips, down her thighs and over her knees. Not until she was completely naked, with the exception of her red leather pumps, did he stand and unbutton the waist of his jeans. Leaving them open, he pulled the T-shirt over his head, exposing the pecs of a guy who obviously spent all his free time at the gym.

Alex finished unbuttoning his jeans and slid them down his legs, pulling them off. He'd gone commando, so there was nothing hiding his enormous package, which he pulled and stroked. The guy had a gorgeous big cock. He stroked it twice more, appreciating the sight of Bob's naked wife, before going to his knees and latching his mouth to Barbara's cunt. Bob watched as the guy's cock bobbed in time to what he imagined was Alex's sucking rhythm.

Barbara flung her head back and moaned. "Oh, god, Alex, you're so good—so much better than my worthless husband." She wrapped her hand around his cock as she kissed him. "God, so big. Not like the tiny, little nothing Bob's got between his legs."

Bob's *tiny, little nothing* had grown to a very respectable length and thickness as he stroked it gently, not wanting to overstimulate himself. He watched as Alex pushed his wife to her knees and fed her his cock. He almost lost it when she gagged a little as Alex pressed her face to his body, but he managed to maintain. He let his cock bob in time, without the use of hands, as Barb sat atop Alex and rode him while her lover squeezed her tits. He saw her shudder with an orgasm a few minutes before Alex pulled out of her, porn movie style, and came on her stomach for Bob's benefit. Bob's painfully hard cock ached as she made him crawl over to lick Alex's come off her skin.

"Good boy. Now go back to your corner while I say good-bye to our guest."

Barb returned to the bedroom, after ushering her fucktoy out the door, to find Bob kneeling on the bed, cock rampant and his eyes burning for her. Letting her robe fall by the door she said, "It seems that got your attention. Not bored anymore, are you?"

She wrapped her hand around him and Bob moaned.
He grabbed her head and kissed her roughly; he tasted
the other man on her tongue and his cock jumped.

"Baby," she said, "I think we found the magic
formula."

COOKIE

Sharon Wachsler

Renata climbs the stairs from the dungeon, brushes aside the leather curtain, and looks around. Tonight she doesn't need a fancy station. She only needs a quiet corner and a chair. This room will do nicely.

She takes a seat against the wall. Like a lioness crouched by a watering hole, she watches the snack table across the room. People come, people go. Then her patience pays off. Vicki's red latex minidress and stiletto ankle boots identify her. She's trying to drink a Coke with one hand while holding a chocolate-chip cookie with the other. It's awkward with the cuffs. Renata strides over and presses herself against Vicki's back.

"When's your break over?"

"Now." Vicki lowers her snack.

"Good. Keep the cookie."

A hand on Vicki's biceps, Renata propels her across the room. Vicki's ass and boobs jiggle under the low-cut latex. The ankle cuffs mean she has to shuffle quickly to keep up. By the time they get to Renata's chair, Vicki's breathing hard.

Renata drops Vicki's arm and sits, facing her. "Are you hungry?"

Vicki's eyes jump to the cookie, Renata's crotch, Renata's eyes, away. She licks her lips. "Yes?"

"Is that a question or an answer?"

"Both."

Renata allows herself a small smile then erases it. "Get on the floor. Don't break the cookie."

Vicki bends her knees and waist until she can gracefully go no lower. Renata offers no help. Cupping the cookie as if it were a fledgling, Vicki tilts, landing on her ass, the cookie aloft.

"Well done," Renata nods.

"Thank you," Vicki lowers her head.

"Come closer."

Vicki rises to her knees, inching forward, wincing at the rug burn. When her knees are on either side of Renata's right boot, she stops. Renata's boots shine with perfection—gleaming black, they show no scuff-marks or nicks. The laces are tied in perfect symmetry.

"Crumble the cookie on my boot."

Vicki jerks as if slapped, stares.

"Did you hear me?"

"Yes," Vicki whispers, but hesitates.

Now Renata does slap Vicki across the face. "Do it," she says.

A tear slides down Vicki's cheek as she crumbles the cookie over Renata's right boot. The chocolate has melted. The crumbs are sticky. Elbows on the floor, she rubs her palms together until her hands are dry and the boot a mess. She sits back, tears continuing to slide down her cheeks as she looks at the ruined boot.

"Good. Now, clean it," Renata says.

Immediately Vicki bends over Renata's right foot. Renata watches the back of Vicki's head bob. She feels Vicki's hair brush her pants leg, the girl's breath on her arch, her tongue caressing her toes and massaging her instep. She imagines the taste of Vicki's lower lip, coated with the sweetness of the cookie and the tang of polish.

She laces her fingers behind her head and leans back, eyes shut. Vicki's warm tongue strokes her through the leather: heel, ankle, arch, instep, big toe to small. Renata relaxes into Vicki's mouth massaging her boot, a sense of peace and power filling her. She feels twice her size, breathing slow and deep.

Then, the rhythm shifts, becomes urgent, repetitive. Vicki's overworking where the laces start. Renata's peace punctured, she slides her foot free of the girl's mouth, pressing the toe hard into Vicki's chest. Vicki stills. Renata moves her foot back.

Carefully, delicately, Vicki again licks where the lower laces cross at the bottom of the leather tongue. Renata now sees the crumb her submissive's been struggling to dislodge—a large piece stuck between the boot's laces and tongue. Vicki's eyes dart up to Renata's face every few seconds as she keeps trying to move the crumb without raising Renata's ire again.

Finally, Vicki sits back, brow furrowed, face flushed and beaded with sweat. There is chocolate at the corners of her mouth, cookie dust on her chin and nose. Renata could eat her.

Vicki nods her head once, apparently having come to a decision, and turns and crawls toward Renata's left foot. Renata sees sweat gleam on the sub's bare upper back and shoulders. That crumb is still stuck in her right boot's laces. A cold fist clenches in her chest. The crumb is like a burr inside her boot—rubbing, raw, insistent. She has misjudged Vicki. She's so disappointed, she has half a mind to stand up and walk away.

From this new vantage point, Vicki stops and sits back on her heels, her hair sticking to her face, lips rubbed red and plump. Both stare at the one remaining crumb, brown against black.

Vicki scoots back and lowers herself between Renata's boots until her breasts, belly and cunt rest on the floor. Legs sticking out, her heels point toward the ceiling. She lays her cheek against the right boot, her head resting on it like a pillow, and Renata feels shivers down her spine at the sight of that soft, pale skin resting on the hard, dark toe of the leather encasing her foot.

Her mouth against the laces, Vicki pulls back her lips, like a doe nibbling at a leaf. Gingerly, she picks at the crumb with her teeth. She nibbles at it, bit by bit, until she swallows the last dot. She sighs and kisses the spot where the crumb had been. Lifting her cheek off Renata's foot, she inches back, rising to her knees. She sits on her heels, back straight, facing Renata with shining eyes.

A ball of heat expands in Renata's belly, zinging fire to her cunt as she sees the adoration and pride in Vicki's upturned face. She takes a moment to savor the pulsing power, rubbing her hand over the dick she's packing, feeling the warmth spread between her legs.

Closing her eyes to slits, she leans forward. She runs a forefinger all along her boot, searching for cookie crumbs or dust. She finds none—no grit, no smears—just soft, warm, supple leather, warmed by Vicki's mouth. Her finger lingers on the place Vicki kissed. A slow grin spreads across her face.

Standing up, she pulls Vicki to her feet and settles the girl in the chair she's just vacated. Vicki leans forward, head lowered, until the top of her head is just an inch from Renata's abdomen. Renata strokes her hair, and Vicki leans in, resting her head against Vicki's belly. Vicki allows it. They stay like that for a few minutes, Renata quietly stroking the girl's hair. Then Renata eases away, and Vicki straightens.

Renata goes to the snack table and finds a Coke, opens it, pours it into a cup, adding a straw. She brings it back to Vicki and, making sure the trembling hands are wrapped around it, places the straw between Vicki's bee-stung lips. As Vicki sips, Renata reaches into her pocket. She pulls out a key and unlocks the cuffs at Vicki's wrists and ankles, then hangs the cuffs on the key chain that goes from her pocket to her belt loop.

She takes one of Vicki's hands and rubs the wrist.

"Are you ready to go home?" Renata asks.

"Mm," Vicki says, nodding sleepily.

"I'll get our coats," Renata says, walking to the coatroom. She stops by the snack table and bites into a cookie. It's rich and buttery, but then, she reflects, everything Vicki bakes is delicious.

EYE OF THE BEHOLDER

Stella Harris

Jason left for work the same way he always did, but instead of following his normal routine he came home two hours later and slipped back into the house. Sneaking through his own house like a criminal felt absurd, but he did it anyway.

When his best friend told him he thought their wives were more than just friends Jason hadn't believed it. Things like that didn't happen in real life. So when Rose told him that Miranda was coming over that day to help her in the garden he knew what he had to do.

As he creeps upstairs, he hears soft voices and sees that the bedroom door has been left ajar. He leans forward until he can see into the room. And there they are, Rose and Miranda together in bed.

Jason watches them. He can't help but appreciate how beautiful Rose is like this, her head thrown back, eyes closed and mouth open. Sure, he's seen her like this before, but it's not the same when he's the one moving above her, when he's focused on what he's doing, what he's feeling.

Now he can just watch.

He'd expected to be angry, jealous, but they are just too beautiful together, they look too right with their limbs entwined, moving, shifting against each other.

Miranda leans forward to whisper something in Rose's ear and Rose smiles. Next thing he knows, Miranda is sliding down Rose's body, disappearing below the sheet tangled around them. Rose's hands flail about for a moment, seeking something to grasp, before settling on the headboard above her.

Even from here, Jason can see her white-knuckled grip, the way the muscles in her arms stand out as she pulls against the headboard with all her considerable strength. Her whole body is writhing now, her knees coming up and then lowering again when her feet fail to find purchase.

Rose's mouth is opening and closing, forming silent words that soon take voice, her *oohs* and *aahs* and *yesses* falling from her lips just as they do when Jason does this to her. He finds that thought strangely comforting.

Her volume increases; she always gets loud right before she comes, and he loves the way she sounds, how unselfconscious she is in her pleasure. Her screams send a shudder through his body, settling deep in his groin. But these cries are not for him. This is not for him.

Jason looks back up, not having realized he'd looked away, just as Rose lowers her still-shaking arms, reaches for Miranda and pulls her up, pulls her close and captures her mouth in a long kiss. Miranda is brushing Rose's hair away from her forehead where it sticks to the light sheen of sweat. The gesture is sweet, tender, and it is this—more than anything he's already witnessed—that makes Jason feel like he's intruding.

He takes a careful step away, then another, then moves more quickly when he's reached a safe distance.

He's changed his mind. He's not going to say anything. He can let them have this.

STRESS RELIEF

K. Lynn

After a tiring day at the office, my plans for the evening included very little aside from falling into bed and staying unconscious for ten hours straight. But, met with the sight in front of me, I was ready to admit plans could be changed.

Wendy was laid out on the mattress, her head propped up on both of our pillows, and the bed made up with what she deemed our "good sheets." The eight-hundred-thread-count set was a gift from her rich aunt and she refused to bring them out for daily use, instead saving them for only special occasions. Apparently a Tuesday night in the middle of January qualified.

She was wearing a matching set of baby-blue underwear: bra, panties, and garter belt to hold up her white stockings. The colors reminded me of *Alice in*

Wonderland and I felt like I had just fallen down the rabbit hole myself. What had brought on this midweek show? I couldn't think of any special occasion I might have missed.

"What's all this?" I asked, my voice low, trying not to break the haze of fantasy she had created.

"Just felt like it," she said, as she ran her fingers along the straps of her bra. "You sounded tense on the phone, so I thought this might help."

I nodded, not trusting myself to say anything. My body was no longer locked in shock and I could move forward, closer to the bed. I slipped off my shoes on the way, loosening my tie and throwing it aside, too. I was unbuttoning the top of my dress shirt by the time my knees hit the side of the mattress and Wendy just looked up at me, amusement evident in her gaze.

"I've never seen this before," I said, waving a hand over her body. "New?"

"Bought today, just for you." Her breath stuttered as I knelt on the end of the bed, beginning to crawl up over her body, between her legs.

I ran my hands up her stockings, my thumb pausing on the clasps where the garter belt held them in place. I could tell she was getting worked up, ready for me. My hands continued their exploration up the straps until they rested on the blue panties she was wearing. The front was completely lace, not hiding a thing underneath. I could see the hair of her pussy pressing flat against the material. She once offered to shave for me, but I forbade it. I didn't want to fuck some prepubescent teenager; I wanted a real woman.

She was wet for me, a circle of moisture already formed on the cotton strip covering her pussy, making the baby blue turn dark. I leaned down and nosed at the material before running my tongue over it. The sweet tang of her scent filled my senses, sending a jolt of pleasure straight to my cock. I shifted back, resting with my knees on either side of her legs as I reached to the clasps of her garter belt once again. With a flick, first one and then the other released, snapping back against her skin and causing her to flinch. I didn't give her time to speak, instead pulling at her panties and trailing them down over her hips, thighs and finally off completely.

I took a moment to consider whether I should strip her the rest of the way, but gave up on the thought. She looked good spread out for me, half-clothed and ready for whatever I was willing to do to her. My cock was straining for release now, pressed against the seam of my pants and aching, as I started moving up her body again.

When I reached her splayed thighs, I gave a kiss to the inside of each one before I lifted up and began undressing myself. When my pants were unbuttoned and unzipped, I could push them down, along with my boxers. I didn't need to take them completely off, and it would seem unfair if I weren't in a disheveled state to match hers. With the hindering material pulled to my knees, my hard cock was ready for her. I leaned down again, draping my body over hers and seeking out her entrance.

She was so wet that I had no problems sliding right in, warm heat enveloping me as I began to move my hips forward and then back. The rough lace of the garter belt rubbed against my stomach every time I pushed into her, a faint irritation that fought against the waves of pleasure I was feeling. Our bodies were in tune, perfected motions from years of practice. Her pussy pulsed around my cock, squeezing me and pulling me back in whenever my hips bucked up. It didn't take me long, already so close to the edge that my body was soon shuddering as I came. Her moans kept time with mine and I could feel her fluttering around me as she neared completion, too, squeezing me until my spent cock slipped from her warmth.

I collapsed to the side of her, gasping to get my breathing under control. I reached out and lay my hand on her covered breast, the rough lace and silky material in direct opposition to each other. I could feel the faint pounding of her heartbeat under my fingers as she turned to look at me.

"So," she said, still panting. "Am I a good stress reliever?"

I hummed, tightening my grip on her breast. It was all the answer she needed.

IF YOU KNOW
WHERE TO
LOOK

Giselle Renarde

I hate being here.

I hate sleeping in this bed, Clark's marriage bed, sleeping on his wife's side while she's away on business and waking up face-to-face with the knickknacks and nail polish on her bedside table.

And the baby oil! Why wouldn't Clark have put that away before I came? Why the hell would I want to be reminded that he has sex with her too? More puzzlingly, why do I jump at every opportunity to stay the night?

Well, that question has an easy answer: it's the wake-up call that keeps me coming back. It's his arms circling my body before the sun comes up, when I'm still warm with sleep. He kisses my shoulder, walks his fingers down my belly, and I'm sold. I'll put up with any amount of heartache if it means getting fucked first thing in the morning.

My pussy's never wet when he finds it, so Clark burrows under the covers to turn me on in the most efficient way possible. Spreading my legs, he situates himself between them and dives at the apex of my thighs. I don't know how he finds my clit in the dark, but his tongue zeroes in on it so fast it makes my head spin.

I'm dizzy with sleep, wanting the pleasure without the work, and he knows that. He licks my pussy languorously at first, careful not to hurl me over the edge too quickly. Every slow, wet caress makes me moan, mumble, like I'm talking in my sleep. I'm telling him, "More, more," and that's what he gives me.

His saliva drips down my crack, wetting my asshole before dripping against the sheets. He'll have to wash them before his wife comes home, but I don't want to think about that right now. I wish I hadn't thought that thought at all, and I close my eyes, focus only on the sensation of Clark's hot tongue against my pussy.

He sucks my clit and I arch off the mattress, gasping, astounded by the depth of pleasure that action presents every single time he does it. There's no preparing for a sensation like that—you just have to take it. The outline of his head between my thighs, like a crystal ball draped in bedcovers, makes me laugh, and that feels good too. My laughter becomes conflated with the orgasm sitting like a buzzing weight in my belly, and pushes me closer to the edge.

Pressing my heels down against the fitted sheet, I

writhe against Clark's face, against the forceful warmth of his velvet tongue. It feels good to move, and when he cups my asscheeks with both hands, I ride his mouth in furious strokes. His stubble stings if I push too hard, but I don't care right now, even if I have to pay for it later. I fuck his face hard, pushing my clit flush to his tongue, making myself come so hard I scream his name.

"Shh!" he says, digging out from under the covers. "Quiet, Beck. The window's open."

God forbid the neighbors should hear.

"Fuck me," I plead, growling the words, and I roll onto my front because I don't want to do a goddamn thing. I want him to straddle my ass, plunge his cock inside my cunt and ram me from behind.

Since I give him no other option, that's what he does. His erection flirts with my asscrack as he finds his way down there, searching through all that juice for the warmth of my pussy. I'm so wet that he enters me in one swift move, an intrepid arch forward. His muscular thighs clamp down against mine, and I know how tight I must feel to him now.

I compress my pussy muscles, milking his dick, and he moans, collapsing on my back. He's hot and hard, covered in a sheen of morning sweat, and his face is in the crook of my neck now. I feel the heat of his breath trapped in the frazzle of my long black hair. It's a curtain across my face and I can't see a thing, but I don't need to. All I need to feel is Clark moving inside me, that big fat dick pulsing in my pussy with every thrust.

He's grunting and yelping in alternation, and I know what this means. He's going to come soon, and I want to be there to greet him, so I push my ass back into the saddle of his hips. There's just enough room for him to reach under my body and play with my clit, which is aching even though I had an orgasm not five minutes ago. I can come until it hurts, and with Clark I often do.

Mashing his finger against my pulpy wet clit, Clark fucks me in smooth thrusts and then jerky shoves. His cock feels huge inside my cunt, and I tighten every muscle in my body, which makes my clit itch for release.

He's almost there and I'm close too. I'm squealing into the pillow, whipping my hair away, trying to see and not see. I can't keep still. I buck back against him while he rams me and scours my hot clit, and I'm so fucking close I can barely breathe. There's hair in my mouth and I try to spit it out, which seems to make my pussy clamp down on Clark's dick. Who knew?

"Yeah, Becky." He's whining against my ear, so hot, wet. His words are everywhere. "Fuck yeah, Beck."

I growl, shoving my ass back against his body, milking his cock with all I've got while he squeezes my mound, compressing my clit.

"Fuyaaaa-ckyeeeeee-aaaah!" The syllables that tumble out of my mouth don't make any sense, but I'm sure Clark's coming too hard to hear me anyway.

My heart is pounding in my ears and his heart is pounding against my back. He lies on top of me, dead weight. I'm moaning, more nonsense syllables, but he doesn't scold me for the noise this time.

I'm dazed and, for the moment, I feel no pain. Everything is good. This is what I live for.

Time goes by, and Clark pulls out of me, leaving a hot trail of cum down my thigh. He walks to the bathroom and I open my eyes and it hits me all over again: the bedside table, the nail polish, the knickknacks, the baby oil.

Every time I spend the night here, I want to leave something of myself hidden in plain sight. Maybe a lip gloss or a bracelet or a hair elastic—Clark's wife has short hair, so she'll know it isn't hers. I want her to find this little piece of me and take it in her hands and look at it, then call out, "Where did this come from?" And even if she doesn't ask the question, she'll know it came from me. Not me specifically, maybe, but some sort of "me," some girl that isn't her.

Mother Bear says, "Who's been sleeping in my bed?"

The shower hisses on, and I roll out from under the covers. Sure Clark came not long ago, but if I suck him he'll get hard enough to fuck me again. I know this from experience.

As I cross the threshold into the bathroom, I remember all the times I've lathered my hair with *her* shampoo and softened it with *her* conditioner, all the times I've rinsed those products out under the flow of that brushed-nickel showerhead. It occurs to me that every time I've been here, I've left a bit of myself behind: I've left thick strands of my long black hair in the drain. I doubt if Clark thinks to clean it after I've gone.

I'm here, Clark's wife. I'm here, if you know where to look.

THRILL THE COMPETITION

Allison Wonderland

It's not much fun giving a blow job," Taryn remarks over the noisy gush of heat hitting my hair. "Although I think every lesbian feels that way, don't you?"

"Only if they can speak from experience," I reply, wincing as Taryn continues to torture my tresses. Taryn winces, too—for an entirely different reason. "And I seriously doubt that the judges are going to inquire about my sex life, oral or otherwise, during the interview."

"Agreed." She puts down the blow-dryer and picks up a hairbrush. "A better question would be: why did you get involved in beauty pageants?"

I smirk. The answer is out of the question. I got involved in beauty pageants because I wanted to meet girls. I could care less about the sash or the cash or the crown that glitters like a dinner plate in an advertisement for dishwashing soap. That doesn't mean I don't take pageantry seriously. It just means that I'm not in it to win it.

I used to think pageants were sideshows, populated with aspiring anchorwomen who were glitzy and ditzy, self-confident and self-conscious. But I've been on the circuit for two years now, since I was nineteen, and in that time, I've met girls with moxie and mettle and razor-sharp minds. Girls like Taryn.

The first time I saw her parade across the stage, her gown sparkling like a Christmas ornament, her teeth aligned like corn on the cob, I wasn't really attracted to her. There was something in the way she moved, her back as straight as an exclamation point; her steps so polished, so precise; that made me think she was hollow on the inside.

But, as the saying goes, first is the worst, second is the best, and Taryn made a much better impression the second time around. We were at a local pageant, waiting outside the hotel's conference room for the personal interview to begin, when Taryn tapped me and said, "I much prefer T&A to Q&A. Do you?"

"I do," I replied, like a blushing bride.

Not surprisingly, she and I became fast friends. Well, not fast friends exactly. If we'd become fast friends, we would have fornicated by now. But... Look, let's not hump to conclusions, all right? I don't want to hook up with her; I want to date her, which I am. It's just that sometimes I feel like she's the tortoise to my hare.

Maybe it's because in the pageant world, scandals are a no-no, so we've had to keep our relationship hush-hush. But I ask you: would anyone *really* be surprised? I'm surprised there hasn't already been a sapphic snowball effect. I mean, here you have a bevy of beautiful women who grin and bare it backstage, treating each other to flashes of flesh and snippets of skin, and—

"You still haven't answered my question," Taryn tells me. She lies down on her bed, beside a new pantsuit that wasn't there a minute ago.

"You're wearing beige?" I query. "That's sort of a noncommittal color—neither good nor evil. You must be in a Mae West mood: you used to be snow white, but you drifted." I tickle her torso.

"Be that as it may," she squeals through her squirms, "I need an answer, Miss Behave Yourself."

"I got involved in beauty pageants because I want world peace and a piece of the pie," I reply, giving Taryn's mussed hair a few fluffs.

She shakes her head, the light locks shifting across her back. "You're going to blow it," she informs me.

"Oh, come now."

"Instant orgasm? Is that anything like instant coffee?"

We look at each other. Her eyes are Bambi-brown and notably enchanting. I get lost in them, in her, in our very unladylike laughter. (We both do a Steve Urkel sort of snort, just one of the many quirks we have in common.)

Taryn takes the pantsuit by the hanger. "Sorry, Mom, but my girlfriend doesn't approve." She walks across the room, to the garment bag draped over the dresser. "I'll exchange it before the pageant."

I watch her walk, modeling confidence that is at once casual and cautious. "Not before you help me find an outfit. You know I like your taste."

"I know you *would*, anyway." Taryn blushes, rushes to hide her embarrassment behind her hands. "Did I just say that with a straight face?" she mumbles into her palms.

"Technically, no."

"Thought so," she says, and laughs a little. "Well, good, I'm glad we're in harmony about that."

"I'm sorry. I don't speak Care Bear." My tone is light, but my heart is knocking against my ribs and I'm more than a little damp with desire. Taryn comes back to bed, her face still red. "Awww, don't be bashful," I tease, hugging her. She hugs back, until we're embracing so tightly we're practically wearing each other. "So...are you a beauty in the streets and a beast in the sheets?" I'm going for husky but my voice comes out high, and I sound like a cross between Frenchy from *Grease* and Jeanette the Chipette.

In answer, I get a kiss—slender, tender lips moving against mine, grapefruit gloss charming my taste buds.

"Maybe," she murmurs, sincerely uncertain.

We keep kissing.

I begin to undress Taryn, to reveal her appeal. Taryn's

body is a potpourri of swerves and slopes and swoops. Her teats pucker like the tips of lemons and her fuzzy swatch of hair curls like the tips of chocolate chips.

I touch her skin, pale and pliant and softer than cashmere.

I kiss her skin, painting her cake-batter complexion vixen red. I don't know why I left my lipstick on. Maybe so I could leave my lipstick on her.

Taryn's spine curves as my tongue loops hoops around her nipples.

My palms shift to her sides, drift to her thighs. I lower my head. She raises her hips.

My mouth cruises along her sex, the color of pink champagne and the flavor of pineapple and red velvet cake.

I tunnel through her cunt, lust glazing my lips.

I seek the perky pink morsel snuggled in the ripples and feel her clit thump against my tongue.

Quiet quivers bolt through Taryn's body. It isn't in her nature to be noisy. But her face is screaming, the features beautifully contorted, like a Picasso.

After she comes, I linger between her legs, enjoying her scent, the perfume of her pussy. "I hope the judges don't ask me about a recent goal I accomplished," I murmur, watching the rapid rise and fall of her chest. Soon, it slows, indicating that her heart has resumed its regular rhythm.

"Tell them the truth," she suggests, as I move to lie beside her. "Tell them that you turned an innocent beauty queen into a slightly less innocent pillow queen."

"Oh, so you're not going to return the flavor?" I challenge, mindful of the clear-colored cloud covering my crotch.

Taryn's smile makes her dimples grin. "Some other time," she says, stretching her lips into a yawn.

"You cannot put lust on a waiting list," I grouse, my sex scraping her hip. "Can I at least get a hint of what's to come?"

Taryn turns to me. "Yes," she says, our limbs entwined, her lips fading into mine. "You."

COSMIC FATE

Angell Brooks

Ten more minutes, I thought, glancing around the carnival. *Ten minutes and then I can get out of this nightmare and go for a drink.* I hauled one of the milk cartons up in front of me, and began stacking the plastic rings from the Ring Toss. This was the last year I'd volunteered for the games. Next year, I'll sell tickets or something that doesn't involve snotty kids screaming because they didn't win a plastic frog.

The sky was several shades of amber in the wake of the setting sun. I loved summer. And despite the disaster of this year's Ring Toss, I always looked forward to the annual Shriners Carnival. I always volunteered. The money went toward revitalizing the parks and playgrounds in the area, places I used to go to when I was a child.

Every year held surprises, from the old friends who came back for the night, to the local celebrities who turned up in support. Last year, we had an Emmy Award winner perform an impromptu concert. This year, my surprise was the very reason I needed that drink.

Jackie Johnson, or JJ for short. A cosmic blast from the past towing a tail full of heartache, confusion and lust. And she was heading right into my atmosphere.

This collision would make the big bang look like a firecracker.

I filled up one milk carton, and started on the other, the meeting playing in my mind over and over on continuous loop...

It had started as a great day. And then, with two hours left in my shift, I turned around to retrieve a stray ring, and when I turned back to my customers, I found myself staring into a very familiar pair of green eyes. Her mouth opened to speak, but before words could emerge, a pair of arms encircled me from behind.

"Hey, honey." A set of lips I knew as well as my own settled on my neck. I shivered as Jackie's eyes narrowed and grew dark. Instead of dealing with it, I turned into Dani's embrace. "Hey yourself, gorgeous. How's your shift going?" Dani was manning the Tilt-A-Whirl. It was where we had met two years ago. Her brown hair was falling out of her ponytail, and it gave her the sexy, disheveled look that made my knees weak.

"All right. But I think I'll be done after you, so how about we meet at the car? And then we can go home and…" She whispered naughty things in my ear. I bit back a moan, my pussy instantly wet. Not one for PDAs, Dani gave me a quick swat on the ass and winked as she walked back to her post.

I noticed that Jackie was gone. My heart sighed a little. Jackie had been my first love, my first real girl-friend after I'd finally accepted that I liked girls more than guys. Jackie's was the first pussy I'd ever tasted. And she'd been my first heartbreak.

It hadn't ended well. There wasn't even a definitive reason for it to end. Just one day—she was gone. But even after five years, JJ still had the power to make me want.

Why was she back? Did it even matter? I was with Dani now, and I was content. And that was enough—wasn't it? Sure, she didn't excite me like Jackie did, and while she was adventurous in bed, there weren't the astronomical fireworks that had happened every time JJ and I made love. But it was enough. It had to be—because I couldn't go down that road again.

I finished packing up and, grabbing my bag, waved good-bye to the night guards. I made my way toward the parking lot, taking a shortcut through the dense trees to get there. I couldn't wait to get home, with Dani, and all the dirty promises she'd made.

I cried out in surprise as I was dragged behind one of the giant oaks. Jackie's soft, supple lips mashed against mine, taking my breath away with a single kiss. The air around us crackled with the fireworks I remembered. There were no words to say, as my camp shirt was ripped open and a willing hand sought my breasts. Jackie's other hand pinned my wrists together, bringing my arms above my head, causing my tits to pop out of the flimsy bra.

I was already aroused, but now my excitement completely soaked through my thong, and was threatening to show through my tiny denim shorts. My chest was heaving as JJ brought my bare breast to her mouth, gently encircling the nipple with her lips. Hot breath mingling with the cool night air was almost enough to make me come on the spot, and somewhere in the back of my mind, I thought I should fight—I should stop this. But then Jackie stuck out her talented tongue and licked the tip. Shivers ran rampant through my body as I moaned.

The bark of the tree was scratching my bare arms, the rough texture adding to my pleasure. JJ's mouth continued its onslaught on my flesh, and tears threatened to spill from my closed lids as she suckled me closer to a delicious orgasm. My groin thrust forward, desperate for contact, any kind. Because I knew that one touch could put me right over the edge. And I fucking wanted it—needed it. From her. With her.

And she knew it.

Jackie's height had her at an advantage, and she just moved out of reach, never releasing the hold her mouth currently had on that supersensitive nipple. The other one stood out, begging for a little attention, and

I motioned with my torso, biting my lip. After years of being together, JJ knew my body language and obliged with a quick flick and a rough suck.

As I was on the brink of coming, my cell phone rang. Talk about timing.

Jackie released my hands for me to find the phone but continued to pay close attention to my breasts, which were still bare. I didn't dare answer. There was no way to explain the quiver in my voice or the breathlessness I was experiencing.

"That's...Dani..." I managed to force out in little squeaks. "Need...to...go..."

And then she spoke. "No, baby." She put my tits back in the bra, and reassembled the shirt. Moving in close, her voice was the husky whisper I loved to hear, the voice I often heard in my dreams. "From where I stand, you need to come."

And with those words, she kissed me gently, her hand slipping up the leg of my short shorts. Her finger found my clit, stroking it lightly as her tongue did the same to mine. She delicately slipped two fingers into my dripping cunt, fucking me against the tree.

I came in waves, mewling against Jackie's mouth. She held me up, grinding the heel of her hand into my pussy. I felt my clit pulsating and quivering as Jackie kept me coming, ignoring my weak protests.

The phone went off again. This time, Jackie released me, pulling me away from the tree, and picking pieces of bark and leaves out of my hair. She looked me in the eye.

"This isn't over. I'll call you tonight."

Legs shaking, I slowly walked toward the meeting spot, pausing long enough to put my phone on silent. I saw the car sitting there, Dani in the driver's seat, with steam coming out of her ears.

"I called you twice. Where the hell were you?"

I feigned surprise. "You called twice? I didn't hear anything." I pulled the phone out. "Two missed calls. Weird. Try it again. Maybe something's wrong." I grabbed Dani's phone and pressed the redial. My phone, sure enough, didn't ring. I checked the settings.

"Shit. It was on silent. How the hell did that happen?" Dani shook her head.

"Doesn't matter. You're here now. Ready to go home?" she winked. With a heavy heart, I slipped my hand into hers, knowing it might be the last night of contentment we'd have.

As the car pulled away, I glanced out the window and saw JJ standing there, gazing after the car, and I knew she was right.

This wasn't over.

Two roads diverged in a wood and I...I'd wind up taking the one already traveled. And for no other reason than that I needed the damn fireworks.

LET ME TIE
YOU UP?

Devin Phillips

et me tie you up?" he asked me, holding up the ropes so I could see them.

At first I couldn't take my eyes off them; they were slim and white and gorgeous. They were looped over one another and tied off beautifully in lengths with colored ends, so he could keep the lengths separate.

I must have stared at those ropes in his hand for half a minute before I brought my eyes back to his and saw the wicked joy in them.

Peter's smile broadened to a grin. His blue eyes brightened. He knew he had me.

He was fully dressed, and I was naked—very, very naked. I'd just gotten out of the shower, and I'd been thinking about him in there—thinking about what we might do when I got out of the shower and Peter took me to bed. I was already very turned on.

He could see everything he wanted to see, I realized—in exquisite detail never before revealed. I'd just shaved, so he could see my sex. He could see the hot flush of arousal through my breasts and my face, see the stiffening of my nipples that told him his plea was turning me on as much as it was scaring me. He could see my lips, parted, my breath coming tight and short and fast.

A ripple went through my nude body. I said, "What will you do once you tie me up?"

"Well," Peter smiled. "That's up to me, isn't it? Once you're at my mercy...I can do anything I want to you, can't I?"

He came in close, till his body was up against mine; his hard, big body in its rough cotton clothes. He came in close till he held me, naked and helpless in his arms.

And he said, "So please let me tie you up and do whatever I want to you."

I shivered. A pulse of sexual heat broke through me like a wave. I felt helpless in more ways than one.

"All right," I said, my voice small and soft and vulnerable.

Peter took my wrist; he turned me around and faced me toward the bed. He pushed me onto it. He spilled me across the big soft California king, forcing me onto my hands and knees.

"Do you want me on my back?" I whined, insecure.

He bent down and put his lips to mine and kissed me

hard, his tongue forcing its way into my mouth.

Excitement flooded me.

"No," he said. "Stay right where you are." He set some of the ropes in the small of my back as if I were a table. He ran his hand up my thigh and felt me up. I was wet. He caressed my ass. "You know how I like this cute butt of yours...and I know how you like it doggie-style. Just spread your legs for me. *Now*."

My eyes fluttered closed and a hot, soft, aroused sound escaped from my lips. That sort of thing was all that Peter had to say to make me lose control, and he knew it.

I obediently spread my legs. I did what he told me to. I wanted to do *everything* he told me to.

He caressed my buttocks.

"Put your ass in the air," he ordered. "Higher."

I leaned forward on all fours, lifting my ass up into the air.

Peter's big hands found pillows, lots of pillows; Peter's house always had zillions of pillows. He shoved them under my belly so my ass was up high.

He opened my legs still farther, planting my knees wide and pushing my shoulders down so that my ass was higher and my belly rested comfortably on the pillows. My shoulders and breasts were flat against the soft, silken bedspread.

As he moved me like a rag doll, the lengths of rope spilled off my back and onto the bed.

Peter plucked them up and tied me.

First, he moved my arms down alongside my thighs into an easy position. Then he tied my thighs, and secured my wrists to them.

I felt the ropes pulling at the flesh of my thighs. I felt the pressure in my sex. My nipples felt hard against the bedspread.

"Comfortable?" he growled with just a hint of irony.

Was I comfortable?

I didn't know; all I could feel was that I was scared and turned on and very badly wanted him to fuck me.

With the pillows under my belly, my back was arched, thrusting my ass up and exposing my sex—and that position always makes me so unbelievably hot. When Peter played with me like this I felt very much under his command—even though he had never tied me up before. The important part was having my shoulders down; that felt far more erotic and exposing. It made me feel helpless.

I liked it.

Yes, I decided. I was comfortable. I still had a hard time telling him, but I managed it. He circled my ankles with rope and tied them to the bedposts. He tied one knot...two knots...three. The ropes felt snug, but not tight; each time he closed a new one, I felt my temperature rising. By the time he finished with my ankles, I was incredibly turned on.

It didn't hurt that after every knot, Peter would take a moment to caress my freshly shaved sex. I had never gone bare before. I had never been tied to a bed—not like this. And I had never been totally controlled by my lover—especially not a new one I didn't even know was kinky until our third date.

Was I kinky, too? I didn't know yet. But Peter was working hard to make me that way.

And those big, smooth fingers of his were doing wonders to convince me I was more than just kinky.

He slid two, then three, up inside me. I moaned. It felt good. He used fingers and thumb to work my pussy and my clit.

I was moaning. I bucked against the ropes, feeling how tightly I was restrained. My pleasure mounted. Peter finger-fucked me until I was close—and then he pulled his fingers out of me.

He came around and opened the nightstand drawer. He reached inside. His hand came out holding a gag—a red rubber ball gag with a black leather strap.

He leaned in, caressed my hair.

He looked in my eyes.

"I'm going to gag you now," he said.

I gulped. I wriggled. I squirmed. I fought the unfamiliar feel of the ropes keeping me firmly in place. I liked it, I decided...I even liked to fight it.

"All right," I said.

He put the gag in my mouth and buckled it. When his hand went back into the nightstand drawer again, I shivered. It came out holding a pair of nipple clamps.

"I'm going to clamp your tits now," he said.

I tried to say "All right," but I couldn't say a thing with the gag in. Somehow that turned me on even more.

The pain was light but intense; he adjusted the clamps and reached back into the nightstand drawer.

This time he hid the item he took out. That made me quiver. It made me tremble. It made me wet.

He went around behind me.

What was going to happen? Was he going to whip me? Spank me?

I heard the rattle of his belt buckle, the hiss of his zipper. I heard the soft rustling sound of Peter's clothes hitting the ground.

He mounted the bed behind me with the tool he'd brought from the nightstand. I heard the buzzing sound as he nuzzled the vibrator up to my clit. Sensation flooded me. I moaned behind the gag. I felt Peter's cock working up and down my freshly bared clit, his cockhead finding my entrance. He tightened his grip on my clit and the vibrations increased to powerful intensity.

I uttered a muffled squeal behind the gag as Peter entered me. His cock slid deep—and at that angle, it *always* hit just about all the right places inside me. I did more than squeal behind the gag; I was mouthing dirty words, cursing in agonized pleasure, tit clamps and vibrator and ropes and cock all driving me into a frenzy. I struggled against my bonds trying to meet each hard thrust of his cock into my helpless naked body. I howled.

The vibrator brought me to the brink, but it was his cock that drove me over the top.

I came an instant before Peter did—my eyes rolling back. I screamed at the top of my lungs; thank goodness Peter had gagged me. Otherwise, our neighbors would have called the cops.

Was I kinky? I guess I had the answer now. Yeah, I was kinky.

And it was far from the last time I'd let him tie me up.

NICE DREAM

J. Sinclaire

There's an indeterminate span of time between asleep and awake. Those bleary moments, waves of thought washing over us as we struggle to gain or lose consciousness. Where dreams blur with reality, taking on aspects and influence from each other.

The shriek of an alarm clock is translated into the cries of some prehistoric flying creature chasing us through Elysian Fields. The scent of bacon spurs a vivid scenario of gorging ourselves on anything and everything within sight.

The slow, rhythmic thrusts of a cock between swollen labia elicits dreams of multiple members in multiple orifices.

This is how I awaken; gradually, with the dawning realization that at least one turgid member from my reveries is truly flesh and blood. Sliding between my thighs from behind as I lie on my side, body curled into the blankets surrounding me. A hand, presumably accompanying the penis in its adventures, is trailing feather soft over the curve of my breasts, fingers occasionally tweaking my nipple.

I hear myself cry out, something between a whimper and a moan. I'm sleepily detached from my body. I feel no association to the sound though I recognize I was the one to make it. My hips swivel back slightly, arching my back so my breasts fill the helpful hand and the cock drifts directly over the simmering button between my pussy lips.

I haven't bothered to open my eyes and decide not to unless absolutely necessary. There's no indication of light; it's likely still night, which is all the more reason to simply enjoy the sensations engulfing me. The slow, gentle prodding against my clit; the head of the cock parting my lips and absently traversing past my ever-dampening slit. It's hypnotic. Not enough sensation to wake me completely, it keeps me at a steady level of arousal. It could still be a dream, though the nagging, rational part of me reminds me otherwise.

The decision to ignore that nag is immediate and the thought vanishes with a swift pinch of my nipple.

Again, that sound.

Again, that warm flush of pleasure between my thighs.

More sensations become apparent to me. The feel of

his thighs against the back of mine. His lips brushing over the base of my neck. His breath, warm then cool against the dampened skin on my spine. His body a soothing presence behind me, apparent yet understated. Softly surfacing, a symphony of subtle sensations.

Alliteration aside, my body is humming with the majesty of an orgasm building with an absolute lack of urgency. The destination is clear, taken for granted, but the moment is awake with possibilities. The permutations of caresses that will achieve their intent. The rocking sway of stiffness on the verge of penetration; against a captive, willing pool of sex and sweat and cunty goodness.

With barely a shift in rhythm, he adjusts his angle and slides inside me on the next stroke. His head drags deliciously against the wall of my pussy, resting with persistent pressure against my G-spot. My breath catches at his incursion and I'm in danger of awakening more when he stills all his motions but the pouty, lingering kisses on my neck. My breathing steadies, my heart beats regularly and I gladly drift back into semiconsciousness.

His cock rests inside, firmly filling me. His hand cups my breast, thumb smoothing along the curve, tracing the hollow of my skin where it extends from my chest. His grip tightens; my flesh cedes around his fingers, taut and tense, but not to the point of pain. We exhale in unison as he relaxes his hold, his fingers brushing across an areola in the process.

I feel my pussy clench around him involuntarily from

his caress, putting more pressure on my G-spot. His grunt is a guttural acknowledgment of sensations I have caused with no intention of eliciting them.

The corners of my lips turn up in what can only truly be called a satisfied smirk before I'm cast back down into the dreamy depths of tactile pleasure.

His hands stay in the vicinity of my breasts but the speed and force of his caresses vary. His lips tease the subtle ridges of my spine to the base of my skull. His cock, solid inside me, keeps still, despite the occasional fluttering of my cunt. My body is humming, taut as a line of piano wire, and the rising pulses of bliss increase the tension.

The areas of focus for his touch are not enough on their own to bring me to orgasm, but the fullness of my pussy, the prodding against the tender, sensitive flesh inside me, are working me steadily to my breaking point.

My surrender comes and brings alertness along with it. Body and mind, fully awake and shuddering with release only achieved through these slow, persistent ministrations. A heat wave surges through my flesh, blanketing me in sticky, simmering joy. No dream could match this ecstasy. In theory, but not execution.

No, this is…exactly what was necessary.

Coming down from the heights achieved is gradual, a process. The brief interlude of lucidity has passed and with him still inside me, I fall asleep once more.

EVA

Donna George Storey

I have about an hour to kill before I can go back to Eva. Walking this town from end to end would take all of ten minutes. I pause at the wine-tasting room, but there are too many tourists inside. Besides I'll have to make the usual inane chitchat with one of the hospitality staff.

"Is this your first visit to the Wine Country?" she'll say, chipper as a Girl Scout.

"Actually, my wife and I come up from San Francisco a few times a year, but not for the wine. We like to play our kinky Dom-sub sex game in your local country inn. Would you care to join us tonight?"

I smile as I continue on down the street. If only it were that easy. Of course, bringing back another woman might be pushing Eva a little too far. This time.

I pass a quaint tavern—everything is quaint here—and peek inside. Dim lighting, a few customers perched at the bar. Perfect. I take a table in a shadowy corner and order a glass of Frank Family Cabernet. You can't get that by the glass in the city.

The wine is delicious, but I plan to nurse it for the rest of the hour. Any more than a glass, and I'll lose my edge. Eva assures me she's not keeping score, but I want each time to be better. On our last visit, I ordered her to shave her pussy for me, but she shied away from the trickiest spots. I made the most of that, believe me. I hauled her back into the bathroom and forced her to lie on the bathmat, legs spread wide, while I did the job right. She was quivering like a nervous filly, so I stroked and soothed her, taking her rosy lips gently between my fingers, pulling the razor across the tender skin oh-so-delicately. Her juice flowed like a river the whole time, and when I kissed her there, my face was literally bathed in her warm nectar. I almost came in my pants right there on the tiled floor.

But this time? Well, I hinted that I wanted her to shave for me again, but I can never predict how she'll respond to my "orders." She might be intentionally sloppy, and then I'll have to be "disappointed"; maybe bend her over the sink for a spanking, get that round bottom all pink and squirming, before I give her another hands-on grooming lesson. Or she might be scrupulously careful, not a hair in sight, and I'll have to come up with another pretext to tie her up to that four-poster bed.

Suddenly, I flash on an idea. What if I "make" Eva write down all her dirtiest fantasies as an assignment? An instant treasury of scripts for future games. I can hear her voice tremble as she reads—*Then you bend me over your desk and lube my asshole with the ointment you keep tucked in the drawer for special "lessons"*... I love fucking Eva in every hole, but nothing turns me on more than slipping deep inside her sweet, dirty mind.

The first time we came up here, we were just an ordinary couple getting away for the weekend. Until, as we sat by the fire with a bottle of good wine, Eva told me about the man inside her head. How he whispered depraved things that made her blush—and masturbate. He took videos of her playing with herself and showed it to his friends while she had to sit and listen to their rude comments. He put her to work as his special assistant, whose duties involved catering to the needs of wealthy clients. Sometimes he'd make her fellate them during meetings, their cocks protruding from their pinstripe trousers. Sometimes he'd bend her over his big mahogany desk and invite a dozen of them to fuck her ass until the stimulation of all those cocks made her come without a single flick of her clit. This dude was one serious pervert.

I found myself getting jealous. And very hard. I wanted to be that man in her head.

Now I am.

The hour is up. I saunter back to our cottage suite, my back straight, my expression uncompromising. Right out of law school, I clerked for a judge named Francis Purcell, the pickiest bastard you could imagine. If only old Frank knew how far his influence reached into his young protégé's private life.

Eva meets me at the door in the hotel bathrobe, bright eyed and gorgeous. I swear I can smell her pussy, like fresh-baked bread. I know that shaving for me arouses her, but something else is afoot. A secret. Almost as if she's had a lover while I was gone.

My cock twitches.

I send her off to bed, and go change into a robe myself. When I join her, Eva's sitting on the edge of the bed studying the carpet and looking guilty as hell.

"You have something naughty to tell me, don't you, Eva? I know that expression on your face."

She stutters but finally admits that she masturbated while she waited for me. My cock gets harder. I can just picture her in the bath, her cunt all dewy, that slim finger jiggling away in the folds.

I ask her if she fantasizes about me when she masturbates at home, behind the back of her poor unwitting husband.

She bites her lip and nods.

"You know you need to be disciplined for this?"

She catches her breath.

I smile. She's handed me the perfect reason to tie her up—to keep those wandering fingers from doing more mischief. It's always easier to push the limits when she "deserves" it. Still I pay close attention to her response as I bind her wrists to the bedpost with the belts of our robes. This was new for us. So far, so good. Her eyes have that dreamy, helpless look, and her nipples are as hard as pebbles under her robe.

She moans when I began to tease her breasts with my lips and fingers. Those beautiful nipples are my best allies. All I have to do is suck and tweak them for a few moments, and she's whimpering for my cock inside.

Tonight I refuse to get near her pussy for a full twenty minutes.

Since we started playing our game, I've learned something about myself, too. I love "breaking" her, using her own arousal against her to reduce her to pure animal desire. I love it when she sweats and pants and begs me to fuck her. There are no sweeter words a man can hear.

Finally I relent, because I'm not sure I can hold out much longer myself. I make her spread her legs so I can examine her. Her lips are as smooth as white chocolate, the inner flesh swollen and moist like strawberries. The vulnerability gives me another wicked idea. I gently slap her right on her clit. She shudders. I wait. Her eyes are squeezed tight, and a slight smile plays over her lips. I spank her vulva again. She spreads her legs wider. Bingo.

It's then I spring my assignment on her—writing down all her fantasies, in a notebook, just for me. I add in an oral recitation in the nude for good measure. I know from the way she arches up and gasps that she likes the idea very much.

Now I can't wait a second longer. I kneel between her legs and slide inside her to the hilt. There's another reason I love these weekends. Her cunt is somehow silkier, hotter, tighter. She pushes up, grinding her shaved slit against me. I realize there's just one thing missing: I want to be inside her head, too.

"Tell me what a dirty girl you are," I choke out, knowing this will drive us both over the edge.

And so she tells me how she loves to get fucked and bound and spanked and forced to admit she likes it all. With each new confession, my cock throbs, and her walls grip me like shrink-wrap. I know she's going to come soon by her ragged breath, the way her left thigh jerks, the low moan rising in her throat. I hold out until she screams, and then finally I let go.

Old Judge Frank Purcell probably never had this much fun in his life.

Afterward Eva laughs and kisses me and thanks me for being such a perfect master. I've done well this time.

But, to be frank, I know for us the best is yet to come.

DRESS CODE

N. T. Morley

We've got a dress code for her when we go out together.

It's not that she has to dress a certain way. It's that if she dresses a certain way, it's acknowledged she's *asking for it*. When she wears certain clothes, she knows things will happen to her.

Things. Dirty things. Very, very dirty things, and things she couldn't ask for. Couldn't *bring herself to ask for*. So she asks for them by wearing what she knows will get her what she wants. And she always gets what she wants.

Fiona and I have been together for eight years, married for five. When you're together that long, your sexual relationship is guaranteed to have its ups and downs. We were having a "down" for a while—I'm not going to speculate as to why; we just were. Then things changed.

Now we have an *understanding*.

We go out together on weekends. We go out to eat—nice restaurants, usually. Never family places. After, sometimes we go to a movie—though we rarely make it that far into the evening. Sometimes we do other things.

We go out together, and Fiona dresses like she wants it.

She wears short skirts, low-cut blouses, fuck-me dresses. High heels. She wears her hair long, now, and it cascades over her bare shoulders.

Her skirts are never very long, but some are shorter than others. The heels on her fuck-me shoes are all very high, but some pairs are higher than others. She can finally walk in heels in relative comfort; all those hours on the stair-stepper gave her something even more practical than having the world's most spankable, lickable, fuckable ass. She knows how to wiggle it. She knows how to show it off.

Just *how* short her skirt is—well, that gives me a hint of what she wants, but I won't know for sure until I know what she's wearing underneath. Sometimes I can see a little hint of what she's wearing underneath—when she's wearing a garter belt, for instance, and sweet sexy stockings with lace tops and seams down the back that lead all the way to heaven. Sometimes I can see her garters, because her skirts are very short, and she's never very careful about not flashing.

She likes other guys to look—and she likes that I know they're looking. When we're at a bar or a restaurant or some other public place, she even goes out of her way to wait until I'm watching her—and I usually am—before she takes a slow circuit of the place, wiggling her ass and letting me track all the bug-eyes that follow her as guys try to be discreet.

She likes the tops of her stockings to show, so when she's wearing a garter belt or even if she's just wearing stay-ups, I get a glimpse of what she's got on underneath.

But I never *really* know what she wants—not until I get a private moment. That's our agreement; I don't get to know what she's wearing underneath until after we're out in public; she even makes me wait in the living room while she gets dressed. I can't feel her up in the house, and I can't do it in the car.

And Fiona's not some drunken teenager; she can flash without flashing. She never shows her pussy—just her legs, her thighs, her ass and everything *up* to her pussy. I'm the only guy who gets to see it, the only guy who gets to feel it. And I don't get to see or touch or taste it until I make a point of doing it in public.

Fiona always chooses public places. Depending on where we are, it might be an hour into the evening; it might be two. It might take a long time before I get enough privacy to nudge my hand between her legs.

The rule is, I've got to do it before dessert, or by our third cocktail if we're just out for drinks. If we go to a movie, the designated feel-up has to happen by the end of the first act. Fiona took a screenwriting course; she can always tell when those fucking acts end, down to the minute—but I can't. So I just make sure that shit happens by the time the credits are finished rolling.

At restaurants, she always asks for a table so I don't have the luxury of hiding what I'm doing in the darkness of a booth. I have to do it out there in the open—under the table, or up against the bar, or sneaking a hug and copping a feel while I'm helping her on with her coat.

Sometimes I do it right there in the full-on open, not under a table or anything—somewhere lots of guys can see what I'm doing. Sometimes I do it that way because my flirty little wife has gotten my dick so hard that I can't put off feeling her up for another goddamn moment. Once, she teased me so bad I shoved her up against the jukebox and shoved my hand up her skirt. She liked it. She pushed her ass back against me and let me slide my fingers into her, once I found out she wasn't wearing any panties. She liked it, all right; she liked it a lot. The other guys in the bar—they liked it too. If anything, *more* than Fiona did.

Most of the time, I'm a *little* discreet, at least. Most of the time I just nudge my hand under the table and slide my fingers up her thighs. I know it's totally nonconsensual of us—I mean, we haven't gotten everyone's permission to do this right out in the open, right?

It's not like we go to family restaurants or PG movies or anything. But yeah, I know it's pretty dirty of us to do it where people might see.

I'll tell you—*you* spend an hour being teased by a girl who looks like my wife, and see if you don't shove her hand up her skirt right where someone might see.

And, see, what happens next is determined by the code. What she's wearing under her skirt is all-important. She goes one of three ways.

Sometimes she's got panties on—always something skimpy, French-cut, revealing. Always very sexy. That means she wants me to take her home and fuck her as soon as possible.

I rarely make her wait. She's always wet; I'm usually hard. We go home and screw; we do it rough and romantic or slow and deep. It's always good; the tease makes the game.

That's one way it can go.

Other times, she wears something even skimpier—G-string style, with no ass at all. Just a thin little thread up her crack, like the butt floss they wear on Brazilian beaches.

That means she wants it *hard*. She wants me to take her home and *do* her—not just fuck her but *do her*. It means I can do whatever I want to her. Bondage. Role play. Dirty talk. If she's wearing a thong, I can even spread her perfect, toned, stair-stepper asscheeks and have my wife's snug little butthole. And when she's up for that, Fiona *always* wants a spanking first. That's how she gets in the mood for sodomy. Hell, could a man be any luckier?

But there's a third way things can go, and you're not going to like it if you objected to the fact that I feel my wife up in public.

If Fiona isn't wearing anything under her skirt—I mean, no underwear, whether or not she's wearing a garter belt—it means she wants something else.

She doesn't want to go home first.

That's where my promise comes in. I always have a place in mind—never knowing whether we're going to use it.

Sometimes it's a park near the restaurant; other times it's a rest stop. We've done it in the car, with people watching. We've done it in a grove of trees. I've shoved her up against a brick wall in a sleazy dark alley.

One time it was a porn shop. I pulled her skirt up and sat her down in my lap right there in the video booth.

She liked that. It scared her a little, but she liked it.

I haven't taken her back there, but I'm trying to think of a dress code she can use…something she can wear under her skirt to let me know she's ready for more sex in a porn shop video booth.

Until then?

Every Friday and Saturday, what she wears underneath tells me just what she wants…and so far I never fail to give it to her.

Because a wife should always get what she wants, right?

CONSEQUENCES

Cheyenne Blue

*T*y:

Ty used to say he liked his chocolate and his women dark. Chocolate that was black with cocoa, bitter enough that it kicked on his tongue, no sweetness to be found. Women so smooth and black skinned that they seemed to suck the light in like a black hole, abrupt and acerbic, no simpering submission.

Met Michelle:

Michelle liked women more than she liked men, but sometimes she craved a cock that was veined and warm, that wasn't strapped on. She wasn't beautiful; she was handsome in an imposing, supercilious sort of way. Men were often intimidated by her six-foot-two frame and haughty expression.

At the hospital:

Michelle was an operating-room nurse, a job that suited her no-nonsense attitude. Besides, as she was fond of telling people, she liked her patients unconscious so she didn't have to talk to them.

Ty and Michelle quite literally bumped into each other when Michelle was coming off shift and Ty had been visiting his idiot of a brother who'd gotten himself beaten up again. They did the *excuse me* dance in the corridor, stepping side to side in unison, unable to pass.

He said:

"Excuse me...excuse me...excuse me..." until they both gave up and stood still and took stock of each other.

She said:

"We must stop meeting like this," accompanied by a smile for the predictability of her words. And then because the first collision had left an impression of strength and hardness, and because she had broken up with her girlfriend two days prior, she said, "I've finished for the day. D'you want a beer?"

He did:

He took her to a bar; one he knew well, but his friends hadn't discovered yet. They drank double-strength mojitos until he'd had enough rum to process the signals she was sending him. He put a hand on her thigh; her smooth, dark thigh; running it along under her skirt, until his fingertips rested on her damp panties.

There was a question in his eyes, but she stared straight ahead, and her expression remained impassive. He was about to remove his hand when her strong one covered his, pressing it firmly to her leg.

Finally, he thought, exultant, and his cock, which had been lengthening, stiffening every time she touched her full lips to the frosty glass, rose to full tumescence.

He took her hand and moved it to his groin.

She did:

Finally, she thought, exultant, and sank lower in the seat so his fingers were pressed firmly against her core. The swelling under her palm pulsated hot promise that thrilled her more than his fingers.

She leaned toward him, seeking his lips, wanting to know the taste of him.

They did:

He met her halfway and they kissed. They both tasted of rum and the sharp tang of lime juice and mint, and his tongue met hers, started the dueling dance that their bodies would reproduce later.

He broke the kiss and stood, his hooded eyes and outstretched hand making his meaning clear. She rose too and took his hand. Together they left the bar, went out into the moist warmth of the Florida night.

"There's a quiet place behind the parking lot," she

said, as she did not know him well enough to take home.

He nodded and they half walked, half jogged, with the urgency of their lust, through the parking lot to where a small park, more an abandoned square of grass, was hidden. They stepped over the outstretched legs of a homeless man, and into the shadows in the corner, the deep wine-dark shadows that would hide them from sight.

He stripped his shirt off, up over his head in one movement.

She flicked the buttons of her blouse, baring her lace-covered breasts to his view.

He thumbed open the buttons of his fly, and hooked a thumb in his briefs, lowering them enough that his cock sprang free, thick and dusky, mouth-wateringly hard.

She took her cue from him and raised her skirt meaning to lower her panties. He dropped to his knees in front of her, and hooked his fingers in the elastic, dragging them down her legs; her long, firm legs; rocking forward so that his nose nudged her mound, and his tongue pushed its way abruptly through her folds into the depths of her cunt.

She wound her fingers into his hair for stabilization in a world that was suddenly quaking and pushed her hips forward. One part of her mind registered that here, finally, was a man who could suck pussy as well as any woman, but the thought flew from her head like a bolting horse as his tongue curled around her clit and reality fractured into a million shining pieces.

He rose, smiling and a little bit arrogant for he knew his skill in that department, and debated the finish line. The ground was damp, the tree was rough, and he was considerate enough to think of her back against the jagged bark.

She made the decision for him, pushing him back down to his knees. Straddling him, she grasped his cock, shuffled into position and lowered herself to meet him. Once inside her, his thick, warm cock pulsated fatly with life, and she stopped the words he was going to say with her mouth and took control, riding him hard and fast, to the edge of pain but no farther.

She came before him, but close enough that she marveled at their synchronicity. His eyes closed briefly, his face clenched, and his cock spasmed inside her.

She rested her forehead against his hair for a moment, remembering other times, other places, other women and men, and with an ungainly movement as her knees were shaky, she levered herself away from him.

He hesitated, torn between the urge to accept the moment for what it was, and the desire to see her again, to learn the different facets of her, to see what they could be together.

The consequence was:

Her skirt floated back down into place and she pulled the gaping front of her blouse together. "Well," she said. "See you around then."

She turned to go.
"Wait," he said.
And she did.

BOOKENDED

Alison Tyler

W hat do you say the morning after fucking a stranger in your bed? Gina had no idea. She wasn't the sort of girl to engage in one-night stands. Andrew didn't know her last name, her favorite color, whether she liked to sleep on her side or her back.

Actually, he did know the answer to that, because he'd punished her ass soundly enough that Gina had spent the night sleeping on her stomach. So maybe there are different rules to waking up with a man who has whipped you with his belt and made you come like nobody else ever has before.

But Gina was still at a loss.

"I work," she said in the morning. "All the time." For proof, she opened her calendar to show him all the blood-red lines of meetings and deadlines crisscrossing the dates.

He sat in bed against her pillows, looking at her. He didn't seem to be in any hurry to leave. She couldn't figure out if he was one-night stand material or something more. She hoped for the latter.

"So you don't date."

"I don't date because I'm always…"

"Booked," he said, finishing her sentence. "I get it. But you'll make time for me."

She wasn't good at this sort of thing—the way you were supposed to behave if you wanted to get a man. One of her best friends bought almost every new self-help book that hit the shelves—Gina made fun of the titles, calling them, "Men Who Think Women Suck… and the Women Who Suck Them."

"I don't want you to think I expect something from you," she said shyly.

"But you should," he said.

Her heart kept speeding up, whenever he spoke. "What do you mean?"

He set her datebook on the bedside table and reached for her. She went to him willingly, but was surprised when instead of pulling her into his arms, he spread her out over his lap. She was wearing only his shirt, half buttoned, and he pushed the tails up to her waist and began to stroke one hand over her naked asscheeks.

"You should expect a lot, because you deserve a lot."

She pushed her face against the covers, embarrassed. He was toying with her, stroking her ass with the open palm of his hand. She couldn't help the way her body responded to his touch. Her hips rocked across his lap, her ass rose up to meet his palm. Her body was talking to him in ways her lips would not. *Spank me*, she was saying silently. He didn't. He stroked her ass again and again, like petting a cat, until she grabbed on to the sheets with her hands and made fists, frustrated beyond all measure.

"What do you think you deserve?" he finally asked her.

She'd been ready to take the spanking. She'd been ready for him to tell her to count, or to stay still, or to behave. But she wasn't ready to speak.

"I won't spank you until you tell me," Andrew threatened.

"Fuck you." The words were out of her mouth before she had decided whether or not she would actually say them. To her relief, Andrew laughed.

"Seriously? You think being a brat will get you what you want?"

He shoved her off his lap, and she moved to the edge of the mattress and looked at him cautiously. Her thoughts seemed to be tripping over each other as she tried to figure out what to do next. In a board meeting, when things took a strange turn, she was always there with the perfect response. But now, feeling her pussy juices slick on her upper thighs, her body seeming to throb with anticipation, she had no idea what to do.

"Bend over the edge of the bed."

Oh, he *was* going to spank her. She felt oddly vindicated as she maneuvered herself into position. He stood behind her, pushed his shirt to her hips and started to stroke her ass once more. She believed he was going to spank her the way he had the night before. Maybe with his belt again. She felt herself preparing for the action, and she thought she might actually come during the punishment, the way her body was angled, pussy pressed against the ridge of the mattress.

"Do you have lube?"

Wait, no. That wasn't the question she'd expected.

He hesitated only a moment before asking the question again, more slowly this time, but not more sweetly.

She looked over her shoulder at him. He was already heading into the adjoining bathroom, rummaging around in her medicine cabinet. He returned with a half-filled bottle. While she watched, he undid the cap and wet his fingers. Then he began to probe between her asscheeks, massaging the lube into her back door.

Her whole body was one tense wire of muscle.

"You wanted a spanking, didn't you?" Andrew asked. She could feel the head of his cock pressing against her from behind. She couldn't speak over the lump in her throat. "Didn't you?"

She nodded. He fisted her hair and pulled her head back. She managed to whisper the word, "Yes."

"Thought I'd heat your pretty heart-shaped cheeks with my hand and then fuck you?"

"Yes, Andrew." It was the truth.

"But you wouldn't do what I asked, wouldn't even answer a simple question."

She got the cadence of the game. "No, Andrew."

"So we'll do something else. And *then* I'll spank you."

The head of his cock rubbed in a circle against her asshole. She sighed under her breath, and Andrew, his voice gone husky said, "You like that."

She wasn't going to fuck up again. "Yes, Andrew."

"Good girl. Tell me what you like."

He couldn't see her face, so he didn't catch her grimace. He was going to make her talk to him while he was fucking her asshole? He couldn't have named a worse punishment. But Gina did her best.

"I like that because it feels dirty."

He moved aside and added more lube, this time dribbling the chilly liquid directly against her rear hole. Gina pushed her head into the mattress while lifting her hips and ass into the air. Andrew parted her asscheeks and slicked her up with his fingertips, working the lube deep into her hole. How had he known? She couldn't guess. Anal was something she'd only done a few times. But she loved the feeling of being taken like that. Her body must have told Andrew everything he needed to know. He splayed her open and pressed the head of his cock to her hole once more.

"You tell me what you're thinking, and then I'll reward you by telling you what's going to happen next."

As he spoke, he rocked the first inch of his cock into her asshole. Gina groaned and bit her bottom lip. But as soon as the head was inside of her, the spark of pain ended and the pleasure began.

"I'm thinking that...that..."

"Say it, Gina."

"That I like being fucked up the ass because it feels naughty. And I've always wanted to be naughty for someone. *With* someone."

He was moving faster now. She could feel how hot and swollen her clit was against the sheets. Andrew reached his hand under her body to stroke her clit as he fucked her asshole. It was almost like being fucked in her pussy. She could not believe how good it felt.

"So this is what's going to happen next," Andrew said, and he was breathless, too. "I'm going to come deep inside of your ass, and then I'm going to take you into the bathroom and clean you up."

He was pounding her now. Fucking her hard to each word, each promise.

"And then I'll give you that spanking you were craving so badly."

She sighed. She was going to come—on his words as much as on his actions.

"Can you guess what's going to happen next, Gina?"

She shook her head. "No, Andrew."

"I'm going to write my name in red on every page of your calendar."

He pinched her clit as he shot inside of her. They came sealed together, her body trembling all over, then both of them still. He carried her to the shower as he'd promised and washed her all over. "I know you're booked," he said, as the water rained down. "But you'll fit me into your world, won't you?"

That was the most gentle he'd been to her, and she saw his eyes were filled with the echoing need of her own. She needed to submit—and he needed to guide her.

"Yes," she said, turning in his embrace under the spray. "I'll make the time."

The water beaded up and ran down her face. He kissed her wet lips and held her to him.

"I always liked books that had a happy ending," Andrew said when they parted.

Gina smiled at him. "Me, too."

ABOUT
THE EDITOR

Called "a trollop with a laptop" by *East Bay Express,*
"a literary siren" by Good Vibrations and "the mistress
of literary erotica" by Violet Blue, **ALISON TYLER** is
naughty and she knows it.

Over the past two decades, Ms. Tyler has written
more than twenty-five explicit novels, including *Tiffany
Twisted, Melt with You* and *The ESP Affair.* Her novels
and short stories have been translated into Japanese,
Dutch, German, Italian, Norwegian, Spanish and Greek.
When not writing sultry short stories, she edits erotic
anthologies, including *Alison's Wonderland, Kiss My
Ass, Skirting the Issue* and *Torn.*

Ms. Tyler is loyal to coffee (black), lipstick (red),
and tequila (straight). She has tattoos, but no piercings;
a wicked tongue, but a quick smile; and bittersweet

memories, but no regrets. She believes it won't rain if she doesn't bring an umbrella, prefers hot and dry to cold and wet, and loves to spout her favorite motto: You can sleep when you're dead. She chooses Led Zeppelin over the Beatles, the Cure over NIN, and the Stones over everyone. Yet although she appreciates good rock, she has a pitiful weakness for '80s hair bands.

In all things important, she remains faithful to her partner of seventeen years, but she still can't choose just one perfume.